yours
TO CATCH

USA TODAY BESTSELLING AUTHOR

HARLOE RAE

Editor: Infinite Well
Cover designer: Harloe Rae
Photographer: Wander Aguiar
Interior design: Champagne Book Design

novels by
HARLOE RAE

Reclusive Standalones
Redefining Us
Forget You Not

#BitterSweetHeat Standalones
Gent
Miss
Lass

Silo Springs Standalones
Breaker
Keeper
Loner

Quad Pod Babe Squad Standalones
Leave Him Loved
Something Like Hate
There's Always Someday
Doing It Right

I'd Tap That (Knox Creek Standalones)
Wrong for You
Yours to Catch

Complete Standalones
Watch Me Follow
Ask Me Why
Left for Wild
Lost in Him
Mine For Yours

Screwed Up (part of the Bayside Heroes standalones)

For Stacey and Candi.
Thanks for everything.

And to giving your smutty side the freedom to go wild
whenever the mood strikes, in whatever capacity that might be.
Read responsibly.

thank you!

Yours to Catch is my twentieth book baby. That's surreal to even type. I think this one is extra special. Garrett and Grace took me on an unforgettable ride that I'll cherish forever. Here's to hoping they treat you to the same adventure.

This crazy amazing dream of mine is a reality because of you. Without you, wonderful reader, this author journey would be a very different road. Thanks for giving me the opportunity to continue doing what I love—writing swoony romance books. Please know how much I appreciate you. Then, now, and always.

I need to thank my fantastic husband and my two adorable children for giving me purpose along with unconditional grace, especially as a deadline nears. Major love to Heather, Renee, Shain, Jackie, and Kate for being there to support me through the thick and thin. To Stacey, Candi, Alex, Keri, Bobbie, Lacie, and Kayla for being such a huge part of my publishing process. To Harloe's Hotties for being the best group ever. To the readers, reviewers, influencers, BookTokers, and Bookstagrammers for everything they do to support us. There are many more who deserve endless gratitude. You know who you are. I'm forever thankful.

And one more thing. If you enjoyed *Yours to Catch*, I would greatly appreciate it if you could take a moment to leave a review. These are priceless and help new readers find my books, which allows me to continue following my passion. You're marvelous!

Cheers to happily ever after and fantastic books.
xx
Harloe

playlist

"Bartender" | Lady A
"Just Breathe" | Pearl Jam
"Shake It Off | Taylor Swift
"World on Fire" | Nate Smith
"A Little Bit Yours | JP Saxe
"Almost Lover" | Jasmine Thompson
"Jealous of Myself" | Tenille Arts
"Falling Like The Stars" | James Arthur
"Dance With You" | Brett Young
"Walk Me Home" | P!nk
"Slow Dance" | AJ Mitchell and Ava Max
"I'll Never Love Again" | Lady Gaga and Bradley Cooper
"Just You and I" | Tom Walker
"Lay By Me" | Ruben
"Open Your Eyes" | Snow Patrol
"Feel Something" | P!nk
"Play Pretend" | Alex Simpson
"That Way" | Tate McRae
"It's Always Been You" | Caleb Hearn
"You Are In Love" | Taylor Swift

yours
TO CATCH

"I know my worth, and it's not measured by fleeting attention or empty promises. I'll only settle for a soul-deep connection since that's not settling at all."—Grace Howard

prologue

Grace

WHO WOULD'VE THOUGHT A PLACE REFERRED TO as 'the cock den' could have potential? Certainly not me.

Yet here I sit, surveying the scene with approval. A relaxed energy ripples across the room even though there's a Friday night crowd. That calm is inviting, which is rare for an outsider to find in a town this small. The welcome feeling extends to the booths along the outer edge that are the perfect size to get better acquainted. But the chill vibe and cozy seating options aren't what hold the most appeal.

Attractive men fill the space in a vast majority. The uneven ratio makes it seem like these guys have been planted on purpose for single ladies such as me. Abbie's preferred location while on the prowl is determined to earn my vote as well. I might be quick to agree if I'm left alone much longer. Maybe that's why my best friend is running late. Or perhaps she's very thoughtful to let me sample the goods prior to her arrival.

Loud laughter draws my attention toward the main attraction in Roosters. Behind the expansive bar that monopolizes the room, a guy is putting on a performance while pouring liquor into a shaker. He flips three bottles at once to earn applause from his adoring fans. Not that I can blame the handful of women currently drooling on the counter for him. His smile steals the breath from my lungs.

I'm openly staring at this point, but the man is irresistible and seductive. Like cuddling by a steamy fire after freezing my tits off in the winter months. That level of smolder results in girls doing unmentionable things in public restrooms. On cue, visuals of him demanding dirty deeds from me pepper my mind. Heat spreads through me and I'm suddenly very thirsty. My fingers blindly pluck the cherry from my drained glass. The sugary fruit soothes my dry throat, allowing me to continue gawking in comfort.

He saunters past his captivated audience at the counter, knowing full well the impact his presence has on them. His broad frame is defined with muscles and confidence. There's just enough stubble on his jaw to chafe after delivering toe-curling friction. Deep dimples appear when he smirks. I nearly sway in my chair at the sight from this safe distance. The ones in direct vicinity openly wilt and swoon from hydration overload to their nether regions.

Dark hair gleams under the overhead lights, the rich chocolate shade streaked with a mesmerizing shine, while blue eyes appraise the room. It's a stark contrast we share, and my imagination gallops off into the sunset. The house has a picket fence—painted sunny yellow because we're not a total cliché—surrounding a grassy yard where our two kids and adopted mutt play. A smile curls my lips at the pleasant visual. In my defense, it's only natural to conjure a fantasy fit for the occasion.

As if hearing the fictitious future I've created for us, he sidles up against the rail to address a customer. His elbow rests on the glossy wood when he leans in. Ropy veins snake along his tattooed forearm—my absolute downfall. I sigh and cradle my cheek on an open palm. Had I met him a few months ago, this would be a very different story.

That doesn't mean I can't appreciate the view, though. At least until an unfortunate blockade cuts the show short. My gaze narrows on the masculine figure, drifting upward until settling on his face. It doesn't take more than a passing glance to determine his boyish features lack the burly edge of the sexy bartender. I raise my brows in question.

His wag in response. "Can I buy you a drink?"

Before I can answer, Abbie appears out of nowhere and drops onto the seat across from me. "I'd love a margarita. Extra salt on the rim. Thanks, beefcake."

He blinks at her timely arrival. "Huh?"

She mirrors his flat expression, then a thought must occur to her. "Oh, gosh. Where are my manners? Please, and thank you."

The guy still looks dumbfounded, his mouth moving silently for several beats. "Um, you're welcome?"

"We'll see." Her acquired tastes give him a calculating once-over. Then my friend glances at me. "Do you want a refill?"

"I'll get it myself." Ulterior motives make a tasty garnish.

"He literally just offered."

"In hopes I'd provide something in return," I counter. I make a slicing motion to indicate my non-interest.

Abbie scoffs and shifts her attention to the guy, only to find him missing. A pout replaces her coy grin. "Do you think he went to get my beverage?"

"Highly doubt it."

"Meh, his loss." A noncommittal noise chirps from her. "There's plenty more where he came from."

I hum in response. My focus travels back to the sex on a stick who's deep-fried in untamed hunger and kinky explorations. He probably delivers multiple orgasms faster than popping caps off beer bottles. His biceps flex while he completes the latter task. The jerky motion sends my mind straight to the gutter.

"Oh, my. Has someone piqued your interest?"

My gaze doesn't stray from the direction that will more than likely lead to a dead end. I manage to string a few consonants together into unintelligible nonsense.

She laughs and swivels in her seat to search for the target. "Who are you ogling?"

I force my focus off the bartender. "Huh?"

Her butt lifts from the chair while she scans the crowd. "Does this mystery man meet the criteria?"

"He probably isn't interested in a serious relationship," I mutter.

Abbie pauses her seeking efforts to study me. "You're really sticking to that?"

I frown at her disbelief. Not that I'm surprised. There are plenty of people who scoff at my desire to settle down at the ripe age of twenty-three. This isn't the first time that the ballbuster sharing this table with me has shared her doubt. It probably won't be the last. But her difference in opinion won't impact my decision. I've traveled down the meaningless fling route, only to discover it leaves me feeling empty.

My shoulder lifts in a lopsided shrug. "Casual dating isn't for me, Abs. Been there, done that, more than ready to break the cycle. I want substance and stability. Someone to plant roots with."

"Throw caution to the wind, fall without fear, and dive into the unknown?"

"That sounds lovely," I coo.

"You wanna get pierced by Cupid's arrow?"

"Um, sure." But my tone is bordering on suspicious.

"A meaty bone you can gnaw on all night long?" She gnashes her teeth.

I scoff as realization strikes. "Very funny. For a second there, I thought you were being serious."

"About losing my fellow freaky fiend to coupledom? It's an adjustment."

"As if I was ever in your lustful league." The suggestion is laughable.

Even during the short stint when I let my expectations slip into no-strings territory, there wasn't a comparison between our exploits. But that's how we balance each other. Unlike me, Abbie's needs are thoroughly satisfied by temporary affections. Her motto is whenever the mood strikes with whatever hot stranger that she deems fuckable. I'll always give her my blessing—along with zero judgment—for doing what I can't.

"Whatever. I still notice the loss." Her hair flutters off her forehead when she forces an exhale. "Your mythical mister still has to prove his worth before I'll approve."

"I have to find him first." Without permission, my eyes drift to the roguish flirt currently passing out shots like candy at a parade.

Abbie follows my stare to catch who I'm looking at. A low whistle escapes her. "Well, shit. That's Garrett Foster."

The trance he's indirectly holding me under breaks as she reveals his identity. "You know him?"

"He's one of the owners," she replies.

No wonder he appears to be in his element. Each move he makes exudes comfort and control. He belongs behind the bar, shamelessly charming his harem. There's probably nowhere else he'd rather be.

A determination solidifies in this moment as I continue appraising him. It's become apparent that his most appealing attribute is how he showers every admirer with equal attention, regardless of her shape and size. That knowledge boosts the comfort I've fought long and hard to find in my own skin. It makes him all the more dangerous.

Abbie prattles on while I treat myself to another not-so-sneaky peek. "The ladies love him. It's no secret that he's the favorite. Ridge and Drake can't compete."

"And they are…?"

"The other owners. Together they're a trifecta of panty-melting temptation. Garrett is the most visible in the front of the house, though. His charm is like a sticky trap for the barflies. People naturally flock to him. It's that charisma. Can't be taught." Her voice is dreamy as she parks her chin on a closed fist and flutters her lashes in his direction.

"He definitely seems to draw attention to himself."

"Magnetic," she muses. "He's a super nice guy too."

"Oh?" My lifted spirits munch on that crumb of intel.

She nods absently. "But unless you're willing to ditch that newfound code of commitment, I'd strongly suggest looking elsewhere. He's the polar opposite of what you're in the market to find."

I suspected as much. That doesn't stop disappointment from slumping my shoulders. "Oh."

Abbie refocuses on me. Her expression is warm with understanding. "Bummer, huh?"

"Meh, I didn't dare get my hopes up. It's safer to assume he's not my type until evidence confirms otherwise. But if nothing else, he's a stellar testament to my willpower."

"Clench that resolve," she groans.

Laughter snuffs out the momentary gloom. "You're ridiculous."

"Me? You're the one denying yourself several orgasms, at the very least. That hottie's talents extend well beyond mixing a cocktail." She blindly waves at the man in mention, as if I'm not already staring at him.

"Speaking from experience?"

"Not personally, but the lucky ladies aren't shy about sharing the sordid details."

My stomach sours and I suddenly feel queasy. "How romantic."

"What do you expect? Gossip travels fast in a community this tightly knit."

"I wouldn't know." Home for me is an expansive city twenty miles north with a population nearing one hundred thousand.

"Well, for your information, bedding Garrett Foster is juicy bragging material."

"Noted. It's probably good that I'm only in Knox Creek during daylight, surrounded by children."

"Unless a certain local convinces you to stay after the nanny duties are done." Abbie wiggles her eyebrows.

I giggle again and allow my concentration to settle on a framed jersey hanging on the wall. "Either way, I'd rather be blissfully ignorant about my future husband's previous relationships."

"Oh, just relationships? Maybe Garrett is still in the running."

"How so?"

"The story I've always heard is that he's only ever dated one girl for the long-term. She broke his gentle heart." Her lips droop into a frown.

There might be common ground to conquer. "Which led to?"

She waves off my question that might as well be rhetorical. "You don't need me to fill in the blanks. Just go talk to him. There's no harm in that. I bet he'd check off several boxes in a matter of seconds."

I grin at her reference to my list of required qualities. It's become somewhat of a joke. "You already told me that he's not the right choice."

"Maybe you'll be the one to flip his permanent bachelor status."

I snort. "Not a chance. Besides, he's too…"

"Sexy?"

A sharp nod is my initial response. "Along with several other shallow traits including, but not limited to, preoccupied."

Abbie glances toward the bar where Garrett is carelessly dumping the contents of an unlabeled liquor bottle directly into a woman's mouth. "Ah, I see what you mean."

"I'm sure it comes with the territory, but he doesn't appear ready to change his feathers."

A crease dents her brow inward. "Huh?"

"Like a tiger and his stripes, but Garrett is a rooster."

She thumps her forehead. "Very clever."

"Thanks." I blow her an air kiss.

"Do you want to stick around for another round or are you throwing in the towel?"

"It's barely nine o'clock. I'm not that picky," I defend.

"You're not. But," she points at me with my discarded straw, "most guys our age aren't interested in settling down. Especially in a place like this."

"This bar was your choice," I argue.

"Well, duh. I wanna get laid." She winks. "Next time, you choose."

"Deal."

"Until then, you should order a Tie Me to the Bedpost from Garrett. Get me one too."

I sputter on my next breath. "Is that an actual drink?"

"Go find out." She sweeps an arm toward a specific section of the room.

"My neglected lady bits won't appreciate the tease."

"Another challenge for your freshly forged chastity belt.

Look but don't touch. Take a long whiff of his manly scent." Abbie pauses for dramatic impact while drawing in a breath. "Or treat yourself to a bang-a-thon, just this once. It's like cheating on your diet."

"No." I shake my head.

"Why not? You can get back on it tomorrow."

"That's how bad habits thrive, not to mention I just started this resolution on the first of the year. It's barely mid-March."

"Far as I'm concerned, you've put in enough of a valiant effort. I mean, aside from your outfit." Her gaze sweeps along my upper half that's in clear view.

"What's wrong with what I'm wearing?" I glance down to see if a stain is earning her distaste.

"Is that a cardigan?" Her tone is steeped in mock horror.

I fiddle with a pearly button. "It gives off a polished impression that suggests I'm classy."

She snorts. "Uh-huh, and the amount of cleavage spilling from your dress pairs quite nicely."

My flat expression reflects how lacking I find her humor. "There's only so much I can do to conceal my generous assets."

"Girl, stop. Your lush thickness is meant to be envied—or worshiped depending on the person leering. Ditch the sweater and flaunt your tatas like the secret weapons they are." Her praise fluffs my confidence as intended.

But still, my priorities don't waiver. "I'm not joking about this, Abs. Casual dating is behind me. Committed relationships only. The more serious the better. I want the real deal with a guy who will appreciate each spare inch my waistline has to offer. It's important to me, especially after..." I let the meaning trail off.

She sighs, guilt splashing across her features. "You're right. I should be more supportive. Mr. Marriage Proposal on the Fifth Date will show up eventually."

My eyes roll at her exaggeration. "That's the spirit."

"In the meantime, I hope you bought extra batteries. Those top-drawer boyfriends are about to come in handy and cause quite a buzz. Pun intended." She cackles in comedic fashion.

"They were a parting gift from my loose standards. I'm well equipped to handle a drought."

"This calls for a toast." Abbie lifts a fake glass in a mock salute. "Cheers to cobwebs in your vagina and more man-whores for me."

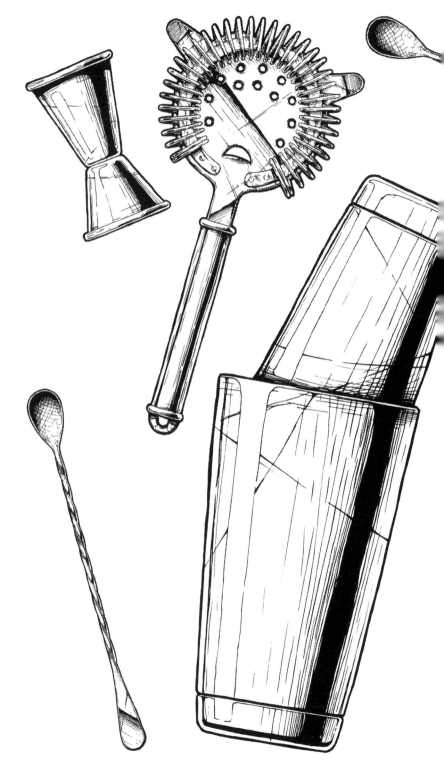

chapter one

Garrett

"How's it going over there, big guy?" I holler across the temporary patio to gain a reaction from the scowling brute who's posted in the opposite corner.

Ridge doesn't disappoint. His expression darkens as he glares at me from behind his portable bar cart. My buddy is known as the least approachable Roosters' owner for a reason. As a former defenseman, the hockey star maintains a steely guard that's fit for a professional bruiser. That harsh shield doesn't slip even while he's slinging drinks at the town's annual spring festival.

"Just grand," he bellows in response.

This isn't Ridge's preferred role. The permanent frown he's wearing lets everyone in the direct vicinity know it. That doesn't discourage a horde of ladies from waiting patiently to try their luck at improving the grump's mood.

His gaze scours the thirsty customers gathered in front of his station. It's almost as if he's searching for someone in particular. Or maybe he's just looking for the end that's no-where near. The line resembles a continuous stream.

I cast my sights on those gathered in our sectioned-off area, and then to the overflow waiting for entry on Main Street. "Damn fine turnout today. Might be the busiest Knox Creek has seen."

Ridge shrugs in that noncommittal way of his and re-sumes taking orders. I do the same in hopes that a break in congestion will magically appear. With that goal in mind, the motions of serving our loyal patrons blur into a seamless flow until I'm lost in the task. Shmooze, pour, shake when necessary, shmooze again, accept payment, leave them want-ing more, and repeat. It's a reliable routine that increases our business with each passing season.

The support from our small community never ceases to amaze me. That's precisely why I convinced Ridge and Drake—the third and final piece in our partnership—to open shop in my hometown. I didn't have to twist their arms too hard to invest. Both have more money than they could spend responsibly. It's still a shock they chose to move here to be involved in the daily grind, though.

A lull in the chaos hits at mid-afternoon to offer a much-needed reprieve. Not a moment too soon as sweat prepares to drip off my balls. Previous experience suggests this relief will be brief, and I don't hesitate to guzzle a bottle of water. Cool liquid dribbles down my chin as I drink without care.

That's when I spot a friendly face laughing at my hasty methods. Harper Wilson is crossing the outdoor space in a hurry, planning to take advantage of the calm as well. Our bar's most beloved booze fetcher is flanked by her long-awaited happily-ever-after. Jacob Evans is nothing short of an asshole, but he finally got some much-needed sense smacked into him.

His little girl deserves credit for bringing the two back together. Rumor had it that six-year-old Sydney was adamant about Harper becoming her real mom. Speaking of the town's gossips, those troublemakers were more than likely involved in the matchmaking too. I'd accept a pat on the back for hiring my sister's best friend while knowing full well Roosters is Jake's favorite place to unwind. In the end, it was a team effort that's now flourishing.

I smile at the approaching trio, but a lone figure snatches my focus before they reach me. The woman is instantly recognizable. She drove me to distraction last month, which led to Harper transforming Roosters into a dance club for an entire night. It's been impossible to forget her hypnotic allure. That trance once again renders me useless.

Harper is talking to her, but I only hear the erratic thrash of my desire. The bombshell that's wrecking my composure is breathtaking in a plain t-shirt and jeans. No frills or fuss, which suits my style just fine.

Her shapely figure commands my full concentration. As if tethered, I'm incapable of looking away. She's lush curves and endless pleasure wrapped in one fuckable package. My mouth goes dry as I treat myself to a languid perusal of those supple lines that connect to create an irresistible form. Somewhere in the recesses of my lust-addled brain, I realize that it's not polite to ogle her this way.

My creeper status warns me to retreat when Sydney joins their conversation. A slow blink does little to alleviate the pressure in my groin. In a weak attempt to sever this daze—and regain control from my cock—I forcefully avert my gaze off her tits. The button on her purse strap halts my decent intentions. I cough to free myself from the stupor.

"Holy shit," I blurt. "You're my other half."

Harper squeaks in outrage and claps her palms over Syd's ears. Then she pins me with a glare. "Can you watch your language?"

The pinch in my features is meant to be apologetic. But

in reality, I'm too transfixed by the raven-haired beauty to notice much else. "We're meant to be."

She raises her hands to strike my wayward nonsense. "I just want a cocktail."

"Hold the tail?" I wag my brows to regain the trustworthy charm that never steers me wrong. "We can save that for later. For now, we need to celebrate. Your number is the same as mine. Fifty-three."

Her gaze narrows on the button I have proudly displayed on my shirt. Then she glances at the identical pin attached to her purse strap. "I forgot about that."

"It's tradition," I hoot and spread my arms wide. "The anticipation of meeting your match keeps you searching the crowd."

My exaggerated reaction makes this casual game sound like the stars aligned to bring us together. Maybe there's a bit of destiny involved. Not that I believe in fate. In reality, every attendee is given a button at the entrance with the incentive of a prize. The festival ritual is forgotten more often than not. I'd been guilty of doing just that until this chick returned to my sights.

"That's quite a romantic sentiment." She gives me another once-over. "Front and center, huh?"

"Didn't want the one meant for me to miss it." I tap the number pinned smack dab in the middle of my chest. Then I tack on a smirk to showcase my dimples. These weapons of destruction have an undefeated record against panties. The protective layer melts off before the ladies know what hit them.

This girl is my latest target and appears caught under the influence. After staring openly for several seconds, she rips her gaze off me. "And now that you've found her?"

"Pretty sure you found me, soulmate."

She snorts at the nickname. "Not on purpose."

"Isn't that how the best love stories begin?" I saunter out from behind the portable bar cart to stand beside her. "What's your name?"

A suspicious brow quirks at my close proximity. "Thought it was soulmate?"

"Oh, you're already agreeing to be mine?" Warmth thrums in a downward trek to stroke my ego.

She presses her lips into a flat line. "Hardly. I'm Grace, and you're not my type."

Sydney gasps, cutting off any chance for me to claim otherwise. "That's my middle name! We're like almost twins."

Grace radiates pure happiness at her remark. "Aww, I feel extremely fortunate. That's really special."

"Do you know what twins are?" Syd leans in before her new gal pal can consider responding. "It's when a mommy has two babies in her belly."

Grace widens her eyes for the little girl's sake. "Bet that gets heavy, huh?"

Sydney nods, sending her pigtail braids flying. "Uh-huh, super-duper. Do you know how the twins get in her tummy?"

Harper suddenly jolts into action, as if running interference on this conversation is vital. "Let's not spoil the surprise, superstar. Grace can research on her own."

She shrugs and snags a cherry from the garnish caddy. "M'kay."

So," I begin to regain the spotlight. "What're you doing tonight, Grace?"

"I have a date." Long lashes flutter at me.

The smile I give her is equally endearing. "With me? That's a tad presumptuous, but I'd love to."

"You're not my type," she reminds in a sing-song tone.

"What makes you so sure?" Because I'm more than prepared to defend my case stating the opposite.

"The performance I witnessed at your bar was plenty, Garrett."

And just like that, she reveals that I left an impression on her as well. My chest suddenly expands to twice its regular size. "I don't recall introducing myself. Did you ask around about me after visiting Roosters?"

Her cheeks flame into a rosy hue that has little to do with the warm weather. "Um, no. My friend is a regular and filled me in on your… tastes in women."

"Is that so?" I bend lower into her personal space, inhaling sweet vanilla and ripe temptation. "Give me a chance to change your mind about me."

Grace's unwavering eye contact could make a weaker man squirm. "Are you looking for a serious relationship?"

"Absolutely not." And never again. Images of my worst mistake still haunt me all these years later.

She imitates the sound of a buzzer. "Wrong answer."

My tongue feels tied as what's meant to be an easy opportunity begins to evade me. "Uh, well…"

"That's what I thought." Her huff might as well be a smack to the back of my head. "I'm in the market to settle down. Period."

And there goes my erection. Damn. I awkwardly shift while my dick shrivels as if dunked in an ice bath.

Still, I can't deny giving her credit for being bold. It's damn impressive. This woman knows what she wants and isn't afraid to voice her demands for all to hear. That's a trait I can admire, even if I want nothing to do with her commitment.

Silence descends on our small huddle. It seems I'm not the only one offering Grace internal praise. Harper's jaw has been hanging slack long enough to catch flies. When she snaps out of the shero worship, her focus swivels from me to Grace.

She taps her lips and I brace for whatever is about to spill free. "This could make for an interesting story."

I chuckle, but tension lingers between my shoulders. "I guess we'll have to wait and see."

Grace cracks a grin, rolling her eyes for good measure. That small gesture releases the pressure valve between us. "For now, how about you fix me a drink?"

I inhale my first decent breath in what feels like hours. My bravado rebounds at the mention of the simple task. "What's the lady's preferred poison?"

"Surprise me." Her voice drips seduction from a bottomless tap that I could get drunk on.

The free rein she innocently provides rouses images that would probably offend her. Instead of sharing my dirty mind, I gulp to pour the intoxicating suggestions into the gutter where they belong. My feet round the counter and I settle into the familiar motions to do her bidding. The urge to keep her talking prods at me while I dump ingredients into a shaker.

"Tell me about this date you have tonight," I say while reaching for the pineapple juice.

Suspicion enters her expression again. "Why do you want to know?"

"I'm curious about your strategy. Most guys I know would fuck off straight to the exit after hearing a girl wants to settle down. Especially if you just started seeing each other. Is this dude aware of your specific desires?"

Grace shivers over that last word. The reaction is small, but I'm too fascinated by her every move to miss a single blink. "We haven't met yet."

"Ah, I see. How long do you wait before stating your expectation?"

She shrugs. "It depends on how things are going. If I'm being totally honest, there hasn't been a need for me to use my list lately."

I notice Harper, Sydney, and Jake wander off. There's also a line beginning to form behind Grace. My gut clenches at the sight. The last thing I want is for her to feel a sense of urgency and leave. A discreet chin lift from me directs them toward Drake's station.

"Your list?" I ask in an effort to get back on track.

"Of preferred qualities," Grace explains.

I suck my lips between my teeth to stifle a laugh. This girl is just too damn cute. "What's included on this list?"

"The most important traits I'm looking for in a husband." She prattles that statement in a flippant tone one would use to recite daily activities.

Meanwhile, I nearly choke just hearing that term leave her mouth. "Well, shit. Why haven't you referenced it recently if these characteristics are that vital?"

The confidence in her posture waivers ever so slightly. "It hurts to admit, but I haven't had a second date since my resolution started."

My hand pauses in midair, the vodka bottle hovering in a precarious position. "Which was when?"

"January first."

I whistle. "Four and a half months?"

"The losing streak stretches well beyond that." Her lush mouth dips into a pout.

"Well, that sucks." Not that I'm all that shocked considering her endgame. "Hopefully this will turn the odds in your favor."

After a final inspection, I set the specialty beverage on the bar top for her approval. An oversized mason jar showcases the tropical concoction. The different flavored layers provide a colorful presentation. In addition to the visual pleasure, there's enough fruit on the rim to be considered an afternoon snack.

Her blue eyes sparkle in appreciation. "How pretty. Is this one of your signature drinks for Swing into Spring?"

"Nah, this is just a little something I whipped up for you."

Grace clutches her palms over her chest. "Aww, thank you. What is it?"

"Let's call it…" I pause to think of an appropriate title. "Ultimate Distraction."

"And why would we choose that?"

"It's inspired by you."

She presses a fluttered hand to her forehead, pretending to swoon. "Are you a closet romantic?"

"Are you trying to flatline my dick permanently, woman?" My balls threaten to shrivel at the prospect alone.

Loud laughter escapes her. "Don't worry, bartender. I'd never do that to your harem. How much do I owe you?"

"This one is on the house. Maybe it will lift your spirits along with your skirt." I drop a cocktail straw into her drink.

"That's sweet. Mostly. But do you have a bigger one?" She frowns at the stir stick like it's offensive.

I bite my knuckles with a growl. "Damn, baby. Why didn't you say so sooner? I can give you a solid nine inches if you're willing to drop the serious relationship requirement for a night."

"Only if you're willing to be my Prince Charming for always. Why should I be the one to sacrifice what I want?" She puckers her lips in an erotic display that gets my blood pumping too hot.

I almost concede before logic smacks me. "Afraid I can't agree to those terms."

Her sigh attempts to convince me that she's disappointed. "Then I guess this is where we part ways."

"Don't be bleak." I grab a regular-sized straw and slide it into her glass. "Our paths will cross again."

Grace tosses me a wink before snagging her drink from the counter. "I'll leave that up to you, soulmate."

chapter two

Grace

JOY FOSTER BEAMS FROM HER SPOT BESIDE ME ON THE bench. "Okay, I've made my decision. The job is yours."

I clasp my hands together in an attempt to corral my excitement. "Really?"

The new mother nods. "Absolutely. There's nothing left to consider. Your references speak for themselves. I'm getting a super comforting vibe from you. My fiancé put me in charge, which means he's on board too." She leans closer to share her final point. "And full disclosure, it's tough to find a reliable sitter to fill random hours in this town."

My heart swells at her faith in me. "Wow, that means a lot. You won't regret it."

"I'm confident in my choice. Belle agrees. Don't you, precious angel?" She simply glows while making googly eyes at the baby girl who's dozing in her stroller.

A mist blurs my vision while I indulge in their sacred bond. It's moments like these that solidify my decision to find a partner to share this life with. Sooner rather than later. And if we're lucky, there will be children included in our journey.

Joy nuzzles her newborn's nose before returning her focus to me. "This might seem like a strange question, but did you set out to become a nanny or was it more of a happy accident?"

"Um, both? If that's an appropriate answer." I take a pause to wipe at my wet lashes and compose myself. "When I only had a few months left of college, a family friend introduced me to Wanda Nelson. She was pregnant with her daughter and had a rambunctious toddler at home. What was meant to be a summer gig to offer a helping hand during the transition turned into a permanent position. And now, here I am, fortunate enough to care for Belle as well."

"We're very pleased to have found you. That's definitely one consistent factor in a small town. Talk travels fast. It just so happened to swing in our favor for once." She rolls her eyes, more than likely thinking about the rumors constantly churning in Knox Creek.

I bob my head in agreement. "It's useful in this case that everybody knows everybody. Abbie was all too eager to pass along the news. She's been trying to get me to move here since I started working for the Nelson family two years ago."

Joy swivels on her seat to face me. "You should. It's such a great community."

With limited dating potential. But I don't voice that concern. I compromise with a truth. "It's being considered."

She chews on her bottom lip. "Do you plan to make a career change soon? Just so I can prepare for how long you'll be available."

"To be perfectly honest, I'm extremely fulfilled with this role. I couldn't have picked a more suitable field whether I stumbled into it or not. The kids are incredible. There's no reason to leave something I'm enjoying, right? At least until I start a family of my own."

"Ohhhh," she croons. "Is that already in progress?"

"Not even close," I laugh. "First, I need to ditch my singleton status."

She squints against the sunlight. "Ah, yes. That can be challenging."

On cue, a figure in motion across the park catches my attention. I turn to see none other than Garrett running along a paved path. He's shirtless, which just isn't fair. Tan skin, sculpted muscles, and colorful tattoos fill my vision. Even from this distance, I can see sweat streaking down his chiseled abdomen. Heat infuses me in a fiery wave that sets me ablaze. My throat is suddenly dry, which is becoming an inconvenient recurrence whenever he's near. I part my lips in a weak attempt to draw in a much-needed breath.

"Do you want to borrow Belle's bib?" Joy's voice is barely recognizable.

"Huh?" But there's no looking away from sinful temptation in the flesh.

A pink cloth suddenly blocks my view. "To mop up the drool."

That wrenches me from the foolish gawking. I swipe at my chin as flames burn my cheeks. "Good grief, I'm sorry. That was extremely unprofessional. Please don't hold this against me."

She's laughing too hard to appreciate my apology. Tears are nearly spilling from her eyes. "Oh, gosh. Don't even. I understand completely. My body is pumped full of enough raging hormones to satisfy an entire hockey team if I desire. Cole can barely handle my sex drive."

"I doubt he's complaining," I joke in an effort to bury my embarrassment.

"Not even a little bit. Who's the lucky duck to get you flustered?" Joy scours the open field for suitable suspects. A loud gag rips from her in the next second. "Ugh, gross."

"What?" I don't dare look at the source of her upset.

"My stupid brother is over there, flaunting his male ego." She makes another disgusted noise.

"Your—?" My voice slams to a halt as realization strikes. "Ah, crud buckets. Foster."

"That's our last name. Don't wear it out," she sings.

"I never would've made that connection." Which pummels me with another punch of humiliation. "You don't really look alike."

"Yes, the attractive genes were saved for me." Then she quirks a brow. "You know my brother?"

"He's my soulmate," I mumble.

Joy lets her jaw hang slack. "Excuse me?"

"Not actually," I rush to explain. "Our numbers matched at the spring festival thing. It's not a big deal."

She studies me for several tense seconds. "But you just called him your soulmate."

"He started it," I defend. "Just as a joke."

"Okay, now you're making sense. 'Cause I was gonna say," she mutters. "That nincompoop has trouble committing strictly to boxers or briefs. He switches off to ensure his detached reputation remains intact. I've been tempted to buy him a dog just to see if he's capable of forming an attachment to something other than family or his bar."

"Is he that opposed to commitment?" Something about the extreme definition doesn't sit right with me.

"Meh, not really. I'm exaggerating. Mostly. He just doesn't want to settle down. As in never ever. But otherwise, he's great. Dependable where it counts, you know?"

I make the mistake of peeking over to where Garrett is stretching against a tree. One harmless glance is enough to render me incoherent. "Uh-huh, I can see that."

"This should be entertaining." Her smile takes a conniving turn that prickles the skin on the back of my neck.

"Please don't—"

Before I can finish my request, Joy is catcalling her brother from where we sit several yards away. She gestures wildly for good measure. "Hey, lover boy! Over here. Yoo-hoo!"

Garrett whips his head in our direction. A megawatt smile stretches his irresistible appeal to a point I might never recover from. Damn those dimples. I muffle a whimper while trying to pretend to be unaffected. The effort is in vain since Joy caught me ogling him not even five minutes ago. She's well aware of my current struggle, not bothering to tamp down a victorious giggle.

To make matters worse, Garrett jogs toward us in all his hulking glory. The smooth pace showcases his reincarnated Adonis physique. No man should look that good, especially one who's determined to remain single. Tack on his charm and wit and seal him as the entire package.

My temperature rises with each foot he erases until I'm set to sweltering. If twat flutters exist, I'm experiencing an episode powerful enough to climax. I force my concentration to focus on counting blades of grass or I'm likely to spontaneously combust.

"Hello, ladies." He's not winded in the slightest. Go figure.

Joy wiggles her fingers at him. "Hey, bro. Didn't expect to find you frolicking about."

"This is my usual route," he explains. His sharp gaze shifts from his sister to me. "How do you two know each other?"

"It's a funny story," I note absently.

"Grace is your niece's new nanny," Joy chirps.

His eyes bulge. "No shit?"

"Language," she scolds.

Garrett grunts. "Belle doesn't understand me."

"Not yet, no. You should change your bad habits before she can. Be proactive."

"Fine, whatever. Why didn't you tell me you were hiring a nanny?"

Joy snorts. "Did you want to apply?"

He scrubs at the dark scruff coating his jaw. Those same thick fingers comb through his damp hair to further tickle my restraint. "I could try to shift my schedule."

"That's very generous, but we've got the situation handled." She gestures at me. "I believe you're already acquainted."

"Something like that," I hedge.

Garrett pins me with the full intensity of his smolder. "Aww, come on now. Don't give our fierce attraction the cold shoulder. We're way too hot for that. I'm willing to bet there's a fire burning just for me in your—"

Joy slices through the space separating us from him. "Grace is off limits."

"Telling me she's forbidden fruit isn't your wisest move." His words are for her, yet he doesn't remove his stare from me. "But don't fret, sissy. I'm aware that I don't meet her standards."

I grumble under my breath about his wounded pride. "You don't have to make me sound hard to please."

His fingers lift, almost close enough to touch, before he drops his hand. "I'd never mistake you as such. If you give me the chance, I'll prove just how easily I can please you. Over and over and—"

"Now that you mention it," Joy cuts in. "You might be of assistance after all."

His attention shifts to her after a delayed pause. "Oh?"

"Reliable sources report that our mutual friend is in the market for a baby daddy." She hikes her thumb in my direction as if there's another sap in our vicinity who's desperate to settle down.

I hold up a hand to ward off any confusion. "No, that's actually not—"

But Joy doesn't take my correction into consideration. "Would you care to donate sperm purely for reproduction purposes? I'm sure your swimmers are adequate. Probably." She suddenly folds in half and pretends to vomit. "Yuck. Why am I talking about my brother's semen?"

"Beats me," I muse. I'm more concerned about the crooked spin this entire conversation has taken.

"Freaking ewwwww," she spits.

Garrett appears unfazed by her theatrics. "If you're done being a drama queen, I'd like to hold my niece."

"She's sleeping." Joy points to where her daughter is snoozing in the stroller.

"I make a decent pillow." He mimics clutching a priceless bundle against his chest.

A telltale clench signals that my ovaries are preparing for the impending onslaught. My nails pierce into the wood bench to stop me from doing something I'll regret, such as volunteering to be cradled in his arms. I'm saved by my new employer's disgruntled huff.

"You're sweaty." She wrinkles her nose.

He glances down at his slick torso. "So? I don't complain when Belle's butt stinks."

"Puh-lease," his sister retorts. "She's two months old. Her poops are still adorable."

"Solid argument. We can smell adorable together." Garrett beckons for his niece again.

Her expression twists into another impressive grimace. "At least put on a shirt. You're dewy and moist."

Try as I might, a whimper escapes to protest her demand. There's little I can do to salvage my feigned indifference. But dammit, I'm not a quitter. "Yeah, do us all a favor and cover that pasty paleness. You're scaring off my prospects."

Joy snorts, which quickly morphs into undignified cackling. "Soulmates indeed. I figured you two would be entertaining, but I'm getting a hunch this will be something else entirely."

"Um, thanks?"

She waves off my uncertain gratitude, managing to stem her laughter into choppy snickers. "No, no. Thank you. This might be the worst best match our town has ever seen. And this girl"—she points to herself with both thumbs—"scored a front-row seat for the fireworks. Let the denial begin."

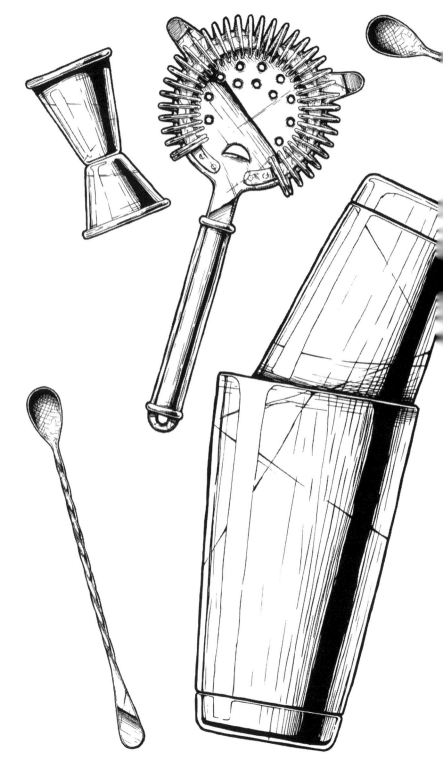

chapter three

Garrett

I SPY A CERTAIN BARTENDER STARING AT ME FROM THE bowels of territory better left ignored. Again. It's enough to derail my progress on polishing the wood counter. My hand pauses the endless task in order to give her the undivided attention she seems damn determined to receive.

"Is there something wrong?" There's even a concerned edge to my tone.

"Why don't you tell me?" Harper grins, not bothering to hide the fact that she's been watching my every move since her shift started.

I straighten and toss the rag into the nearest sink. "Nothing new. Just doing my job."

She props an elbow on the bar to indicate this will be a lengthy conversation. "You seem distracted."

"Me?" I grumble a few choice phrases about nosy employees and scrub over my stubbled jaw. "You're the one standing around doing nothing while on the clock."

"I'm checking on my boss. That's important."

Disbelief scoffs at her flimsy excuse. "Just spit it out, Harps. We have work to do."

My sister's best friend makes it a point to glance across the bar where only a few stools and tables are occupied. "I think we can spare a few moments to chat."

Ridge appears beside me from the shadows or wherever he's been lurking to avoid social interactions. "Are we discussing Foster's lady friend?"

The finer sex is quite fond of me, but there's only one who's left a lasting impression. On all of us, it seems. "Ah, the truth comes out."

Harper flattens her lips at the intrusion. "I was getting there, Brewster."

He snorts at the nickname. "Why beat around the bush?"

She bends at the waist while hacking up what I can only imagine is a lung. The coughing fit quickly transitions into giggles. "Damn, that was a good night."

I lean forward to pat her back. "You all right?"

"Fine," she croaks. "Just reminded me about Jake. He's fond of diving right in."

Bile churns in my gut. "I don't want to know."

"You really don't." Her wink is over the top.

"Fucking Evans," Ridge grunts. After a sharp jerk of his head to undoubtedly clear that horrific image, he refocuses on me. "Is this chick different from the rest?"

"Depends on your definition. This one in particular is in a hurry to walk down the aisle."

His brows bounce to his shaggy hairline. "The fuck?"

"That's not entirely true," Harper counters.

My gaze narrows on her. "How do you know?"

She shrugs. "Joy spilled the tea."

I wait for her to share more. When she doesn't, I roll my wrist to motion her onward. "And?"

"Oh, now you wanna talk?"

"He doesn't know what he wants," Ridge drawls.

I raise my hand. "He's right here, and wasn't aware we added barbecue to the menu. Are you planning to grill all night? Or is there a gangbang portion I can look forward to? I hope there's enough lube to go around."

"Don't worry your pretty pucker, Foster. I'm always prepared." His conviction clenches my butthole, even though there's zero threat of him swinging that way.

Harper hisses in a breath. "I better warn Callie that the backdoor isn't off limits if that's how you play. Sheesh, she's in for a crude cherry poppin.'"

He pins her with a glare. "What about Callie?"

"Be careful with her."

"What's that supposed to mean?"

She brushes off his worry. "We'll discuss it when you make your move. That is if you ever make an honest woman out of her."

"Deserves far better than me," he mutters.

"Chivalry at its finest. Anywho," Harper pivots the topic with a glance at me. "All joking aside, what's with your blatant refusal to even consider a serious relationship?"

Ridge rubs his chin. "Now that you mention it, he hasn't told me either."

And that's how I plan to keep it. The past is buried, along with my trust in fidelity. "I don't think it's fair for only one cowgirl to keep me saddled and ridden for the rest of my virile years. It's not considerate to the female population. More so, I'm not interested in being a prize pony. Period."

Harper's stare narrows into a shrewd point, peeling away more layers than I'm comfortable with. "Who broke your heart, wild stallion?"

I pinch the bridge of my nose. "We're done dissecting my nonexistent belief in love."

"Maybe it'll just take the right girl to restore your faith," she muses.

"Doubt it."

Harper swivels to the entrance in a purposeful action. "Why don't we ask her?"

As if staged, Grace opens the front door. She struts into my cock den like the last hen who has any clucks to give. A single once-over has me dizzy with want. Her tan skin glows under the dim lights. Long hair cascades in glossy waves, tempting me to fist the strands and bend her over the rail. I widen my stance to conceal the evidence of what that visual does to me. Grace's piercing stare meets mine as if my filthy imagination is whispering in her ear. A coy grin curls her painted lips, revealing that I'm busted either way.

My gaze drops again to appreciate the entire package she presents. Black fabric clings to her body in a seamless line. The tight dress is made for sin, along with each luscious curve it accentuates. Her figure is full and juicy, dripping with seduction. She reminds me of a ripe peach. Motion on my left reminds me that we're not alone in the room.

"Holy hotness," Harper praises from her stooped position beside me. "That woman is certifiably bangable. I'd totally wife her."

"You're already engaged," I remind.

"Jake won't care, but I suppose he did claim me first." She snaps her fingers. "Aw, shucks. But my loss is someone else's gain. She's gonna get hitched real quick."

That thought doesn't sit right with me, which I immediately smother. Especially when Grace slides onto the empty stool in front of me. Her keen awareness sweeps across the open space. A deep crease forms between her brows as she completes the inspection.

"Where is everyone?"

"Just waiting for you to arrive, soulmate." I wink at her.

Ridge and Harper exchange several murmured words. Their chatter draws Grace's attention away from me. Her eyes gravitate toward the retired hockey star. The urge to shift and block her visual path to him flexes my muscles. It's a pointless instinct, mostly because Ridge is only interested in one girl who's more than likely already tucked in bed. But more than that—Grace isn't mine. She never will be.

The reminder injects another dose of reality into me. I cast my most flirtatious smirk at her, the one reserved for big tippers. "Sit tight. Marriage material candidates will flock faster than we can serve them."

Her doubt peers at the empty seats surrounding her on every side. "I'll believe it when I see it."

"Such little faith," I scold.

"Hypocrite." A muffled cough calls me out.

A glance over my shoulder exposes the guilty party. I'm not sure when Drake wandered from the safety of his office sanctuary to join the peanut gallery. Now isn't the moment to evaluate his strange habits. A delicate throat clearing draws my attention back to where it belongs.

"Are you doing deals on specialty cocktails? Joy told me there's an event." Grace tucks some dark hair behind her ear.

I track the simple motion, my fingers itching to repeat it for her. "Is that so?"

"Uh-huh. Something like"—Grace leans in and lowers her voice—"Pussy in Paradise. I'm assuming that's your version of a ladies' night."

The whispering behind us grows in volume thanks to Drake's involvement. I'll never regret opening a bar with my two best friends, especially when they let me rule the roost, but this sudden hovering is making me wish their partnership was silent. These grumpy bastards need to get laid and leave me to handle business.

It's easy to ignore them when Grace spoils me with a

shy smile. "I'm getting the impression that your sister was stretching the truth."

"Just the clit." I spin a fingertip against my palm to mimic pleasuring that elusive bundle of nerves. "Tuesday evenings are notoriously slow. The entire day actually. I wish I could take credit for that creative title, though."

Harper smacks my arm. "We should have themed activity nights!"

I rub my forehead. "If you were left in charge, our casual sports bar would be renovated into a frilly dance club."

"So?"

"You already have one of those." I hitch a thumb at the building saturated in pink across Main Street. "Over there."

"No harm in spreading the goodness," she chirps.

"Roosters is just fine without additional fluff," I reason.

"Sure about that?" Grace gestures at the obvious lack of customer traffic.

"Hey," I chide. "You've been here when the place is packed."

"That's true. I've seen it get very busy." She waves at the loyal patrons that we've come to depend on.

The handful that are currently belly-up to the bar occupy a spot rain or shine. Harper takes that as a cue and trots off to check on them. Her motivations are more than likely spurred on by wanting to stick around for whatever happens next. Otherwise, I might be tempted to send her meddling ass home.

"I'd heard a newbie managed to get Foster's boxers in a twist. Or is it a briefs day?" Drake cuts in at my expense.

Unfortunately for him, my feathers are far from ruffled. I'll gladly take whatever shit they dish out if it leads to him getting out of his recent slump. "Commando, thanks for asking."

Grace audibly gulps, and I catch her focus lowering to my jeans. One downward tug at the zipper and my cock would spring free for her taking. I angle my hips forward in invitation.

"Hold the fuck on. Is this the chick you met that Harper keeps talking about? The one that distracted you to the point of agreeing to everything?" Drake nods at Grace while addressing me.

Her lips twist to the side. "Well, we didn't technically meet until the festival."

"So, you just drooled over each other from across the room? How adorable."

My features go blank as I gape at him. "Did you just say adorable?"

"Would you prefer another term?" Ridge almost cracks a grin. "Like soulmate?"

Grace's gaze shifts between my so-called friends. "Is this heckling normal?"

Drake shrugs. "Only when he shows a genuine interest in someone."

"We gotta get our rocks off somehow," Ridge adds.

I chuckle. "Yeah, the women in this town are wise enough to keep a safe distance."

Grace's expression beams brighter with each taunt we fling. "Should I feel honored?"

"Yes," they say in unison.

"Well then." She flips her hair. "Yet Garrett doesn't do relationships."

Drake tosses his hands in a defeated gesture. "Not every guy is built to be a love machine. Sex fiend? Absolutely." He points at me to eliminate any confusion. "At your service."

I bow for everyone's benefit and amusement. "It's a tough job, but I do my part for the good of humanity."

"Yes, you're extremely noble." He snorts and slaps me on the back. "We embrace his bachelor lifestyle. It's just fun to give him shit when he doesn't get the girl of his most recent desires."

"Ah, so I'm more of a challenge." There's no question in her tone.

My loud scoff draws her attention to me. "Nah, sweetheart. We're not meant to be fuck buddies."

"We could just be buddies," she offers in compromise.

I choke on the sharp denial slicing at my throat. "Whatever blows your skirt up. And we can begin our purely platonic arrangement by getting you a proper date."

Grace blinks at me. "You want to be my wingman?"

"Sure, why not? The clock is ticking. And it'll get these assholes off my case."

On cue, Ridge and Drake amble away to make themselves scarce. Plans of retribution are already brewing in my brain. But revenge will have to wait.

A breeze from the entrance resembles a monumental quake. Four guys saunter inside like their shit doesn't stink. The douche quad has no clue what's about to hit them.

"Well, well, well. Look at that." I jut my chin in their direction. "Fan the flames, Gracie. Eligible candidates are already catching a whiff of your smoldering loins."

chapter four

Grace

I t's been an hour since I pranced into Roosters under false pretenses. What I originally believed was a night I'd potentially get swept off my feet turned out to be a ploy. I can't find it in me to be the least bit upset with Joy, though.

Pussy in Paradise might be a farce, but Garrett's undivided attention is very real. His fierce stare makes me feel like I'm the only woman in this bar. Hell, maybe even in this entire town. That heady sensation launches into swoon territory when he slides a carefully crafted concoction across the wooden counter toward me.

"Oooooh, how pretty." I squirm on my stool, eager for a taste.

He parks a bent elbow on the bar. "Better be, considering its inspiration."

My cheeks warm from the implied compliment. A casual remark from him renders me speechless. I focus on his most recent creation in an attempt to gather my composure. Just like the cocktail he made for me at the festival, the drink is layered in multiple colors. An assortment of fruit accompanies sugar on the rim.

"Thank you," I murmur after a pause. "Does it have a name?"

"Let's call this one…" He inspects his handy work with narrowed eyes. "Wife Material."

There's a forceful lurch in my chest, as if my heart is desperate to break free. "Now you're just teasing me."

"Why would I do that?" His smirk exposes those devilish dimples that make me want to do wicked things.

I toy with my straw to stop myself from fondling the charming divots. "You think I'm silly for wanting commitment."

"Nah, sweetheart. I'd never toss shade onto your dreams. Aspire away. You do you, and I'll do me. We can meet in the middle to discuss our trials and tribulations."

"You want to hear about my dates?"

"Isn't that part of our friendly agreement?" His voice holds a raspy edge that curls my toes.

"I guess." My nose wrinkles to reveal layers of uncertainty. "In all honesty, this is uncharted territory for me."

"You and me both," he mutters.

"Really? I assumed you were an expert at dumping girls in the friend zone."

Garrett thrusts his head back, loud laughter booming from his depths. I'm struck by the sight of his bulky form shaking with the action. His stubbled throat moves to amplify the joy for everyone to soak in. My eyes feast on the view while drool threatens to spill free.

Amusement glitters in his gaze when he refocuses on me. "You're a fucking riot, Gracie."

"Thanks?"

"Trust me, women aren't usually interested in my friendship." Passion sizzles in his unwavering stare.

The temperature spikes and I almost fan my face. "Oh?"

"Would you like a private demonstration?" The intimacy in his tone is almost my undoing. But his suggestion reminds me of our uncommon ground. If only we shared a mutual appreciation for love and romance.

"Pass, playboy. I kinda like where things are going."

"Me too." He grants me a lopsided grin that's too endearing.

The dryness in my mouth becomes unbearable. Tangy sweetness bursts on my tongue when I finally take a sip of my beverage. Each flavor profile hits my palate separately, then blends together in a yummy wave. An exaggerated moan offers compliments to the cocky bartender.

I smack my lips after swallowing. "Wow, this is delicious. What's in it?"

Garrett straightens to his full height, appearing pleased with my praise. "Booze."

A brow quirks at his basic explanation. "And?"

"Fruity shit," he mumbles.

"Whoa," I note dryly. "If I didn't already have one, I'd order another from that endorsement alone."

"How's the girth for you?"

Precious liquor dribbles down my chin when I choke on his question. "Excuse me?"

"Does that width satisfy your needs?" He points at the straw pinched between my fingers.

It's only then I notice the size. "Did you give me such a big one on purpose?"

Lust pools in his eyes. "I did."

Warmth spreads through my veins, which has little to do with the alcoholic contents in this glass. "The hole is very adequate. Shoots a lot in my mouth at once. I don't have to suck that hard. Just keeps coming."

He curses under his breath. "Damn, that backfired."

"Now you're thinking about me sucking on something else, huh?"

His groan is pained. "Don't tease me, woman."

I stick out my bottom lip purely for his benefit. "You brought this on yourself."

"Hey, Fuckable Foster. I need you," a feminine voice croons from a spot down the rail.

Garrett turns toward the greeting, a charming smile already plastered on his lips. "Hey, sweetheart."

My stomach curdles at the familiar—and apparently frequently distributed—nickname. It's another much-needed reminder that I'm nothing more to him than one of the many. In truth, I'm probably even less valuable since I won't sleep with him. Shame is quick to slam down on me. It's unfair to judge my new friend when he's been nothing but considerate.

"Give me a moment, yeah?"

It takes me several seconds to realize Garrett is talking to me. "Do your job, sweetheart."

He chuckles at what I thought was clever petulance. "Don't miss me too much."

An equally witty response evades me. Instead, I watch him strut toward the woman who beckoned. She's skinny and blonde and everything else I'm not. Their exchange is an even flow, revealing the comfort between them. Garrett spoils her with shallow compliments that I've witnessed him pay to countless others. Her fingers dance along his inked forearm while she absorbs every word.

The scene creeps along my skin in a torturous crawl better reserved for spiders. My mood sours with each passing moment. It's an irrational reaction, and more disappointing than I care to admit.

I wrench my gaze off their flirtations to scan the rest of the bar. Cheerful voices serenade the relaxed atmosphere. To my surprise, half of the tables are occupied. Others stand in clumps to mingle and circulate freely. The influx in attendance went unnoticed thanks to my fascination with an unavailable bachelor. Time to fix that.

My true purpose begins to search for a spark in the growing crowd. Men create a large majority similar to my first visit to Roosters. Maybe there's some truth to Joy's claim after all. Restored confidence thrums through me as I swivel on my stool to evaluate the potential.

"Find anyone yet?"

I peek over my shoulder at Garrett's reappearance. "Maybe."

"Which one?" He pauses to inspect his customers like matchmaking is a top priority.

"Aren't your services required elsewhere? You looked busy." My head tilts in the blonde's direction.

He doesn't spare her a glance to catch the daggers she's aiming at me. "Nah, Harper has this section covered. My attention is solely focused on this task."

The preferential treatment releases misguided flutters in my belly. It's difficult to concentrate on a love connection whenever he's nearby. I stare at a football poster on the wall to stop myself from suggesting a compromise.

"Want me to get him over here?" There's no telling who he's referring to since I'm not looking at anyone in particular.

I tease apart his motives instead. "You're serious about helping me?"

"Why not?"

"What's in it for you?"

"Aside from diverting unwanted attention from myself?" He nods toward the woman from earlier.

"Didn't look unwanted from where I'm sitting."

He winks. "I'm very good at what I do."

There's no stopping my eyes from rolling skyward. "Okay, fine. What else do you get from being my wingman?"

His shrug is lazy. "I want to see you satisfied. That's what friends are for."

"If you say so."

"I do," he boasts and rubs his hands together. "Now, back to business. How about that bloke? Does he make your beef curtains tingle?"

I sputter over his choice of phrasing. "My what?"

"Penis fly trap," he hollers too loud.

A fierce blush heats my entire face. "What's happening right now?"

"If you're questioning it, the answer is no. Moving on." Garrett skewers the unsuspecting bunch with a calculated squint. "That guy by the dart boards is a decent choice. I grew up with him. My mom tried to marry him off to Joy. It didn't work for them, but he could be a happily ever after for you."

My gaze trails to where he points. Confusion instantly follows. "You think we would fit together as a couple?"

"Yeah, why not?" Only genuine curiosity bleeds from his tone.

It's once again apparent that Garrett doesn't see weight as an issue. Toxic negativity rips at my throat, demanding to ridicule his unawareness. But those are my insecurities. I can't fault him for overlooking a factor I'll never be able to ignore. It's one of his many endearing qualities.

"He's very thin." As in a strong gust could tip him over. Guilt threatens to suffocate me just for voicing the reason aloud. I can't deny the facts, though.

Garrett reviews his pick through narrowed eyes. "Yeah, twigs aren't my favorite either. But I pride myself on being an equal opportunity lover for all the ladies. It's the person, not the package."

"Which I admire, but it's not that easy for me."

"How so?"

"You don't see how disproportionate we are? Really?" I gesture at my plus-sized figure.

"Does that bother you?"

"Unfortunately. It's deeply ingrained." Not to mention a permanent scar outlined in a traumatic memory. I blow out a heavy sigh. "I'm sure he's a wonderful man, but I'd be constantly concerned about crushing him."

Garrett drops his jaw. "Seriously?"

"Yes," I insist. "He's tiny compared to me."

His Adam's apple bobs with a thick swallow. "Am I being ignorant?"

"You're not. It's my problem." I avert my watery stare, unable to take the regret in his.

"Grace, look at me." His stern tone demands to be acknowledged. He draws in a sharp breath when our eyes clash. "You're the hottest woman I've ever seen. Period."

For whatever reason, in this delicate moment, that compliment doesn't sound like a cliché line to pacify me. I sniff and force a smile to hide the wobble in my lips. "Thank you."

He scrutinizes my acceptance through narrowed eyes. "You don't believe me?"

I pause to collect my thoughts and contemplate an honest reply. History screams for itself in a relentless loop. This is a weak side of myself I prefer to ignore. But she's a part of me whether acceptance and confidence have overruled her or not.

As a heavier gal, the number on the scale is a sensitive subject. If given the power, it can cripple my self-esteem on a daily basis. I've fought hard to not let the pounds consume me. But it's a battle not everyone understands.

My pulse calms as I allow his presence to soothe me. "It's a constant struggle. I'm comfortable in my body. I have a healthy relationship with food. Don't get me wrong about that. But there's only so much I can control."

Garrett rests his arms on the counter to bring us closer. "Such as…?"

I focus on the earnest curiosity in his blue stare. "How people look at me. I try not to let my weight define me, but others do. It's an automatic reaction."

He scoffs. "That's bullshit."

"And that's your opinion, which I appreciate." My hopeless romantic heart is especially grateful.

"For the record, any man worth the oxygen in his lungs would gladly take his final breath from between your thighs."

"I'll keep that in mind." But not really. Even my imagination doesn't run that wild.

"You still don't believe me," he notes with a frown.

"It's fine," I laugh. "Maybe I shouldn't be so picky."

He fixes me with a fierce stare. "Knock it off, sweetheart. You can be as picky as you damn well please."

"Please don't call me that." My voice is brittle under the pressure of this topic.

"Why?"

"I don't want to be lumped in with your other ladies. I'm not one of them." I shouldn't care, but I do.

"No, you're certainly not." Garrett shifts until our noses are inches apart. "You're much more. If you're willing, I'll prove just how sexy I think your body is. I'll worship every delectable curve until you beg me for mercy."

I gulp to trap a whimper. "Does that mean you're willing to consider a serious relationship?"

"No, but I'll give your twat tassel something to quiver about."

And that comment douses the flames in my core. I huff at the abrupt change in his demeanor. "Are you ever serious for longer than five minutes?"

"Believe it or not, soulmate"—he gathers my hands in

his for a reassuring squeeze—"I'm realizing our friendship is getting very serious for me."

Wishful thinking attempts to skew my logic in a rosy hue. "You're just saying that."

"I better improve my strategy." Garrett straightens to stretch for this so-called game-changer.

My gaze makes a meal of devouring his flexing muscles. "And how might you do that?"

He twists from left to right in comical preparation. "Tell me about your list."

"It's not really a list."

His mouth firms into a terse line. "You told me it was a list."

"Call it whatever you want, but there isn't a physical copy to reference." I groan and cover my blush with a flat palm. "It's not that complicated. I just want to meet someone who shares an appreciation for commitment. They should be kind, loyal, and considerate. Chemistry and compatibility are important too. Similar interests would be nice. It shouldn't feel like a chore to be with them. Is that too much to ask? I don't know at this point."

"Why are you embarrassed?" Garrett tugs at my wrist.

"This conversation has been a lot," I admit.

"We've barely scratched the surface."

"Which is even more concerning."

"Don't fret, Gracie."

"Easier said than done," I chide.

"Give me your phone." He holds out his palm.

"Why?" But I'm already reaching into my purse.

"We need to exchange numbers. Then I can text you."

"About what?"

"Dick pics."

The hand clutching my iPhone pauses in midair. "Umm…"

Garrett laughs and snatches the cell from my grip. "Just

fucking with you. The guys will be fully clothed. You can tell me if they pass the vibe check. Consider me an initial screening process."

"Okay?" I find myself wondering, yet again, what he's getting out of this.

He types on the screen and a muffled alert dings from his pocket. Then he's holding up my phone with the lens pointed at me. "Now, say splooge-a-palooza and smile wide."

Before I can question him, he snaps a photo. A panty-melting smirk approves the shot. Another tap to the screen sends the picture to himself.

I quirk a brow. "What's that for?"

"Your future admirers. They don't know what's about to hit 'em." He yanks on a stray lock of my hair. "You'll be off the market in a few months. Maybe. Just be patient. This is my first time."

Silence follows as our eyes lock. Even my lofty standards can't compete with the idea of him. Especially when sexual tension smolders from his expression. Mine is eager to reciprocate. An electric charge thrums and crackles to fill the lull. That magnetic attraction suggests this arrangement will fail. Probability aside, I don't have it in me to discourage his efforts.

I park my chin on a bent fist. "True love is worth waiting for."

Garrett winks, letting his dimples dazzle me for good measure. "I'll take your word for it."

Call me pathetic, but I wish he wouldn't.

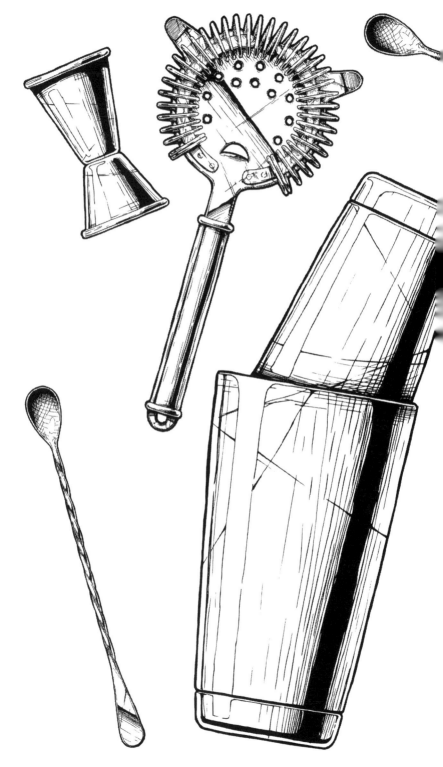

chapter five

Garrett

JOY GLANCES AT ME FROM ACROSS THE DINNER TABLE. There are only a few things that can distract me from my mother's homemade apple pie. The gleam in my sister's gaze is at the top of that short list. It might as well be a warning flare. I brace myself for whatever nonsense she's about to spew.

"Garrett has a girlfriend," she croons.

Mom's fork clatters to the wooden surface. "Thank the heavens. I never thought this day would—"

"It hasn't," I cut in. "She's a friend who happens to be a girl."

Disappointment wrinkles her weathered features. "Oh, darn."

Dad snickers from his devoted spot beside her. "Just let the boy be, love."

"He isn't a boy," she argues. "Our son is almost thirty."

"The reminder really isn't necessary," I mumble.

Mom purses her lips at me. "That's what it takes to needle you into action?"

"My youth is slipping away. It's just not fair," I bellow and shake a fist at the ceiling.

She pats my hand in a placating manner. "Quit the theatrics, kiddo. There's still plenty of time to give your darling mother the grandchildren she's desperate for."

I recoil from the suggestion. "That's not my department. Joy and Cole already have one fresh out of the oven. I bet another will be baking shortly."

My sister shares a look with her fiancé. After a silent exchange, Joy plasters a wide grin on her face. "This conversation isn't about my ability to reproduce."

"Well, it should be. You make adorable babies." I gesture at Belle, innocently babbling in her swing.

"We do," she agrees and peeks down at her daughter.

Cole loops an arm around Joy to join in the admiration of their offspring. "Yeah, we did really good. She's perfect."

On cue, little Belle toots loud enough to amuse her captivated audience. We coo and sigh as a unified group. Mom dabs at her misty eyes, as if a baby fart is the most precious sound.

"Such a blessing," she gushes.

"See? Problem solved." Even if I have to choke on bile at the thought of my friend impregnating my little sister. Again.

My mother turns the full intensity of her stare onto me. "You're not interested in experiencing such a miracle?"

"What do you mean? I'm sitting right here, smelling the stink bombs like everyone else."

"Can't you take this seriously for once?" Her statement is eerily similar to Grace's accusation from last week. The reminder threatens to unravel my overall indifference to this topic.

"How about we change the subject? Dirty diapers don't pair well with dessert." I motion to my untouched pie.

"Or just circle back to Grace. We got sidetracked, which is

super easy to do with this cupcake nearby." My sister blubbers over Belle, immediately distracting us again.

"This could go on all night," I mutter.

Mom wrenches herself free from the baby trance with a shocking demonstration of willpower. "Who's Grace?"

"Garrett's girlfriend," Joy reiterates.

I grunt at the purposeful misconception. "She's just a friend."

"Who you've been texting nonstop."

A sudden urge to check my phone for new messages has me shifting on the chair. "I'm trying to find her a decent guy to date."

"Have you looked in the mirror?"

"You're the one who told me she's off-limits," I remind.

"Only if you're sticking to the hump and dump habits."

Our mother groans and rubs her temples. "Please stop. This is too reminiscent of your teenage bickering. It's giving me horrible flashbacks."

"Sorry." We recite the simple apology in tandem just like our younger years.

"Accepted," she chirps. "Which one of you is going to tell me about Grace?"

"She's the nanny we hired for Belle."

"You hired a nanny?" Mom's sharp tone bleeds with offense.

I slap a sympathetic palm to my chest. "That's exactly what I said. It's a shock that she didn't ask you first. I even tried to volunteer, but she shot me down."

Joy glares at me. "Real nice. I appreciate your support."

A mulish snort escapes me. "Suddenly you want to be on the same team?"

She presses her lips into a firm line before forcing a smile purely for our mom's sake. "I didn't want to be a constant burden. You already watch Belle most mornings. Grace is available during the evenings as needed. It's a random schedule and very inconsistent. Just when I'm at the studio and Cole is held up in meetings."

After several tense seconds, Mom nods her acceptance. "All right, I understand your choice. We do keep ourselves busy most nights."

Dad winks at her. "Can't keep this social butterfly home for too long without her getting antsy."

My sister makes a mushy noise better suited for a cheesy movie. "Don't you want to grow old with a special someone, bro? Look at their love. It's unconditional."

Cole hauls her against him, whispering what I can only imagine to be pure filth into her ear. Joy's rising blush confirms my assumptions. Unfiltered devotion wafts off them to turn my stomach. A sideways glance at my parents finds them in a similar embrace. I'm surrounded by proof that fairytales exist. The outpouring of adoration in this room would have most reconsidering their stance on commitment. I prefer to consider myself immune, but this is a bit much. Not to mention the temptation from a certain raven-haired beauty.

My appetite vanishes and I push my plate away. "Who needs dessert when you're serving sweet nothings and sappy sentiments? I'm going to be sick from the excessive sugar content."

Mom clucks her tongue. "There's a simple solution."

"Drink the syrupy potion. It's better than Kool-Aid." Joy nods at my glass.

"I'm not thirsty." The curt response reflects my frustration about the sudden influx of meddling I'm receiving from everyone. I figured that a family meal would be safe, but the opposite is proving to be true.

My mom's expression softens. "We're not trying to pry, sweetie. It's just that you used to be much more carefree and passionate. You let possibility stand a chance."

"I still do."

"Not like before," she argues.

"Like when I was five? Pretty sure everything is sunshine and rainbows at that age."

"Don't be a smart ass," Mom quips. "I'm talking about what's happened since you graduated college."

The reminder of my so-called glory days delivers a bitter taste to further sour my mood. Football was my first true love. I lived and breathed for the game. Sweat, blood, and tears poured down on a daily basis as I pushed myself harder. Too bad that dedication wasn't good enough to earn me a spot in the draft. It wouldn't be as devastating if I hadn't been so close. They teased me with the opportunity, gave me hope, just to rip it away.

That loss cut deep, but it was expected in a sense. The odds of playing pro ball are slim. Only a very select few get chosen. My football career hit its peak and I accepted that. What I didn't see coming was my girlfriend betraying me in the dark hours when I needed her most.

The league didn't want me. She didn't either. And people wonder why I have commitment issues. A hollow scoff escapes me. Those two consecutive blows altered my path. Permanently.

I rub at the ache lodged in my chest and shake off the memories. "A lot has changed since then."

Cole scrubs over his mouth, muffling several expletives. "Don't let that jersey jumper ruin you for the rest. She wins if you do."

"Yeah, what he said." My sister hitches a thumb at her fiancé.

My only response to their attempts at encouragement is a dry chuckle. "That tactic is the oldest trick in the book."

Joy shrugs. "Worth a shot."

My mother hums in a tune that raises my guard. "It would

put me at peace to see you settle down and get serious about someone again."

I frown at her. "Really, Mom?"

She blanches as if her manipulation tactic stems from pure innocence. "I'm your mother. It's my job to badger you about marriage."

"I'd prefer you didn't."

Her sigh has the power to spear me with guilt. "That mess with Hillary was years ago, dear. Aren't you ready to move on?"

My ex's name is a punch to the gut. "Already have."

She quirks a brow. "With this girl who's just a friend?"

It's my turn to expel a defeated breath. "No, with my business. I own a bar, remember?"

"Ah, yes. How could we forget the cock den?" My father's eyes crinkle in the corners.

He's always supported my brand of debauchery. Meanwhile, my mother wishes for the day my wild oats will be shackled to a ball and chain.

"Please don't encourage him," she chides on cue.

I laugh at the predictable exchange. "Roosters is thriving, thanks for asking. Our revenue from Swing into Spring could carry us until the summer festival if needed. But we're serving more customers than ever. Best decision I ever made."

"Aside from adding a ladies' night." Joy winks.

"That was clever." And beneficial for Grace's resolution.

Although, my success rate remains at zero. Not for lack of trying. I've sent her at least a dozen guys. Her responses have been lukewarm at best. I'm beginning to suspect she's noticed they're stock photos.

Mom furrows her brow before swerving us back on track. "We're glad business is booming. Truly. But those are just professional goals. What about your personal life?"

"I'm doing just fine in that department."

Joy snorts. "Depends on your definition."

My patience frays into a thin strand. "What's with the sudden interest in my relationship status? It's been the same for years and will remain that way indefinitely. Or did I miss a town meeting where everyone decided to try to convince me otherwise? Spoiler alert: you're wasting your time and mine."

The stubborn tilt to my sister's chin might as well be a warning flare and I brace for impact. Again. "You and Grace belong together. It's obvious to anyone who's seen you with her. You're meant to be."

"No, we're not."

"You are," she counters immediately. "Chemistry that crazy amazing doesn't come around too often. Why aren't you willing to explore that?"

I shrug, more than ready to excuse myself from this pressure cooker. "We want different things."

"But she's not just any girl. This is *the girl*." She clearly emphasizes the distinction. "Don't waste your chance."

"Not a problem since I never had one to begin with."

Her jaw unhinges. "You're really planning to help her meet some other dude who's half the man you are?"

"Already in progress, and thanks for the compliment."

She scowls. "Consider it rescinded. I didn't realize you're actually a spineless—"

"Okay, that's pushing far enough for one evening. Garrett is about to bolt as it is." Mom puts her hand on my shoulder, offering a gentle squeeze. "We just want you to be happy. The pestering comes from a good place."

My gaze moves around our small gathering. Warmth spreads through me despite the recent discomfort. "I appreciate your concern, but I'm happy with my choices."

"Then we'll drop it," Dad cuts in. His stern gaze levels on the group, daring anyone to speak against him. "Let the boy enjoy his dessert."

"I suppose," Mom relents. A loud exhale slumps her

shoulders. But in the next breath, a sparkle brightens her gaze. "Will you tell us more about this friendly arrangement with Grace? She wants you to find her a date?"

"Oooooh, yes. Give us the dirt as a compromise." Joy leans in. "Straight from the ground source."

There's no stopping a smile from growing, even though I'll catch hell for it. "Just don't make me regret it."

"We won't." Their unified response reveals that they most certainly will.

chapter six

Grace

I DIDN'T SET OUT TO BECOME A NANNY, MUCH LIKE I TOLD Joy when she interviewed me. My degree in communications and psychology was a strategic pick to open a variety of doors. In fact, when I was a freshman in college, I pictured myself in an office alongside other adults. We'd attend morning meetings before going our separate ways to complete our daily tasks. It would be simple and clean and polished.

But as I sit with these two messy kiddos at this adorable coffee shop that serves dessert, it couldn't be clearer that I'm right where I'm meant to be. Warmth spreads from my chest in a comforting wave. I can't imagine not seeing them five days a week.

Amusement brightens my already sunny mood while I watch Bradley and Violet attack their ice cream with the ferocity of a competitive race. The siblings I look after definitely share an ambitious spirit. Maybe they're trying to see who will get a brain freeze first. It's bound to happen at the pace these two are eating.

The idle chatter in Bean Me Up does little to drown

their enjoyment. Pleased hums accompany the metallic clink of diving in for another bite. One glance at their sticky faces further proves how much they appreciate the surprise treat. My lips automatically lift at witnessing such pure delight.

"Yum yum yum in my tum tum tum. It's soooo yummy in my tummy," Bradley sings the cheery tune around a mouthful of ice cream.

"Cure the craving?" I smile at the little boy who's been in my care for the past two years.

He smacks his lips. "Super duper."

A peek at his sister finds the toddler living her best sugarcoated life. "Is it yummy in your tummy too?"

Violet bobs her head with extra enthusiasm. The fast motion dribbles chocolate goodness down her chin and splatters her shirt with a fresh layer. Gooey brown covers most of the front at this point. It's worse than when she gets ahold of a bag of Cheetos. She's going to need an entire pack of wipes to make a dent in the slop, but I've discovered the biggest messes usually equal memorable fun. These stains are a badge of honor to her.

"Do you want help?" I lift my hand toward the spoon in offering.

"No!" She whips the utensil, sending a blob of hot fudge flying. Thankfully it lands on the floor rather than an innocent bystander in the splash zone.

I hold up my palms in a peace offering. "Okay, Miss Independent. Just making sure you didn't want more to actually make it into your mouth."

Violet's forehead crinkles in effort as she scoops a huge chunk. As predicted, only a small dollop reaches the target destination. The rest paints the lower half of her face. She shows off chocolatey teeth with a megawatt grin that claims nothing but success.

"I do good," the little girl boasts.

My smile reaches new heights to match hers. Any improvement should be celebrated. "Yes, you're getting much better at using silverware."

Just last month, she still preferred to eat with her hands. That was another battle entirely. A shudder rolls through me at the reminder of those countless tantrums. I'm calling this a win, sloppy or not.

"It's almost the weekend." Bradley makes that connection while finishing his ice cream.

I tap my phone to check the time, and promptly ignore the swoop in my belly at the notification on the screen. "Only two more hours until your mom gets home. We should get going soon."

The kids exchange a rowdy cheer that ends with a sticky high-five. Nobody in the cozy establishment appears shocked by the random outburst. Violet boomerangs back to her dessert and Bradley tilts his head at me.

"Whadayuh do when you're not with us?"

"I spend time with family and friends."

His nose wrinkles. "That's it?"

"Read. Knit. Water my plants. Go for walks. Enjoy the quiet." My wink is paired with a cheeky grin.

He sticks his tongue out at that last point. "That's laaaaame. You must miss us lots."

"I sure do." Which is why I avoid thinking about him starting kindergarten in the fall. These two have become a vital part of my routine. At least I'll still see him in the morning and afternoon. It will just be... different.

Bradley hasn't lost interest in the topic, his gaze fastened on me. "Why don't you have kids?"

"I don't have a husband." Not that having a partner is a requirement. But in this case, it's a simple and safe answer to appease young curiosity.

But the little boy isn't satisfied. "Do you wanna get married?"

"Once I meet Prince Charming."

"Pwetty pwinshess." Violet toys with my hair, no doubt gluing several strands together.

Meanwhile, her brother is scanning the room. His search noticeably lands on a man sitting alone. "Hey, mister!"

Mortification preemptively scorches my cheeks. "Bradley, you're not supposed to talk to strangers."

The stubborn five-year-old isn't hearing me. He only has eyes for his intended audience. I dip my chin, preparing to hide my flaming face if necessary. When the guy glances toward our table, Bradley begins flailing his arms in an unmistakable signal for attention.

"Wanna marry my nanny? She's suuuuper nice and fun and needs a husband. Really bad. I guess she does boring adult stuff on the weekends. But I think you'd like her." His voice might as well be spoken through a megaphone.

"Oh, my gosh." I peek through my fingers to see the little troublemaker point at me, just in case the entire room isn't already staring.

The man waves in a kind gesture, then points to the wedding ring on his left hand. He mouths an apology before returning to his coffee.

"How embarrassing," I grumble.

"That's poopy," Bradley huffs.

"No potty talk please." But my muffled tone doesn't hold authority.

His lower lip juts out. "I did my bestest, Grace. It looked like he coulda used some company. How was I s'pose to know he's married?"

The urge to bury my head under a pile of napkins is strong. I'm not even sure how to respond to that. But as it turns out, I don't have to.

"Thought I recognized you," comes an amused voice.

I straighten in my chair at the sight of Harper and Sydney. "Oh, hey."

"Quite a performance.

"Caught that, huh?"

The spunky bartender laughs. "Pretty sure the entire town did."

My shoulders hike to preserve what dignity remains. "A new level of desperation has been achieved."

"Don't get too bent out of shape. Kids are clever. They have a sneaky ability to read the fine print we assume they can't comprehend. That intuition can come in handy at the right time. Just air out the laundry." Her smile is directed at the little girl attached to her hip.

Before I can respond, Harper's daughter takes the notion as an opportunity to be acknowledged. Sydney bounces on her toes until she's next to me. "Hi, Grace. We're twins, remember?"

Our conversation at the spring festival several weeks ago floats to the present. "You have a great memory, Sydney Grace."

"Well, duh. I'm very smart," she preens.

Laughter bursts from me in a fluid stream. Harper joins in, shrugging to indicate this is precisely what she meant. Five minutes in her presence would confirm the same. In addition, I've heard rumors about this cutie pie's accomplishments. Her confidence is definitely well-earned.

My grin reflects the natural ease between us. "It's a fabulous name, even stuck in the middle."

She beams at me. Then her focus moves to the siblings, specifically narrowing on Bradley. "Who are you?"

He gapes at her with cartoon hearts in his eyes. If he hadn't already finished his ice cream, the frozen treat would be forgotten. The sight of him instantly smitten is precious. I slouch in my seat while watching the inevitable unravel. This boy doesn't have a clue about what's in store for him.

Sydney blinks at his prolonged delay. "Why aren't you answering? I know you can talk, and I don't think you're shy. You just yelled super loud at that guy over there. Did a cat get your tongue? My daddy says that can happen. It's never happened to me. Maybe 'cause people call me a chatterbox. Does it hurt? Do you need help?"

The kid is struck by a rare silence, too enamored to find his voice. Only a soundless squeak escapes him. Not that I can blame him. Sydney possesses an endearing quality that leaves the rest of us speechless.

"Are you gonna tell me your name?" She waits for a breath. "You have one, right?"

A loud whir from the espresso machine knocks him from the stupor.

"Bradley," he finally sputters.

"It's nice to meet you, Bradley." She thrusts her hand toward him. "I'm Sydney Grace Evans. You can call me Syd."

He stares at her outstretched palm for a second before jumping into action to accept the gesture. "Nice to meet you too."

Her attention pivots to the toddler at our table. "Oh. My. Gosh. Is this your baby? She's adorable! Her pigtails are perfect. How'd you get 'em so straight? Daddy always makes mine crooked. Eeeeep, I wanna squish her chubby cheeks." The energetic word flow pauses. "But maybe later. She looks sticky."

My brain snags on one portion of her excitement. "Violet and Bradley aren't my children. I'm their nanny."

Sydney gasps. "Really? I told my dad I needed one of those once, but I really just wanted him to fall in love with Harpy."

"Totally worked." The blonde remarks while flashing the bling on her ring finger.

Sydney snuggles against her. "Uh-huh. She's my real mom now."

"You'll have to tell me more about that story when there's more time. I have to get these troublemakers home soon." A thought occurs to me as I glance at the thinning afternoon crowd. "Aren't you supposed to be in school, Syd?"

"Nope. The teachers needed the day to be students." She shrugs.

"Staff development," Harper explains.

Sydney skips to the empty chair next to Bradley and plops down. "Do you go to Knox Creek Elementary too?"

His throat works with a thick swallow. "Um, no. Not yet."

Syd's eyes go wide. "Oh. My. Gosh. You're younger than me?"

"I guess?"

"Bradley starts kindergarten in the fall." I sniffle in exaggeration purely for his benefit. The little turkey loves to tease me about how fast he's growing.

"Uh-huh, I'm getting really super big." He wiggles his brows in my direction.

"That means you're ready for school," Sydney says. "I'm in kindergarten now. Miss Tiffany is the best. Make sure you're in her class. Oh, oh! On Tuesday afternoons, we get free time. But only if we're good listeners. And then…"

She proceeds to tell him everything he needs to know to survive. From the tastiest lunch options to shortcuts in the hallway. Even Violet is captivated by the animated intel. The siblings gobble every crumb Syd is willing to drop.

With the kiddos distracted, I point to the remaining chair for Harper to occupy. "Take a load off."

"Aren't you leaving?" But she accepts the offer to sit.

"In a few. I'd hate to cut off Sydney while she's on a roll."

Harper laughs. "If you don't, she'll just keep going."

"Five more minutes won't hurt." I check the time on my phone.

It's only then that I remember Garrett's text from earlier. The unread message notification dominates the screen. Curiosity gets the best of me. A quick swipe and tap exposes his latest phony find. My eyes roll at the image. Harper catches my reaction and raises her brows.

"It's from your boss. He's been sending me pictures of guys."

"As potential dates?" Disbelief shades her voice to a muted gray.

"Apparently."

"Why do you sound skeptical?"

"See for yourself." I show her the most recent decoy that Garrett expects me to believe is a legitimate candidate.

Harper glances at the photo. A snort is her initial reaction. "Isn't he a model?"

I bob my head at the correct assessment. "Uh, yep. He's on the cover of several romance novels that I have at home."

"That's where I recognize him from." She smacks the table, rattling the dishes to make an awful racket. The kids barely react.

"Garrett probably didn't think I would notice," I clip.

"Has he done this before?"

"A dozen or so." I scroll along our thread to expose his previous attempts.

"Wow, he's totally catfishing you. What a nincompoop."

"I just don't understand the point."

"Me either. It's not like he's interested in dating you."

My flinch is a pitiful reflex. "He's made that perfectly clear."

She must hear the guard I slam into place. "Oh, crud. I didn't mean you specifically. Garrett doesn't want to get serious with anyone. Ever."

My eyes narrow on her. "Weren't you encouraging him to settle down with someone just last week?"

"Yeah, but he turned into a grump about it. Joy told me their most recent family dinner was bumpy at best after confronting him. We have to accept that he's a complex fellow who's highly unlikely to ever take a wife."

I cock my head at the familiar line. "Did you just make a *Friends* reference?"

"It was called for."

My jaw goes slack. "I think you just became one of my favorite people."

"Instant bestie at your service." She brushes her palms together after a job well done. "How do you usually respond to his nonsense?"

"Um, I haven't."

Harper just stares at me for several beats. "Why not?"

"What am I supposed to say?"

"You could start by telling him he's got competition." She nods toward Bradley. "This tiny wingman is already proving to be more authentic in his methods. The guy your little dude picked might be married, but at least he's local."

A cramp seizes my stomach muscles from laughing so much. "I'm not sure if that's better or worse."

"Eh, whatever. Respond to the supposed matchmaker." Harper nudges my phone awake.

"And say what?"

"He better up his game or someone else will see that the task is done right."

Hot air puffs from my cheeks. "I dunno. He's already giving me model material."

"Exactly." A wicked glint sparkles in her eyes. "Ask when you can meet this handsome stranger. That ought to make him sweat."

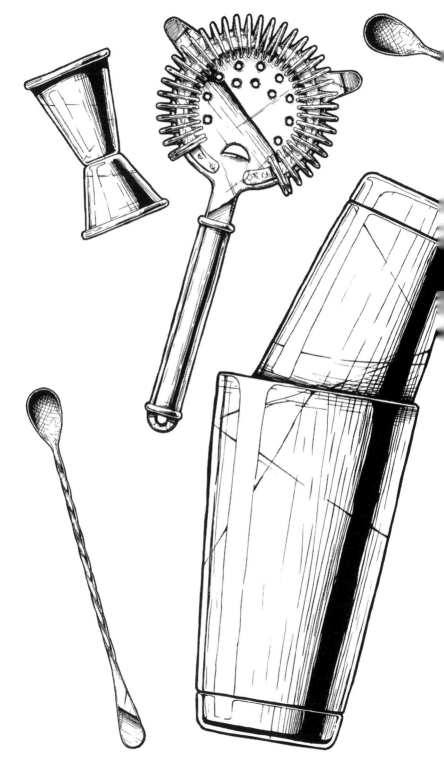

chapter seven

Garrett

MY DAY OF RECKONING HAS OFFICIALLY ARRIVED. It was only a matter of time before Grace called me out. I'm honestly shocked that it took her this long. There's some leeriness lurking as well, and for good reason.

The initial hunch that she had been aware of my scheme since the beginning has blossomed into an indisputable fact. Her sudden demand to meet the latest phony I sent is nothing short of a red flag. Choosing a picturesque scene to reveal the deceit in my actions seemed appropriate. The mid-morning sky even features fluffy clouds for an Instagram-worthy background. It's almost as if the weather is telling me not to admit defeat.

Unfiltered sunshine threatens to blind me as I preemptively search the outdoor space. There's a real possibility that I can find a decent guy for Grace in this crowd. I'm not sure why I was faking it before. That's not helpful to either of us. It's not like we're going to end up together. She has her desires and I have mine.

A smirk tugs at my lips. Look at me offering the perfect

woman to some other man. On a silver platter suited for a wedding registry no less. How selfless. I snort at the misplaced trait. Idiotic is a much better fit.

"Well, if it isn't my loyal matchmaker."

I turn on my heel to face the beauty responsible for that cheeky greeting. The swift motion doesn't give me a chance to rouse my defenses.

A breeze ruffles Grace's dark hair while her blue eyes sparkle from the natural light above. Temptation is already suckling at my dick from that sight alone. I fight the urge to surrender while simultaneously appreciating her shapely figure accentuated in that clingy dress. It would take the will-power of several disciplined gentlemen to shift my focus off her lush hips. Instead of looking away, I wonder how offended she'll be if I request a taste.

Not that I'm about to let my knees hit the pavement. The fantasy she presents nearly has my tongue lolling out, though. Sweat prickles my forehead and I'm flooded with heat. My voice is impacted next, lost to the lust pumping me at a furious pace.

A hand sweeps across the space in front of me. "Garrett?"

I blink out of my horny stupor. "Uh, hey. Thanks for coming."

"It would kinda defeat the entire purpose if I didn't, right?"

"Yep, this is where the magic happens." My gaze still doesn't leave her.

Grace's squint has little to do with the bright sun. "At the farmers market?"

Which serves to remind me of exactly where we are. This wholesome location suddenly appears like the worst idea. Good ol' boys create the very foundation of the town's seasonal pop-up shop.

Regret clenches my gut. But I have a mission. One I'm better off completing for her sake and mine.

"Your true love is right over there." I wave in a random direction. There are a dozen or so booths arranged in a square at the rear of the grocery store's parking lot. One of them is bound to have a single guy behind the counter.

Her eyes roll. "Simple as that, huh?"

"Absolutely."

"You're awful sure of yourself, Cupid."

I can't fault her disbelief, considering this is a total sham. Based on her previous lackluster responses, I figured it was safe to continue sending pictures of models. Just a bit of messing around. Although, once again, I'm not entirely sure why I decided to dupe her in the first place.

That flimsy excuse is weaker than my mother's coffee, which might as well be water.

Denial is just as pointless. I'm done playing games. If we're gonna find a guy to fill her specific requirements, this Knox Creek staple is the best place to start. That's my cue to get her on board the enthusiasm wagon.

"Romantic possibilities are ripe in the fresh air, Miss Matrimony. Take a whiff." Meanwhile, I scoff at the cheesy nonsense spewing from my mouth. What a crock of shit.

Grace takes a deep inhale just to humor me. "Uh-huh, yummy. Where is… what's his name again? I can't spot him when there are so many *possibilities* to choose from."

I'm beginning to sweat a bit, but I don't want her to catch the stress seeping from my pores. "There isn't a gent you can pluck from the barbarians? Well, crud. Maybe we should check elsewhere."

"But you told me this guy was here." She whips her phone out and proceeds to show me the most recent picture I sent.

I don't need to look at the screen to tag the image as a

phony. Guess we aren't quite done playing pretend yet. "Isn't that him at the fudge stand?"

"Um, no."

"Are you sure? Filters are all the rage these days. Take a closer peek. He might have a few more wrinkles than the edited version."

"AI is more likely in his case. That's a total facial reconstruction," she clips.

"Weird. Maybe he left."

"Didn't you tell him I was coming?" Now her arms are crossed, ready for a banter battle.

"Sure did." *In another dimension where I'd actually follow through on this fucked plan.* "Maybe that's not him."

"Oh, so you're not even sure who he is. Are you ready to admit he doesn't exist?" Amusement bobbles Grace's voice, almost cracking into a giggle.

"Nah, the sun is just in my eyes. I'm sure he's around somewhere." I make a grand production of searching the area.

Her scrutiny burns into the side of my face. "Yeah, I bet he is. Which reminds me, what's his name? Don't think I missed how you dodged that question earlier."

Determination rises to the surface. I hitch my thumb at a random dude selling organic fertilizer. "That's John. He's full of shit."

"John?" She doesn't bother sparing him a glance.

"That's what I said." It's common enough to set the odds in my favor.

Her narrowed eyes flick to where I'd pointed. "Seriously?"

"Such little faith." I cup a palm around my mouth to call out across the lot. "Hey, John!"

Several heads turn, none of them the dude I singled out. So much for my upstanding reputation.

As if agreeing, Grace releases a dry laugh. "Nice try."

"That doesn't mean he isn't the one for you."

A snarky hip cocks out at me. "Based on what criteria?"

"Are you questioning my methods?" I inject a hearty dose of offense, purely for my benefit.

She gives Not-John a more thorough appraisal. "Can you blame me? He doesn't look like any of the pictures you sent either."

"That's because I haven't had the chance to take one of him yet." It's not a total lie. I very well could've snapped a shot while waiting for her to arrive.

"How convenient." The grit in her tone reveals that she's definitely not buying what I'm selling.

"Fine, I don't know his name."

"And?" Her wrist rolls to encourage the confession dam to burst.

"That can easily be rectified. Would you like me to handle introductions?"

Grace tips her head to the sky, requesting patience in a silent plea. "Just come clean, faker."

"About what?"

She moves into my space until we're almost touching. Her finger jabs into my chest, but I barely notice. Sugary vanilla and filthy suggestions that lead to hours between the sheets drift on a gust to tease my senses. Once again, I fight to stave off the baser urges demanding I give her several orgasms to remember me by. Grace quirks a brow when I do a shit job stifling a groan. Almost as quickly, she remembers her outrage.

"You're not helping by sending false advertising. These men"—she waves her phone—"aren't realistic candidates. They're models and stock photos."

"I figured you wanted the cream of the crop."

"Quit with the antics." The flush coloring her cheeks is a sultry shade I'd prefer to admire in a different setting.

"Fine, but my actions weren't completely dishonorable," I grumble.

"Says you."

"Did you actually believe me?"

"Not even for a second," Grace mutters.

"See? No harm was caused. I'll do better from now on."

"That won't be necessary."

"Giving up so soon?" I'm such an insufferable prick.

"With you in the driver's seat? Just about."

An unfamiliar sinking sensation tugs at my heart. "Ah, soulmate. Don't be like that. Give me another—"

"Oh. My. Gawd. Fuckable Foster is at the farmers market?"

I cringe at the shrill voice, not needing to turn to recognize the speaker. Grace's brows shoot for the stars while she mouths the ridiculous nickname. Her lips curve into a saucy grin and I flex to shield myself from the onslaught. But her attention shifts to the rude interruption that's approaching on our left. I shadow her lazy pivot as if choreographed.

Jasmine Poe descends in a flurry of too much perfume and desperation. She's a loyal regular at Roosters, but an overall pain in my ass. Her recent mission to perform a hat trick maneuver—also known as sleeping with all three owners—is served with relentless pursuit. Drake almost fell for it once. Ridge and I have steered clear ever since. That hasn't stalled her efforts in the slightest. If anything, our evasive tactics just provoke her to chase us faster.

"Shit," I curse.

Grace startles at my abrupt expletive. "What's wrong?"

I don't think. Basic survival instincts have me reaching for her hand, threading our fingers in an intimate embrace. "Just follow my lead."

She gapes at me for a pause that's pregnant with twins. "Huh?"

But there's no time for an explanation. Jasmine reaches us in the next frantic beat of my pulse. Her stare immediately drops to where our palms are locked. The spark in her gaze has me taking this charade one step further. I ditch the hand-holding to cinch an arm around Grace's waist, tugging until she's flush against me and staking a more significant claim. She comes willingly, but there's no disguising the tension in her stance.

The smirk I paste on lacks its usual charm. "Hey, Jasmine. Crazy running into you here of all places."

Her eyes narrow into sharp points. "I was going to say the same thing. Is this your first trip to the market?"

There's no point denying the obvious. "It just took the right woman to make me realize what I've been missing. And on that note, this is Grace."

Which reminds me that I don't know her last name. That's a mystery to solve later.

My partner in this façade wiggles her fingers in a cutesy wave. "Nice to meet you."

Jasmine falters for several seconds. "Hold the hell on. Is this a… date? It can't be. Nope. No, that's not how you oper-ate. It must be a quick stop before you bang her in a bathroom somewhere. Pump and dump, right?"

Grace glances at me. There's no hiding the disgust curling her upper lip. "Uh, thanks for that delightful visual."

That's my cue if I plan to maintain a sliver of dignity. "We're shopping. For our dinner. That we're making. Then we'll eat it. Together. As a couple."

Fully formed sentences would've been preferable. Instead, my tone is disjointed with that feeble explanation. Guess I'm not earning any awards for being a fast thinker.

But my lame bumbling seems to do the trick.

"You're in a relationship"—Jasmine's shrewd focus slides to Grace for a once-over that feels purposefully critical—"with *her?*"

Between her snide tone and the dismissive emphasis she

places on that final word, my composure is frayed to a single strand. My grip tightens to pull Grace impossibly closer.

"I'm a lucky bastard, right? It was love at first sight."

Jasmine's eyes bulge while Grace chokes on her exhale, prompting me to continue. I press my nose to her temple and take an audible inhale that ends in a groan.

"Still can't believe she agreed to be mine," I croon.

"And I can't believe you're trying to convince me that you've been domesticated." There's a harsh, defensive edge in Jasmine's retort.

"Why wouldn't you? Our love is pure devotion and commitment and… tenderness in the flesh." Someone needs to cut me off. I send a pleading look to Grace.

She blinks, then seems to recognize her role with a jolt. "Oh, yeah. He begged me to give him a chance. I was skeptical, but he wouldn't take no for an answer. Just kept giving me more without expecting anything in return. This guy really aims to please. A true giver with a bottomless appetite. He doesn't leave a single crumb. Isn't that right, munchie bear?"

A mental image of her spread wide as an all-I-can-eat feast assaults me. My arousal is swift and potent, the blood draining from my brain at a speed that leaves me dizzy. I'm hard for a woman only meant to be my friend.

"Can't get enough," I grit through the desert in my throat.

Grace leans forward to address the other woman. "He's such a snuggle puff. I never pegged him as the overly affectionate type. He also loooooves nicknames. Don't you, snickerdoodle cookie crumble?"

"Yep," I croak.

Damn, she's laying it on thicker than chunky peanut butter. Jasmine still isn't swayed, if her jutted jaw is any indication. It would be wise to tread carefully. She's spiteful and vindictive and likely to spiral into a jealous fit that will give the town gossips something juicy to chew on. Too bad I've never been known for my sound logic.

This calls for drastic measures. I cradle Grace's chin between my thumb and forefinger, lifting until our eyes lock. My unwavering stare is meant to reassure her and beg for the trust that I haven't earned. The permission I seek bleeds from my gaze in what I hope is a sincere request. Before she officially grants it to me, I'm swooping down to brush my mouth over hers.

She goes rigid in my grasp, almost to the point of concern. Doubt creeps in the next second, immediately followed by her melting into my impulsive display of affection. I get lost somewhere between the gentle press of her lips against mine. Everything fades, at least until a perturbed huff intrudes on our moment.

Jasmine's reaction isn't unexpected. I make it a point not to kiss women in public. It's somewhat of a standard for me ever since my ex shoved my heart into a meat grinder. That's what makes this simple gesture a bold, undeniable statement.

Grace is the one to pull away after a final shared breath. I don't miss the dazed confusion swirling in her eyes. That uncertainty clings to her expression until guilt peppers me. But there will be time to explain later. For now, I want to ensure the deed is done.

My thumb traces the smooth shape of her jaw. "What did I say, huh? The farmers market is full of romantic possibilities."

"Uh-huh," she mumbles absently.

"Do you think she's convinced?"

The gleam in Grace's gaze hasn't faded. "I don't see how she couldn't be."

chapter eight

Grace

"STARE A LITTLE HARDER. I BET THAT WILL MAKE him actually fall for you."

I wrench free from my Garrett-induced stupor at Abbie's words. Thankfully, he's busy with other customers and hasn't noticed my blatant ogling. My friend sure has, though.

The remaining fog clears from my brain as I focus on her. "Can you repeat that?"

Her pinched expression has me pitying myself. "You're being painfully obvious."

"What do you mean?"

But I already know. I haven't been able to quit replaying our kiss and it's created somewhat of an obsession where the popular bartender is concerned. My lips are still tingling a week later, which sounds pathetic. Even to me and my hopeless romantic outlook. That doesn't make it any less true, though.

Meanwhile, Garrett seems to be just fine pretending our minor lip lock didn't happen. Either that or he wasn't impacted by the smooch in the slightest. Probably the latter. His reputation suggests that it requires far more than a chaste peck to leave a memorable impression on him. My growing attachment is only encouraged on the rare occasions I watch his adorable niece. I find myself daydreaming about him taking care of blue-eyed babies.

Abbie's sigh is drawn out to punctuate her exasperation. "We've discussed this."

"Okay?"

She rolls her eyes to the wood beams along the ceiling. "Forget Foster, fuckable or not."

I snicker at the nickname lovingly bestowed upon him by Jasmine. Zero regrets sharing the tale with my bestie. "Careful or he might hear you. He's right over there."

Her palm whacks the counter. "Consider him off-limits. He's not relationship resolution material."

"But he volunteered to find me a guy who is," I use as a weak defense. In all honesty, I'm not mentally or emotionally available for the dating market. Again, how pathetic.

"Didn't you fire him from that position?"

"Um, I guess?"

"Then it's settled. I'm taking charge of this romance mission. You'll be living a fairytale in no time." Abbie flutters her extremely fake eyelashes at a speed that might stir up a tornado.

"Or we could just enjoy each other's company."

She scoffs and brushes off my evasive attempt. "Have you cheated on your diet yet?"

"Other than that measly lip-lock with Garrett, my dry spell stretches on."

"Not for much longer. It's Friday night. There are countless cocks to choose from."

"How appealing." But I take a glance just to humor her.

The stage is similarly set from my first visit several

months ago. It's strange to think how much has changed, but also how little. June has arrived and summer officially starts in a few weeks. I'd be tempted to assume the season is already in full swing based on the skimpy outfits. Roosters is definitely giving off a steamy vibe tonight. Suddenly, my knee-length dress doesn't feel that sexy.

"How about him?" Abbie waves to the left where a guy is standing alone while perusing the crowd.

"Seems to be on the prowl," I mumble absently.

"Which is perfect," she chirps.

A cursory glance suggests he might be my type. He's not bad to look at. The smile he's wearing reaches his eyes, crinkling at the corners. His tall frame is broad with plenty of meat on his bones. Yet the giddy flutters from instant attraction are noticeably absent. But I need to kick this doomed crush sooner rather than later.

"Sure, why not."

She lifts a brow at my limp tone, but slides off her stool to test the waters. "Super. Try to inflect a tad more enthusiasm when I bring him over, yeah?"

"If he's even interested," I mumble.

"Hey," she snaps. "Any man would be a lucky bastard to snag you."

A thrill zips through me at the familiar words. Garrett said something similar at the farmers market. My hopeful heart doesn't care that he was playing pretend.

I watch Abbie skip off to the lone wolf on a hunt for his next meal. She points at me, and his gaze follows. What I assume is a pleased grin tilts his lips when our eyes connect. Not a single flip flop in my belly. That doesn't mean there's no chemistry. It could just be hidden under unrequited feelings for a perpetual bachelor.

The man saunters toward me. He isn't shy about checking

me out while erasing the short distance between us. "Is this seat taken?"

I peek at Abbie hovering over his shoulder, flashing me a double thumbs-up. My gaze shifts to him. A smile that feels wrong rests on my lips. "Nope, it's all yours."

"Brent," he offers as an introduction.

"Grace," I say in return.

"It's a pleasure to make your acquaintance."

Cheesy line aside, I manage to keep my mouth from losing its upward curve appeal. "Likewise."

"You're very beautiful." His gaze burns straight through my clothes as he gives me a suggestive thrice-over.

"Thanks. You're not so bad yourself." The compliment tastes bitter.

A lull I'm not overly eager to fill makes itself cozy for an extended snooze. Brent drags a hand through his hair. The disheveled tresses are thick and begging to be tugged on. Even that prospect doesn't stir a tingle.

"Nice straw." He juts his chin at my drink.

I can't help the laugh that bubbles up at the reminder. Garrett provided me with a fun curly version that's more commonly seen in party favor bags for kids. It got a cheerful giggle out of me just the same.

"The bartender is a… friend. He spoils me with goofy straws and personalized cocktails."

His brows rise at my slight hesitation when slapping a label on Garrett. Before Brent can reply, a shadow appears over us. My favorite flirt at Roosters is looming from his usual post behind the bar.

Speak of him and he'll appear.

Although, Garrett doesn't look like himself. Gone is his signature golden retriever smirk and carefree spirit. Instead, he resembles a thunderstorm ready to strike a very specific target.

My gaze boomerangs between the two men. One is oblivious to the nearby threat while the other prepares for battle.

"Hey, you." I wiggle my fingers at Garrett.

But he doesn't remove his hostility from Brent. There's a fire in his glare that only needs a tiny spark to set the entire building ablaze. "Can I get you something to drink?"

"Miller Lite." Brent places the order without taking his eyes off me, completely unaware of the danger facing him.

"Tall or short?" There's an unmistakable growl in the formerly friendly bartender's tone.

"Tall. I have a feeling I'm not going anywhere for a while." He winks at me.

A peek at Garrett reveals his jaw clenching into stone. If he grinds much harder, his molars will crumble into dust. He blindly whips a glass fresh from the washer and fills it with beer from the tap. Then he slams the Miller Lite on the counter. Golden brew sloshes over onto the wood surface from the agitated motion. Brent doesn't notice.

"Anything else?"

"Nah, man. We're good." Then he proceeds to shoo Garrett away with a flick of his wrist.

My jaw drops at the dismissive action. Even if I'd been hanging on this dude's every word, that disrespectful jab would've slaughtered my piqued intrigue. As it sits, I'm prepared to tell him off in Garrett's defense.

But, as it turns out, my noble sheroism isn't necessary. Water shoots out from seemingly nowhere to soak Brent's lap.

He leaps off his stool with a stream of curses flying from his foul mouth. "What the fuck, man?"

Garrett has the audacity to appear very satisfied, his familiar smirk returning in stunning clarity. "Whoops. The gun got away from me. Finger slipped on the trigger. Faulty pipes. You know how it is. Right, *man?*"

I barely stifle a laugh as he swings the handheld soda dispenser by the hose like a floppy dick. "Simple mistake."

Brent swipes at his drenched jeans. "Complete bullshit. I want to speak to your manager."

"You're looking at him," Garrett drawls. "Unless you'd rather deal with him."

He points at Ridge slinging drinks a few paces away. His fellow owner turns on cue to scowl at Brent. Menace oozes from his features. The former hockey player is terrifying on a good day. This scare tactic is something else entirely. It's enough to make my spine straighten.

The warning gives Brent reason to pause his erratic—and useless—attempts at drying his drenched pants. "What am I supposed to do about this mess?"

"There are paper towels in the can." Garrett hitches a thumb behind him.

"Dammit," he spits. "I was about to smash this pussy. Now I gotta stick my junk in the spin cycle."

"Gross." My gasp at the vulgar description gains Brent's glare. The wince tightening my expression is apparently a next-level offense.

"Don't give me that wounded look. As if I wanted anything more from you other than a juicy fuck."

The slap of his comment strikes directly at my pride that's only sensitive to a select few topics. I suck in a sharp breath that sputters, much to my embarrassment. The past I've tried to leave behind races onto the scene with an onset that's so sudden it's painful. I can't mask the hurt. My smile slips into a rejected flat line. Heat stings my vision until the bar is a blur.

"Get. Out." Barely restrained fury vibrates in Garrett's bellowed command.

Brent reels back as if he's actually bothered. "Excuse me?"

Drake and Ridge materialize to flank Garrett for the

parting blow. "We don't want your business. You're not welcome here. Show yourself out."

"Whatever. Fuck this." Brent slinks off like the soggy crotch he is.

Even with the douche canoe gone, my mood plummets. I curl inward against the pressure caving in. The excess weight on my figure becomes encased in iron. I'm a heavy lump wasting too much space. Someone skinnier and looser should take my spot. The ugly insults form a relentless attack until I crumple under the force. It's more than I can handle.

I don't need a man to validate how I feel about my body. But it really fucking sucks when someone spews hateful words meant to attack my character.

Garrett vaults himself over the counter to land in front of me. His palms rest on my shoulders, rubbing soothing circles into the tension there. Then he goes and hauls me in for a hug that's nothing short of electric. His touch sends my stomach into a somersault routine fit for an Olympic gymnast. Of course, the guy who's made it perfectly clear he's not relationship material is the only one I respond to.

"Don't let that asshole get to you," he murmurs into my hair. With this casual embrace, he's shoving my insecurities back into the dark corners where they belong.

My nod is jerky against his chest. "I'm trying not to. It's just… hard to hear."

"Not to mention a brazen lie. He doesn't deserve to be in the same area code as you."

"Thanks." I grin, but the edges wobble. "My ex spewed similar venom when I had the audacity to ask where our relationship was headed. Turns out he was just stringing me along as a sidepiece. He never intended for me to be anything more than a thick and chunky screw." I shudder. "His words, not mine. Brent reminded me of him just now. Hit too close to history."

"Fuck both of them." He releases me to stare directly into my eyes. "What can I do to make you feel better?"

Other than tumble head-over-heels desperately in love with me?

I laugh at my own pathetic musings, though the tune lacks humor. "Get me good and drunk."

Garrett's smirk is already working to restore my spirits. "You got it, soulmate."

chapter nine

Garrett

RIDGE AND DRAKE ARE BEHIND THE BAR WITH ME TO ease the heavy load of a Friday night. That's allowed me to focus on a particular customer. Grace hasn't left my sight due to the amount of alcohol pumping through her system.

True to my word, the booze is flowing on an endless tap. I haven't let her drink hit bottom. Her hydration became my main priority when she tasked me with getting her intoxicated three hours ago, and the proof of my diligent productivity is currently swaying in her seat.

This quality time together is beneficial for our blossoming friendship, but a real bitch on my resolve to keep us strictly zoned as such. Especially when she stares at me in a dreamy trance like I'm her hero. Although, that misplaced worship could be blamed on the liquor. Her gaze holds a telltale sheen that suggests she's about two and a half sheets to the wind. My mission is almost complete.

I lean on the rail, putting our faces a few feet apart. "Hey, Gracie Lou. How's it going?"

Her smile is lopsided to match the droop in her eyelids. "Just dandy."

"Want something to eat before the kitchen closes?"

"Maybe a bratwurst that I can chop into tiny pieces for minced meat." She pounds a clenched fist onto the counter in rapid succession.

I wince at the visual. "Sounds… therapeutic."

"Men are jerks." Grace swipes her glass from the safety of a stable surface, generously slurping at the fruity contents. It's a tangy combination I affectionately dubbed The Peak is Near.

"Not all of them."

"Only the vast majority I've met," she sighs. "You're a rare gentleman. Too bad you don't want to date me."

An unfamiliar pang strikes my chest. "Don't take it personally. I won't date anyone."

"Yeah, yeah." She swats a sloppy palm through the air. "It's just such a shame. You're smart and sexy and successful and smell like seduction. Yummy."

My brain knows that this is mostly the alcohol talking, but that doesn't register with my dick. A dull throb accompanies the warmth spreading in a downward spiral. The flush rising on Grace's cheeks only spurs the arousal. It's too easy for me to picture her spread out beneath me, quivering in the throes of pleasure only I can deliver. Her vanilla scent surrounds me as I thrust in and out at a relentless rhythm. That visual strokes my cock until I'm ready to hump the bar.

Instead, I tug at my shirt collar in a weak attempt to stifle the heat. "Um, thanks."

Grace is oblivious to the fire in my blood, stumbling onto boner-killer territory in the next breath. "My ex was the worst. He strung me along for almost two years. The saddest part is that I believed he wanted a future with me. Foolish."

Any trace of flames is snuffed as I envision the bastard

who dared to do her wrong. "He's a moron. I hope he's suffering from a special brand of torture."

"You won't hear me disagree," she laughs.

"Same with that douche from earlier. I'm still pissed at myself for letting him through the doors."

She sips at her cocktail, pouty lips sealing around the straw like a fantasy. "You didn't know. Besides, he's not the first. He certainly won't be the last."

"If anyone else has treated you as less than a queen, they better hope we don't cross paths."

"Plan to defend my honor?"

"Indefinitely." I raise my arms and flex, showing off the strength behind my vow.

Grace flutters a palm to her forehead. The pose is too practiced to be authentic. "My very own knight in shining armor. How romantic."

"Wouldn't go that far," I hedge.

"Oh, duh. There's a limit." She blinks the stars and hearts from her eyes. "Just like how I used to be insanely attracted to you."

I almost stagger sideways as the implication hits me. "As in not anymore?"

Her shrug is crooked. "Why bother crushing on someone when you know it's not leading anywhere?"

That notion doesn't sit well with me when it comes to us, not that there's an alternative. "Never hurts to stroke my ego."

"You have plenty of girls who do that," Grace teases.

"Not that I take seriously."

Her expression sobers. "Are you saying this is serious between us?"

Now I do stumble while standing upright. "What? No. Why would you think that?"

The blank mask cracks, her entire body shaking with laughter. "Wow, your face is priceless. Don't worry, I won't mistake you for marriage material. But that makes me wonder if you're truly afraid of commitment."

"I have plenty of attachments," I argue. Then I force the strain from my stance in an attempt to appear casual. In reality, my body slumps against the bar in an uncoordinated heap.

"Do any of them include platonic relationships with women who aren't family?"

"Maybe I was saving that honor for you." I bounce my brows as if that's convincing.

As if staged, Grace rolls her eyes hard enough to tip backward, catching herself at the last moment with an impressive pinwheel maneuver. "Whoops."

I chuckle while reaching forward to assist in setting her straight. "Wanna hear a secret?"

"Obviously." Her attempt at a snide tone in her current condition is nothing short of hilarious.

My stomach muscles twinge from laughing so hard. "If I was going to date anyone, it would be you."

"Pssshhhh, you're just saying that." She brushes off my declaration with a limp gesture that looks like a dead fish.

I snatch her floppy hand in midair. "It's true, soulmate. Please believe me. I think you're the perfect catch."

Grace's stare bores into mine. Time is suspended as we exchange silence. Neither of us looks away. My thumb traces a line along her inner wrist. She gasps as my touch wanders to explore more skin. Her pulse hammers, giving a furious beat to this moment. I think it might be too much until she bursts into a fit of giggles.

"Yep, you're messing with me." She slips her hand from mine to wag a scolding finger at me.

I clear my throat. "Just trying to lighten the mood."

"And you're doing an excellent job overserving me."

"At your service." I tip an imaginary hat.

"Keep 'em coming. I could use it after another botched

blunder without the thunder." She squints while repeating the sentence under her breath.

It's impossible to trap a smirk. "Yet you're not jaded on love."

"Nope. I'm determined to find a connection that lasts forever. Even from the grave."

A low whistle escapes me. "Damn. That sounds tragic."

Grace nods, the motion disjointed. "My mom passed away when I was thirteen. That didn't stop my dad from keeping her memory alive. He never wanted to remarry. Well, not again. They'd both been married and divorced before meeting each other. I have three half-siblings that are older. Two from my dad and one from my mom. We've never been that close. Not even my brother from my mom's first marriage. He took off after the funeral and I haven't seen much of him in the last decade. I still have my little sister. Layla is my only full sibling. She's normal. Mostly. I think it was better that she was younger when my mom passed. Wanna hear something wild? She was an aunt before she was born. Crazy, huh?"

Just when I think she's coming up for air, her story rambles ahead. "But it is what is. My father is literally the best. He could've crumbled and checked out after my mom passed. Nope, he did the opposite. A real super dad. It's no wonder me and Layla are searching for a fairytale. We have high expectations thanks to him. So… yeah. The entire point of all that was to say I'm not settling for less than soulmate status."

It takes several seconds for me to process and digest that long stream. "That's… um, a lot to unpack."

"Uh, yeah. Wow, talk about an info dump. I didn't mean to blab your ear off."

"It really fucking sucks that you lost your mom. Do you wanna tell me more about her?"

"Hard pass. I don't need to cry. Again." Grace fans her face.

My gut clenches at the thought. "Noted."

"Sheeeesh, Mister." She points her straw at me, but it swerves with her unsteady grip. "You've accomplished your duty. I'm hammered."

"And just in time. This is your last call for alcohol."

"Ah, crud. It was fun while it lasted." Grace spins on her stool, almost toppling off the leather seat completely, to address the empty room. "Helloooooo, ghost town. Where is everyone?"

I grip her shoulders until she stops wobbling. "We close in thirty minutes. Most clear out once the booze is cut off."

She whirls to reconnect our gazes. "Did Abbie leave?"

"About four drinks ago," I chuckle.

"Well, shit. She was my ride."

"Guess you'll have to trust me to take care of you. How about a final round?"

"Yes, please." She tries to purr, which mostly sounds like a lisp in her slurred state.

My fingers dance over the nearest liquor options. "Any special requests?"

Grace taps her lips. "Something with peach? It's my favorite."

"Coming right up."

A trial recipe takes shape. I begin gathering ingredients to create a unique twist on a Fuzzy Navel. A generous serving of vodka, peach purée, pineapple juice, peach schnapps, and lemonade get tossed into a shaker. Grace watches me do her bidding with her chin propped on a flattened palm. Her undivided attention puffs out my chest. It also encourages me to bridge a nonexistent gap for the sake of bonding and share my own sordid past. Or at least a watered-down version.

"I have an ex from hell too."

"It sucks, huh?" Her eyes don't stray from my fluid motions as I dump ice in the blender.

The fact I'm willing to use the mess maker just goes to prove my limits are nonexistent where her happiness is concerned. If this frozen delight earns me a genuine smile, the added effort will be paid tenfold.

I transfer the combined fruity liquid from the shaker into the mixer. "She's the reason I'm done with romantic relationships. Permanently."

"Did she cheat on you?"

"Big time." The hollow pang behind my sternum thumps in reminder.

"What a bitch."

"My thoughts exactly."

"She didn't deserve you, but what about the girl who does?"

I choose that moment to power on the blender to bypass that quicksand pit. Grace's eyes widen at the whir and grind of the machine. The frothy creation gets poured into a hurricane glass. But there's something missing. I grab the whipped cream and spin the can in my grip. Grace watches that practiced move with keen interest.

"Do you play football?"

"Used to. Past tense."

"Touchy subject?"

"Not really. I just wasn't good enough for the big league."

"That's a bummer." Her throat bobs with a hard gulp. "My brother is a major jock."

"Present tense?"

"As far as I know. We don't keep tabs." Her voice drops with that admission.

I wince. "Ah, right."

Grace shrugs, her spirits rebounding almost immediately. "Football is my favorite to watch."

"Keep spouting like that and I'll flip the channel to highlights from last season."

She swirls her finger in a puddle of condensation. "I wouldn't mind."

"Fuuuuuck, that's some damn good foreplay." Before I suggest licking whipped cream off her tits, I squirt a thick spiral on her frosty cocktail. I can't resist adding a cherry as the final touch.

"Wolf in his element," she murmurs.

"What's that?"

"You're very sexy." Grace bites her bottom lip.

It's my turn to swallow roughly. "I thought you weren't attracted to me anymore."

"That was a lie."

"You don't say," I drawl.

"And this is what I have to say about your hot buns." She blows me a noisy kiss. "Mwah!"

A loud chuckle bursts from me in response. "I like you liquored up. You speak your mind, which reminds me…"

That whimsical glint returns to her gaze when I slide the finished product in front of her. "This is all for me?"

"I made it just for you."

"Looks like dessert."

"Try it and find out, Peaches." The nickname gets me thinking about her juicy ass, which leads my mind into filthy territory.

Grace stirs the tropical concoction with the bendy straw I included. "Peaches?"

"Has a special ring to it."

The hum she releases after a small sip tightens my balls. "Ohhhhhh, this is sinfully delicious. You're a genius."

"Anything else?" I croak.

"I'm all set." Then she proceeds to guzzle down the icy blend as if it's a race. Her arms launch straight to the ceiling when the slurpy echo signals that her glass is empty. "Done!"

My brows fling upward. "That was impressive."

Grace hisses and rubs her temples. "Owwwie, I have a brain freeze."

"Could've predicted that," I chuckle.

"Shut up. It hurts. This is your fault for rushing me."

"I've done no such thing."

She blows out a thick exhale, buzzing her lips in the process. "You said the bar is closing."

"It is, but that doesn't mean we have to leave immediately. I'm the owner. We can sleep on the floor if you'd like. You can also keep drinking after hours, but I'm pretty sure you don't need another drop."

"You're right about that." She closes one eye, glancing from right to left. "That last one went straight to my head. The room is spinning."

"And that's our cue." I turn toward Ridge and Drake, who are busy cleaning their stations. My section is already spotless, seeing as my solo customer wasn't too demanding. "Hey, I'm gonna take Grace upstairs. I'll be back down in a bit to help with the rest."

Ridge waves me off. "Nah, get outta here."

"You sure?"

"Positive. Your focus is needed elsewhere." He juts his chin in Grace's direction.

I glance at her, only to find her already staring at me. She puts forth a valiant effort to wink, but it just looks like she has something in her eye.

"Yeah, you're probably right," I mumble.

He snorts, but it almost resembles a laugh. "Good luck, Foster. Don't do anything you normally would."

"Fuck off." I step out from behind the bar and sidle up beside Grace. "Ready?"

Bleary eyes blink at me with unmasked hunger. "Heyyyyy, you."

With a hand pressed at the base of her spine, I gently ease her off the stool. "C'mon, Gracie Lou. Time for bed."

Her expression brightens as she sways into me. "Together?"

"Not quite. I'll take the couch. You can have my bed." I guide her to the exit with gentle pressure on her lower back.

"Oh, my. You're taking me to your place?" She leans in and cups a palm around her mouth, as if sharing a secret. "People are going to talk."

I laugh at her poor attempt at a stage whisper. "Let them blab. If anyone is rumored to be my girlfriend, it might as well be you. I'm more committed to you than anyone else."

She straightens, almost appearing to have a moment of clarity. "What was that?"

"Nothing." I hadn't meant to say that. Here's to hoping she forgets most of what happens tonight, including that dumbass who hurt her feelings to begin with.

"It was something," she retorts.

"Doesn't matter. It's almost two o'clock in the morning. Anyone awake right now isn't the most reliable source."

A chill greets us when we walk outside. Relief washes over me and I don't bother stifling a sigh. The cool air tames my feverish desire. Grace notices the drop in temperature and takes the opportunity to cling tighter to me. A breeze carries her scent on a wave of temptation. She smells like an exotic vacation and lowered inhibitions.

As if listening to my inner turmoil, Grace snuggles impossibly closer. "This is nice. You're warm and toasty and hot."

Instinct reinforces my grip on her. "It is."

"You kissed me," she blurts.

"I did."

"Do it again." Grace puckers her lips.

"That's not a good idea." But I feel myself bending like a willow branch.

The nearby traffic light showcases the disappointment flashing on her expression. "And it was before?"

"That was different," I reason.

"You were just using me."

My stride falters. "Don't phrase it like that."

"How would you prefer I twist your logic?"

"We can discuss this later. You're drunk." And I'm in a sudden hurry to get home.

"So?"

"I'm not going to give you a reason to hate me."

"I could never hate you."

"You say that now, but come morning and the return of your sobriety? Totally different story."

"But I'm horny." The petulant whine isn't aiding her case.

"That's just the liquor slurring your good sense. Get some sleep and you'll be thinking much clearer about who you want to scratch that itch."

"The answer will be the same," she whispers.

Ignoring that comment hurts me more than I can properly describe. The painful clench in my gut does a damn decent job, though. It's worse than indigestion and food poisoning combined.

"This way." My voice is gruff even to my own ears.

But I don't hesitate to steer her around the building. The metal steps straight ahead glint under the streetlamp. Just the climb remains.

Grace slams to an abrupt halt. "You live above the bar?"

"It's very convenient." I get us back in motion without much resistance.

She slaps a sluggish palm on my chest. "No shit. I'm super jealous of your commute."

Which involves a moderate set of stairs. Our pace is steady, but careful. Grace doesn't trip once during the ascend. We share a mutual sigh of relief upon reaching the landing.

I slide the key into the deadbolt and usher us inside. "Welcome to the bachelor pad."

Grace crosses the threshold to enter the dark space. "Seems cozy."

"Let me flip a switch."

My meaning registers very differently for her. Once the door slams shut, she lunges for me. Grace suddenly has a dozen limps, all determined to haul me into a passionate embrace. That singular goal has me suctioned to her until there's no escape. I'd surrender if the odds were even slightly better that she'd remember this in the morning.

"Grace," I wheeze while managing to unravel myself. "Think about what you're doing."

She claws at my shirt. "That's easy. You're all I think about."

"Let's pump the brakes," I urge.

Her grip on me loosens enough to provide wiggle room. My fingers blindly search for the table lamp. It takes several seconds for my eyes to adjust. Grace is still struggling based on the way she's shielding her face.

"You should go to bed." I shuffle sideways to point her in the right direction.

"And you should kiss me," she breathes against my jaw.

"Nah, you don't want me."

"I do. Badly."

"Not like this, Grace." The plea in my voice borders on pathetic. In all honesty, I'm a weak man. There's only so much resistance I can enforce.

"We can pretend it didn't happen. That shouldn't be too hard for me." She hiccups.

I trace her upturned jaw with my thumb. "But it would be impossible for me."

The fight leaves her. "Ah, crap. You really are perfect."

"I'm a long ways away from earning that title."

"Then prove it. Take advantage of what I'm offering." Grace thrusts her breasts at me and shimmies to make the supple flesh jiggle.

Flames billow under my skin, a wave of heat I can't combat. "I'll be no better than those men who've treated you poorly."

She's already shaking her head. "That's where you're wrong. You're nothing like them. No guy has ever gone out of his way to do a fraction of what you did for me tonight. I feel appreciated and beautiful and *seen*. Do you know what that means to a girl who has battled confidence issues most of her life? Let me tell you. It means everything, Garrett."

"Fuck," I curse. My restraint crumbles faster than tissue paper in a rainstorm. "Just a peck."

She bounces up on the balls of her feet to bring our mouths closer. "Uh-huh."

But those polite intentions instantly evaporate.

Our lips slam together in a rabid chase. Her tongue whips out in an attempt to choke me. It's sloppy and wet and arousing as fuck. I've never been harder. My arm circles her waist while both of hers lift to link at my nape. Then I take the liberty of palming her ass. She moans and bucks into me.

Our hips are pressed flush in this position. There's not a doubt she misses how hard my cock is. Even in her bleary state, she can rest assured that I'm extremely attracted to her. That reminder is a slap of clarity. We're on opposite ends of the sobriety scale.

I break our kiss before she can prove how tonsil hockey is won. "Okay, that's enough."

"Just a little more." She tugs from where her wrists are crossed at the back of my neck.

"Tomorrow," I compromise. "When you're sober. I refuse to take advantage of you."

Grace must hear the finality in my tone. Her shoulders slump. "Fine."

The static energy calms into a muted thrum. I turn on the overhead light to illuminate more of my small apartment. The sparse furnishings lack warmth and comfort, but the main purpose is served.

"Let me show you to my room. No funny business."

"Yeah, yeah," she grumbles. Her feet slap on the hardwood as she follows me down the hall to the open door.

"Ladies first." I motion her inside.

She trots forward and swan-dives onto the bed. I scrub a palm over my mouth, but there's no masking my chuckle. This woman is just too much. Then she rolls over and spreads out like a starfish.

"I'm in your sex palace. Why don't you join me?" She crooks her finger in a come-hither gesture.

My steps are measured as I stroll to the mattress and park my ass on the edge. "Do you want a shirt to sleep in?"

She glances down at her dress, then begins to yank the garment up and over her head. A black bra is slingshot at me in the next instant. "Nothing beats naked skin against cool sheets."

I avert my eyes, but the image of her curves bared to me will forever be ingrained. "Uh, okay. Need anything else?"

"Just you." Her lashes flutter at me in a lazy formation. "My knightly hero."

"Yep, that's me. A real wiener."

Her eyes roll at my playful pun. "Thanks for getting me wasted."

"Not sure that's something you should be thankful for."

"I asked for it."

"Doesn't make it right."

"Well, if nothing else, thanks for proving that nice guys still exist." She pats my chest as I tug the blankets over her.

"You give me too much credit."

"And you don't give yourself enough," she mumbles.

Warmth spreads through my chest while I watch her burrow deeper under the covers. "I'm gonna get you some water. Be right back."

She mutters something incoherent as I leave the room. I take my time in the kitchen. There's no rush. Personal experience has me snagging a few ibuprofen for her as well. As predicted, Grace is snoring softly when I return.

I set the items on the nightstand for her to find whenever. Then I surrender to impulse and kiss her forehead. "Sweet dreams, soulmate."

chapter ten

Grace

"RISE AND SHINE, SLEEPYHEAD."

That gravel voice and the decadent scent of caffeine rouses me from a dreamless sleep. Insistent throbbing against my temples suggests I resist the lure. I crack an eyelid open to see Garrett perched on the edge of the bed, wafting coffee fumes at me from a steaming mug. He sets the freshly brewed temptation on the nightstand and waits for me to formally acknowledge his presence.

"Morning," I croak. That's about all I dare to say. My mouth tastes like a full dumpster of poopy diapers after baking under the sun for hours.

"Almost afternoon," he returns with a chuckle.

"My head is pounding. Need. More. Sleep," I groan.

Garrett's lips curve into a devilish smirk made for sin. "Regrets?"

"Heck no." I prop myself up on a wobbly elbow. Even the slight motion drives a spike through my skull. "How else would I gain your undivided attention for an entire evening?"

His eyes become a blue inferno set on incinerating the

differences in our dating expectations. "I could think of several ideas."

The sheet drifts along my bare skin, which alerts me to my state of undress. I grapple for the covers before I provide him with a peepshow. That sets off another internal alarm. My mind is a mushy abyss as I scramble to find missing pieces. Only blurry snippets appear through the fog. And now I'm sweating.

Garrett grunts at my continued fumbling. "Nothing I didn't see while tucking you in."

As if that's reassuring. I fling an arm over my face and gnaw on a foul curse. "Crappity crud buckets. Ohhhhh, shoot. Please tell me we didn't—"

He holds up a palm, effectively cutting off what might've bloomed into hysterics. "Nope, don't fret. I was a perfect gentleman. Mostly. Even when you tried to seduce me with promises of anal."

My breath whooshes from me. "I would never."

"Okay, fine. You didn't offer to let me in the back door. But you did beg me to take the edge off for you. Several times." His wink is too flirty for this conversation.

"Whatever. There's no way that's accurate," I mutter.

Although, my memory remains splintered. There's a solid chance he's right.

His broad grin says he damn well knows it. "You most certainly did, but I'll let you pretend you didn't."

My denial comes to an abrupt halt. Clips of my desperate advances from last night replay in a blooper reel, and I hang my head in my hands. "Aw, shit."

His laughter is a smug tune fit as confirmation to his claim. "Yep, totally happened. You were like a boa constrictor trying to devour me."

I whack him with a pillow. "It wasn't that bad."

"Nah, it wasn't. I'm flattered."

"You should be." The blanket shifts to almost reveal my boobs again. I wrench the fabric to my chin in a white-knuckle grip. "Dammit."

Garrett tosses a soft lump at me. "Put that on if you're worried about a nip slip."

"What—?" I unfold the bundle to reveal a sweatshirt. Stamped on the front in big letters is the phrase 'Hangover Hoodie', and by the softness of it, it's been used for quite a few rough mornings. "Clever, but it's not gonna fit."

"Just try."

I tug the well-worn cotton over my head and discover that it does in fact fit. Before I celebrate that small victory, Garrett's rumble steals my focus. Primal hunger flares in his gaze to warn me that I'm the one about to be devoured.

"Perfect," he rasps.

"Um, thanks."

"Before I forget, I put a pause on your sexual propositions until morning arrived. Still interested?" He begins to lift the hem of his shirt.

Warmth rises in my cheeks. "Are you interested in these relations extending beyond the bedroom?"

"That's kinky, soulmate. I like your adventurous spirit."

"You know what I mean." Then I grumble under my breath about obtuse bachelors.

"No strings," he confirms.

"Afraid I'll have to pass. Maybe you should've taken advantage when the mood stuck."

Garrett's smile appears naturally, as if he predicted my response. "Besties we remain then."

Another moment resurfaces through the haze. "Ah, yes. I'm your first female friend who isn't family. Try saying that five times fast."

He does, just to humor me no doubt. "Impressed?"

"That you're more committed to me than anyone else? Sure am."

A grunt accompanies his cringe. "Remember that, huh?"

"Just a wee bit." I pinch a sliver of space between my thumb and forefinger.

The sleeve of the hoodie brushes my nose and I make the mistake of inhaling. Crisp laundry detergent can't mask the embedded traces of woodsy cologne and carnal lust. Damn, Garrett Foster smells yummy. It's only then I realize that I'm surrounded by him.

Just as I'm about to recline against the headboard and enjoy my coffee, a vivid memory from the night before appears in startling clarity. I lurch upright as the thought occurs to me. Regret instantly follows the fast motion. An ache spreads across my entire body to protest further movement.

His brows wing upward. "Problem?"

"We kissed again," I recall in a hushed whisper.

He licks along his bottom lip in a purposely lazy drag. "We did. It's becoming a habit."

My focus latches onto his mouth. A needy clench in my lower belly has me squeezing my thighs together. "Strange how that happens."

"What's a few kisses between friends, hmm?"

"Completely meaningless." *Liar.* I've barely recovered from the one a week ago and now there's a refresher to contend with.

"You can be my fake girlfriend whenever the need arises. Keeps the barflies off my shit. Want me to thank you again for that?" Garrett shifts into my space until we're close enough to add a third tally to our smooch total.

Too bad I have dragon breath, or I might go for it. Instead, I shove a reminder into the gap separating us. "Will that help me find a real boyfriend?"

It works. A little too well. He moves from his hovering position, and I feel the loss like a physical blow.

"Mr. Monogamy will appear when you least expect him," he clips. "Until then, your knightly hero will swoop in and defend your honor. Isn't that right, Peaches?"

The endearment rushes over me in a comforting embrace. It also sparks a craving for something much sweeter than what's currently rotting in my mouth. "You didn't name that final drink. It was my favorite."

Garrett wags a finger in my direction. "Did you actually drink any of them? Your memory is crystal clear."

"Or my tolerance is higher than you gave me credit for." Another lie. I was properly hammered.

His narrow squint pretends to assess my honesty, but there's no containing the amusement twitching his lips. "Let's call that last one Peachy Bottom Grace."

"Seems very personal," I muse.

"As it's meant to be. I'm keeping the recipe a secret for lonely nights."

"When the only thing in this bed with you is the fantasy of me offering my anal virginity to you on a drunken platter?" I flutter my lashes at him.

Garrett audibly chokes, thumping his chest to regain composure. "Fuuuuuuck, that's just mean. I'm gonna need a cold shower."

"You're welcome."

"As if the sight of you in my hoodie wasn't already premier spank bank material. You're making it hard to be decent." He bites his knuckles and releases a throaty groan.

"This old thing?" I poke at the frayed edges.

"Hangs off your shoulder just right." The need smoldering from his gaze convinces me.

I maneuver to pull the hem as low as it goes. "It covers my rump. Shocking."

"Speaking of your peachy ass," he rasps. Our eyes lock and hold for several seconds. Garrett rips from the trance to stare toward the hallway. "Get up. I made breakfast."

"You cook?" I flop down onto the mattress with a drawn-out exhale. "Go figure."

He pats my leg that's still hidden under the covers. "C'mon, it's already lukewarm at best."

"Let's hope you never meet my dad. He'd give you his stamp of approval, and then you'd be stuck with us."

He stands, stretching until his back cracks. "Doesn't seem like a bad deal. You told me about your family. I'd love to meet them."

"Really?" I sit upright to meet the honesty in his expression.

A sharp nod confirms it. "Your dad and sister sound great. Not sure about the older half-siblings, though. They're more like wild cards."

"That's a good way of describing them. I'm sure he would invite you over for dinner in a heartbeat."

Garrett pauses to study me. "There's something I've been meaning to ask you."

I freeze as well. "Cryptic much?"

His chuckle cracks the tension locking my muscles. "What's your last name?"

"Oh." The leftover strain deflates from my stiff posture. "Howard."

"Well, Grace Howard"—he proceeds to whip the blankets from my clutches—"get your butt out of my bed. We have a big day ahead of us."

It takes four rapid breaths for me to realize my bottom half is now on display. I cross my ankles in a feigned attempt at modesty. "Um, excuse you."

He's openly staring at my shapely thighs. "Great view, soulmate."

I squirm under his blatant ogling. "You shouldn't look at your friends like that. It's impolite and gives the wrong impression."

"We could be more than friends," he mumbles absently.

"This again?"

He snaps from the stupor, scrubbing a palm over his gaping mouth. "Uh, right. Let's go."

"To the kitchen for"—I check the clock beside me—"brunch?"

His head bobs. "And we'll go from there."

"Where exactly?"

"Well, it's Saturday before noon. The farmers market is open until two o'clock."

"Very funny." Laughter bursts from me until I notice he's not joining in my amusement. "You're serious."

"Why not? It can be our thing, like a weekly tradition. We'll find something else during different seasons." His Adam's apple quivers with a thick gulp. "Just as friends."

The slight edge in his tone piques my interest. "Sounds good to me. I just have to go home and change first."

"Nope, there's not enough time for that. You can borrow a pair of my boxers. I have a spare toothbrush too."

My nose wrinkles at the idea. "You must be joking."

He crosses his bulky arms. "Do you have a better solution? We just agreed to start this tradition and it's already wavering."

"I have shorts in my gym bag. Just have to get it from my car." I scoot off the bed to set this plan into motion.

"And you parked…?"

"At Abbie's house," I admit.

"She lives across town. The clock is ticking, Peaches. What'll it be?" There's a starved gleam in his eyes that demands to be fed.

Now it's my turn to swallow hard. I weigh my options,

along with the obvious want that he's aiming at me. Tingles erupt from unmentionable places. A sinking realization quickly follows. Disappointment will replace the fire if I reject his offer to prance around in his clothes. A defeated slump hunches my shoulders.

I hold out a hand, curling my fingers in a beckoning motion. "Let me see the boxers."

chapter eleven

Garrett

THE DOOR FLIES OPEN BEFORE I HAVE THE CHANCE
to knock. Joy is there to greet me with a wide grin.
"Hey, brother! You've arrived. Welcome. Thanks for
coming over on such short notice."

"Didn't give me much choice." I step over the threshold
when she ushers me inside.

"Where would you prefer to watch my daughter? Your
beloved cock den doesn't even have a changing table."

"It's on my list to order," I retort.

But she isn't done. "Don't get me started on your sex loft.
It's littered with sharp objects that aren't safe for the conquests
you haul up there. Let alone a baby."

"Yeah, yeah. Your place is best. Mine sucks. Message received. Can I hold my niece?" I move to cradle Belle in a careful
and supportive grip.

"Yep, she's all yours for the next two hours." Joy plops the
precious bundle into my arms like a sack of flour.

I turn to stone at the rushed motion. The chubby angel

just settles against me like this is a normal occurrence. "Um, okay."

"Don't look so scared. She's much sturdier now."

"Really?" My movements feel robotic as I begin to sway.

"A lot changes in three months." My sister beams at her daughter resting in my arms.

I drift a bent knuckle along the baby's soft cheek. "Where does the time go?"

"Beats me," Joy muses. "I swear it was March just yesterday. Next thing I know, it's mid-June and my newborn is now an infant."

"She's still very little," I murmur.

"And she'll always be my baby." My sister swoops down to pepper Belle with kisses. "I'm glad you were free to take care of her. We're doing this mini showcase performance for parents at the studio. It's too late to cancel."

"I'm shocked you deem me worthy of the task. It's an honor. Am I your last resort?"

"Oh, stop. You're not that far down the list," she argues.

"Everyone else is busy, huh?"

Joy doesn't bother denying it. "Cole's meeting is running late. Mom and Dad have dinner plans."

"What happened to your nanny?" My reason for asking might serve a selfish purpose.

"Grace was supposed to be here, but she isn't feeling well. She called after leaving the Nelson's house. I guess her throat is sore and getting worse."

"You talked to her?"

My sister narrows her eyes at the desperation in my voice. "Well, yeah. How else would I know she isn't coming?"

"She could've just texted you," I grumble. Not that I'm jealous or anything. It doesn't matter that we've never spoken on the phone.

"That's not nearly as professional."

I grunt. "As if you care."

Her squint turns into a sharp point determined to stab at my irritation. "You haven't heard from her lately?"

"Not since the farmers market, and that was several days ago." The reminder of our newfound tradition pumps warmth through me. We didn't kiss, but she let me hold her hand when another clingy barfly crossed our path.

"Have you reached out to her?"

"No."

My sister pinches the bridge of her nose. "And why not?"

Prickles spread across my nape from her direct scrutiny. "I dunno. She's supposed to message me."

"What happened to you sending her potential boyfriends?"

My stiff rocking motion stalls. "Grace told you about that?"

"Harper found out and mentioned something to me," she hedges.

"Of course she did."

She waves off my dry tone. "Like you don't expect us to blab about your business, especially when you're being ridiculous. Did you really think she wouldn't notice the guys are models?"

"They looked like decent options. I don't see the issue." I'm full of enough shit to turn my eyes brown.

"Why can't you just admit that you want her?"

"I do want her, but I'm not who she wants."

Joy scoffs. "Only because you refuse to be in a relationship."

"Why should I be the one to sacrifice my ideals and preferences?" Grace said something similar to me when we first met. I couldn't agree more.

"Fine, whatever. You're just friends. That means there are no dating rules to skirt around. Call her if you want to talk."

"Nah, she's probably resting. I don't wanna bother her."

She groans. "You're such a man."

"Thank you?"

"That wasn't a compliment," she gripes.

"Didn't really figure it was."

Belle wiggles in my arms, swatting at me with a tiny hand. I take that as a hint to resume swaying. Her responding smile is a rich reward.

"You're good with her." There's pride in my sister's voice.

That encourages me to keep the question from mine. "Thanks."

Silence envelops us for several beats. Her unwavering focus has me bracing for whatever she's about to say. "Don't you want kids of your own someday?"

"Didn't we already discuss this? On countless occasions?"

"You'd be such a great dad," she whispers.

"I don't need a wife or girlfriend in order to be a father."

"Well, no. But it's nice to have a partner in the experience." Joy is speaking from her own. Cole—her fiancé and my so-called friend—appears to be an ideal half of a perfect parenthood equation.

"I'll just babysit Belle more often."

"If that fulfills your paternal urges." Her expression is too cheery for my liking.

"Or I could be a sperm donor."

She clenches her eyes shut and quietly begs for patience. "That's not what I meant, and you're missing the point."

"Depends on who I give my swimmers to."

"Such as Grace?" A coy smile curls her lips.

"If she's interested. We could make one of those pacts."

"Yeah, or you could skip the delay and marry her tomorrow."

I blow out a harsh breath. "Isn't there somewhere you need to be?"

My sister laughs at my evasive maneuver. "Just consider

it. You're already committed to her from what I've seen and heard."

There's that claim again, one that I accidentally on purpose spouted as well. Maybe I've brought this on myself. More than likely. That doesn't mean I have to admit it.

"We're just friends," I repeat.

"Right," Joy mumbles. "You can be faithful to someone without slapping on a label."

"Not sure what you're blabbering about." But the knot tightening in my gut suggests otherwise.

A spark flashes in her gaze. "How long has it been since you've had sex?"

I damn near swallow my tongue. "What the fuuuu—dge?"

"Do I actually need to repeat myself?" Subtlety isn't one of my sister's best qualities.

"Gross, Joy. You're my sister. Not to mention that I'm holding your daughter. We're done discussing S-E-X."

"Just as I suspected," she chirps. "You're firmly attached and loyal to Grace. Still referring to her as your soulmate?"

"That's a joke between us." But my excuse is flimsy.

The gleam in her gaze tells me she's well aware. "Denial and delusions aside, your *friendship* is raising eyebrows around town."

Her emphasis on that label doesn't go unnoticed. The whispers circulating Knox Creek don't either. Not that I expected a different reaction after kissing Grace in public. The entire point was to make a statement.

"What can I say? We have an arrangement of sorts. I'm tracking down her Mr. Right and in exchange, she swats unwanted attention off my tail."

"And how does she do that?"

"It doesn't take much," I evade. "Grace is a crowd pleaser. The whole package. I'm not afraid to admit that. People stop and gawk and make assumptions. Not my problem if they jump to conclusions."

"But you won't date her," she deadpans.

"Badger me all you want. My answer won't change. We should concentrate on this little lady," I croon at Belle. "Is there anything vital I should be aware of before you leave?"

My sister is silent for almost a minute, but decides to let me off the hook. "There's a detailed list on the counter for your reference. Belle just pooped so the tank should be empty. You never know, though. She'll be hungry soon. There are bottles ready to go in the fridge. You just have to put them in the warmer."

"Do you have gloves? It creeps me out to touch your breastmilk."

"Then make sure you don't spill any, weirdo. You should be careful regardless. It's liquid gold."

"Yes, ma'am." I nod rather than salute.

"You've got this?" She eyes me holding Belle too stiffly.

"Totally. If all else fails, I'll give her candy."

"Not funny," she mutters. As if needing reassurance, she smothers Belle in more kisses. "Mama is gonna miss you. Don't get into trouble."

"Quit worrying." I settle on the couch with Belle securely tucked against me and flip on the television. "We're gonna watch ESPN. Is our girl a baseball fan?"

"That'll definitely put her to sleep. Good thinking." Approval shines in Joy's gaze as she gathers her stuff. But she still pauses before leaving. "Call me if you need anything."

"Like a pizza? Because I could eat."

"Ugh, you're impossible."

"You make it too easy. Get to work and trust me to be a responsible adult." I shoo her off.

"Okay, thanks again. Bye!" After a parting glance, Joy manages to rip herself from the scene.

The door slams with a resounding bang to signal it's just me and my tiny chaperone. It's so quiet. Belle appears comfortable so I don't move. I try to focus on the Twins game, but my mind instantly wanders. There's an itch in my front pocket that I can't ignore.

"What do you think, Belley button? Should we text Grace? Just a quick message to check on her. It would be the friendly thing to do."

She coos and blows a few spit bubbles.

"My thoughts exactly," I respond.

It takes some careful juggling to retrieve my phone. The anticipation crackling under my skin requires zero encouragement. Several notifications appear on the screen. None are from the one I want but can't have. That doesn't discourage me from typing out a message.

Me: Hey, Peachy Bottom Grace. 🍑

I immediately groan at myself. The emoji was over the top. Too late. Might as well make my craving for contact known.

Me: Joy said you're sick. Need a pick-me-up?

When she doesn't immediately respond, I take the initiative and snap a duo selfie of us. She won't be able to resist replying. Belle is grinning in the shot, which I'm choosing to believe is her approval of my plan and not a warning that she's about to fire one out.

Me: *image attached*

A weight is lifted off my chest and I sag into the cushions. A calm soon floods over the rest of me. "There. Now we can relax."

chapter twelve

Grace

I n my fever-induced daze, I barely register the unmistakable jingle of keys from somewhere nearby. That alerts me to the deadbolt flipping to unlock. A creak from that squeaky floorboard in the foyer suggests someone just entered my apartment. Denial cinches on tighter than this insufferable illness. There's a good chance this is a dream and I'm just hallucinating, too desperate for human contact.

As if mocking my loneliness, the front door clicks shut to slam a lid on any traces of doubt. This is real. A vise clamps around my windpipe. I couldn't call for help if I wanted. Icy threads lash along my spine as footsteps approach from the main living area. I attempt to sit up, but immediately collapse into my sweaty sheets.

"Grace?"

Comfort swells through my sore muscles. Even with panic crawling over my logic, I recognize Garrett's voice. "In here."

His unexpected—although welcome—presence brightens my doorway a moment later. A grin that's warm and gooey and rivals a tropical vacation is aimed at my rumpled form. "You're okay."

My swollen eyes sting at the relief in his voice. "For the most part."

He strides toward my bed in a hurry. "I was beginning to take it personally that I hadn't heard from you."

"Wasn't by choice," I croak.

"That silence was deafening, but now I see why you were avoiding me." Garrett's eyes trace over every part of me that isn't burrowed under layers. "You sound miserable."

"Look it too." I pat the nest that my hair has become over this past week.

"Didn't say that."

"Don't have to. I can feel the grime and crust on my skin." A shudder racks my weary limbs at the thought.

His unwavering focus doesn't miss my reaction. "Need a hand getting to the shower? Or maybe a bath would be better."

My lump of tangles catch on the pillow when I manage to shake my head. "Thanks for the offer, but I'm conserving my energy."

"All right, we'll stay put." He parks his ass on the edge of my bed.

My stuffy nose wrinkles, knowing full well my blankets smell worse than a boys' locker room before they discover the miracle of deodorant. Although, he's probably used to the stench as a former athlete. That doesn't mean I want to repel him with my odor.

"I'm probably contagious. You should stay away." The fresh beads of perspiration dotting my forehead reveal I'm still feverish.

"Your germs don't scare me, soulmate." That statement offers too big of a dangling carrot to ignore.

"What does?"

"Believing you came to your senses and found a better

friend than me." The hurt in his voice would wobble my knees if I had the strength to stand.

"Unfortunately, I'm just sick." A cramp chooses that instant to seize my stomach and I wince. "For the record, I'm not the type to cut and run. I'd at least flip you the bird first."

"Glad to hear you didn't ditch me."

"Not yet," I wheeze. "But the breaking and entering is a tad concerning. How'd you get in?"

"Abbie let me borrow her key." He shares that tidbit like it's the current weather report.

"Did she tell you where I live too?"

"Part of the rescue mission. Which reminds me." He settles deeper into the mattress, making it clear he isn't going anywhere. "You should move closer to Knox Creek. This was quite the drive."

I shift to get a better view of him sprawled out. "It takes no more than thirty minutes."

"That's an hour round trip."

I sputter, which morphs into a rattled cough. "Seriously?"

"Yep, it's simple math." Garrett holds up a few fingers to demonstrate.

"Thanks for the lesson." My puffy eyes roll to the ceiling.

"I'm just saying, you could do me a favor and move. Then visiting you wouldn't be such a long haul."

"Nobody is forcing you to drive all the way out here to Timbuktu," I grumble.

"I had to make sure you were alive," he reminds me in return.

"And now that you have?"

He winks at me. "We're forming another habit. You're lounging like a queen while I sit vigil at your bedside."

"I'm happy to trade places." Yet I snuggle lower into the cocoon I created.

"Aren't you hot?"

"Kinda? The chills come and go. I'm probably due for more ibuprofen." A glance at my nightstand shows that I could use a water refill as well.

"Nothing stronger?" His grimace is for my benefit, or that's what I'm choosing to believe.

"There's no cure other than rest and plenty of fluids."

Garrett launches to his feet to do my unspoken bidding. After grabbing my Yeti bottle, he disappears toward the kitchen. Ice clinks against metal a moment later. A whimper escapes me at the impending relief.

Heat blurs my vision when he reenters my room. He reclaims his spot beside me, going so far as to putting the nozzle against my lips. I guzzle the cold water greedily. As the burn eases, I pull away for a full breath.

Garrett has two pills in his palm. "Open."

I don't hesitate to stick out my tongue. He pops the medicine directly in my mouth. If I weren't out of commission, I'd open my lady business wide for this man.

"Good girl," he rasps as I drink more from the raised bottle.

Our gazes lock and hold until I'm burning again. "Thank you."

"You're welcome. Want more?"

"I'm okay for now."

His focus tracks over me as if to double check my assurance. "You went to a doctor then?"

I swallow in a weak attempt to soothe my throat. "My dad took me after I started throwing up. They did all the main tests, but the results were negative. I either have a bad bug or it's food poisoning. Maybe both."

His jaw goes slack. "It's been almost two weeks since Joy told me you weren't feeling well."

My shrug is more like a fumbled slump. "I took a home

test a few days ago just to be extra sure. Still negative, and still battling symptoms."

"This is bullshit," he mutters.

"Miss me that much?" I try to flutter my lashes, but it takes too much effort.

"Fuck yes. You've gotta be near the end of the tunnel." The hope in his statement sparks my own.

"I'd like to believe so, but this virus or whatever is a real bitch. She's a stage-five clinger."

"Is there anything I can do to make you feel better?" Garrett's gaze lingers on mine, reflecting an unfiltered desire to be needed.

A loose sigh escapes my chapped lips. "Other than sending adorable pictures of you and Belle? If I hadn't already been overheated, that would've done the trick. But no, just you coming over to check on me is more than enough. It means a lot that you were willing to drive suuuuuper far to do so. I guess that makes up for you almost making me pass out from fear."

"You weren't answering my calls or texts."

"Not intentionally. I've been occupied."

"Either way, we've gotta quit meeting like this with you wearing that. It's giving me the wrong idea." He isn't shy about checking me out with a thorough once-over.

It's only then I remember that I have his sweatshirt on. "I'm so cozy."

"As you should be during a lockdown."

I tug on a frayed seam. "Do you want it back?"

"Nah, it's yours. I like seeing you in my stuff." His smolder is an inferno searing me from the inside out. Then he gulps and takes a visual sweep of my room. "What's with all the books?"

"I'm a bit of a collector."

"It looks like your shelves exploded."

And that's putting it mildly. An entire wall is reserved for the custom unit, but I've gone overboard with buying lately. The floor has become somewhat of a temporary storage.

"It should come as no surprise that I'm obsessed with romance novels," I reason.

He leans forward to admire the stacks. "But there are several with the same title."

I struggle to flick my wrist. "Different covers. Special editions are the rage right now."

His brow furrows when he peeks over at me. "Um, okay."

This is the point where I half expect him to abandon me. "Do you still wanna be friends?"

"Psssssh, duh." He proves his dedication by moving closer to my side.

My breath stalls, ending in a shallow rasp. There's a fuzzy texture on my tongue that reminds me I haven't brushed my teeth in… well, I don't even know how long. I clap a palm over my mouth and speak through my fingers. "If germs don't chase you away, my breath probably will."

He tugs at my hand until I release the makeshift mask. "Could've brought that spare toothbrush you borrowed. It's in the bathroom cup right where you left it."

It hurts to laugh, but that doesn't stop me. "Thanks but I have my own. I just haven't been able to get up for much more than dire needs."

"Well, I'll see to your more personal needs for a bit."

My heart lurches, which has nothing to do with the sickness that plagues me. "How might you do that?"

His lips crook into a smirk that spears my depleted passion over a toasty flame. "I could read to you."

"Oh." Now my exhale whooshes out in a lusty wave. Just the idea kindles a slew of illicit fantasies.

He leaps off the bed to peruse my smutty collection. "Any suggestions?"

My head pounds while I rise onto an unsteady elbow. "That's like asking me to choose a favorite child."

"How about this one?" Garrett snatches a familiar spine from the bunch. "What's with the sticky notes?"

"That copy is annotated."

"Ah, right." He inspects the paperback, flipping through it to catch my highlights. "You must really like *Leave Him Loved*, and the author. There are a lot of Harloe Rae books."

My nod is disjointed but visible. "I'm a big fan. She's also local, which is cool. That one in particular is an excellent choice. It's a friends-to-lovers small-town romance."

"Sounds"—he pauses to glance at me, the delay leading me to believe that he's going to make a connection—"interesting."

"I'll gladly listen to you perform a swoony rendition of Reeve Colton."

His smolder heats to a temperature that gives my fever competition. "Would that make you feel better?"

"Couldn't hurt."

Garrett returns to his reclined position beside me. His arm stretches to tuck under my pillow. The smooth motion jerks to a sudden halt. There's a five-second lag where my brain struggles to comprehend his reaction.

Fire rises to my cheeks. In my stupor, I belatedly realize what he's discovered. "Shit."

"What's this?" Glee is thick in his voice. "Were you giving yourself an endorphin boost before I arrived?"

My face flames hotter. "Ugh, no. Shut up."

"Do you always keep a magic wand under your pillow?" He taps at the air like he's casting a pleasure spell.

"If you must know, I forgot Roger was there." I stare longingly at my most beloved vibrator. It's been too long since we've been acquainted.

"You named it?" He inspects the purple silicone with a shrewd stare.

"Of course," I scoff. "They all have names."

"All?" Garrett sputters over his exhale. "How many do you have?"

"That's none of your business."

"Do you want to use this beast while I whisper sweet nothings in your ear?" He waves the dildo in the space between us.

"Can't touch me yourself?"

"Roger can join us. I'm a team player, baby."

"Quit talking crazy." I snag the toy from his grip. Roger lands on the carpet with a thump, but Garrett's suggestion isn't that easy to toss away. My pulse thunders as I try to calm the itch stirring beneath the surface. "I prefer individual sports unless the goal is to score together on a permanent, committed basis."

He whistles low. "No wonder you have so many erotic novels in your bedroom."

The action of fanning my face is purely to get a rise from him. "I do get hot and bothered between the pages of a girthy fantasy."

"Now you're trying to make me jealous."

"Is it working?"

Garrett licks his lips. "Too well."

"Just wait until you meet my fictional boyfriend." I point at the discarded romance on his lap.

He scoops up the book, taking several moments to silently judge the model on the cover. "Should I start from the beginning?"

"No, I'll probably fall asleep before anything spicy happens. It's a bit of a slow burn, you know?"

"Not really."

I thumb through the tabs I've used to mark my favorite scenes. "Read this part."

"Am I going to blush?"

"Doubtful. I chose a sweet spot. This guy is so romantic," I exhale. "He plans the best non-dates."

"Non-dates?

"They're just friends," I remind with a hint of teasing. "Reeve volunteers to show Audria the best parts of living in the country, all the while getting to spend plenty of quality alone time together."

"Smart man," Garrett muses. "When you've made a full recovery, I'll take you somewhere fun to celebrate."

I gasp and don't even choke afterward. "Our very own non-date?"

"Just you, me, and quality alone time."

"Sounds dreamy," I sigh.

"For now, get comfy. Rest your head on my shoulder." He pats the spot that looks too inviting to deny.

Once I've maneuvered myself into the designated nook, his woodsy cologne wafts over me. It serves to remind me just how bad I smell. "It's probably for the best that we're not going to actually date because my stench will forever disgust you."

"I'm not complaining. In fact, I think you smell great." He buries his nose in my hair, and I just about burn up from mortification.

"Liar," I whisper. Secretly, my stomach is doing an acrobatic routine fit for the circus.

"Do you want me to regale you with this charming tale or not?"

I cuddle against him, forgetting my troubles. "Yes, please. Don't let me stop you."

Garrett clears his throat and dives in. His voice fluctuates for the different characters. Talk about swoon-worthy. He goes above and beyond for my listening pleasure. I shove off the desires, distracting myself with the budding romance he's reading.

His deep timbre lulls me into a blissful trance. My eyelids

get heavy just as Reeve and Audria settle in the back of his truck to stargaze. I find myself drifting off to the sound of Garrett's gruff tone spouting the internal conflict from another hero. The one in this story presses his lips to my forehead before I lose the battle against sleep.

"Sweet dreams, soulmate."

chapter thirteen

Garrett

GRACE IS PRACTICALLY VIBRATING IN THE PASSENGER seat beside me. "Are we there yet?"

"You're worse than a kid," I joke. The urge to cover her wiggly fingers with mine almost makes me fidget.

"Can you blame me? I've been pent up for two weeks. Another day in bed and I would've jumped out of my skin. Isolation isn't for me."

"We can agree on that. Not seeing you at the bar or around town was a real buzzkill." The forced separation sprouted unwanted feelings about our... friendship. I'm choosing to ignore those impulses for both of our sakes.

As if listening to my emotional turmoil, Grace smiles sweetly and recites, "Distance makes the heart grow fonder."

Rather than admit the truth, I scoff at the notion. "Nah, I was just bored. Drake and Ridge aren't nearly as entertaining. They didn't appreciate my creative drinks or goofy straws."

Her eyes narrow at my transparent bullshit. "Then I guess you're lucky I agreed to hang out with you."

And it's about damn time. Much like her, I've been itching

to do something fun. Her clean bill of health happens to overlap with numerous Fourth of July festivities. I chose the option most suitable for a non-date based on the standards set by that romance she had me reading.

My thumb taps the steering wheel, matching the beat of the country song crooning from the speakers. "Just a few more miles. I will say that there's lots of space for you to run wild."

Grace rubs her palms together. "Good, I have plenty of energy to burn."

I peek at her from the corner of my eye. "Did you ever find out what you had?"

"Nope, not really. Just a nasty bug that wouldn't leave. On the positive side, I lost ten pounds."

"Didn't need to lose an ounce," I grumble under my breath.

"According to you, bestie. Other guys might choose to see my figure differently." She turns toward me. Sunlight streams in the open window to brighten her dark hair. Fucking breathtaking.

"They can kick rocks if your weight is a factor for them. Your body is beautiful and built to fulfill the most sinful fantasies."

She snorts. "Spoken like a true gentleman who avoids commitment as if it's a flesh-eating disease."

"Yeah, yeah," I mutter.

Before I can argue further, my attention is stolen by a small object crawling across the pavement. A quick glance ahead confirms there's oncoming traffic. The cars show no signs of slowing down. I tap on the brakes, easing over onto the shoulder.

"Little guy is gonna get hit. Be right back," I reassure.

Then I hop out of the cab to rescue the stereotype attempting to cross the road. Once he's safely plopped in the ditch, I return to my spot behind the wheel. Grace is gawking at me while I buckle up and resume our journey.

A minute passes and she hasn't moved. It's the longest she's sat still since I picked her up thirty minutes ago.

I chuckle at her frozen state. "What's on your mind, soulmate?"

Her mouth works soundlessly for several beats. "You stopped to save a turtle."

"Yeah?"

She flails her arms. "Gosh, of course. You're the type of guy who cares about defenseless animals, as if you aren't perfect enough."

I furrow my brow, keeping my gaze trained through the windshield. "Who wouldn't?"

"Most," she retorts.

"Savages."

"That's precisely the problem," she mumbles.

My heart races faster at the hidden meaning. "Is that on your list?"

Grace blinks. "Huh?"

"Of preferred qualities in a potential husband," I remind.

"Oh, right. I almost forgot." She thumps her forehead. "It needs updating."

"Must stop for turtles." I pretend to write, earning me a giggle.

"Top priority," she agrees.

I release a low whistle. "Mr. Monogamy is a tall order to fill."

"Any luck finding him?" She props her elbow on the center console to bring us closer.

My gaze slides in her direction. It takes heroic effort to ignore how round her tits look in that shirt. "Somebody got sick and paused the search."

"Couldn't do the task without me?"

"Why would I bother sending you pics of dudes when you wouldn't even return my regular messages?"

"Still grumpy about that?"

"Just had me worried," I mutter. Examining the depth of that concern is an invasive procedure I prefer to avoid by any means necessary. Somehow, this woman has become very important to me. My plan is to storm onward until it blows up in my face.

Grace's fingers dance across my forearm to rip me from that impending destruction. "How can I make it up to you?"

That sultry rasp almost has me swerving into the opposite lane. "Road head would be nice."

She swats at me and flops back into her seat. "You're such a man."

"Not sure how else you expected me to respond to an open offer like that." I pull into the grassy lot, finding a middle row with open spots. "You're off the hook, though. We've arrived."

She stares at a banner posted near the main entrance. "Wild West Days?"

A sense of pride burns through me as I shift the truck into park. I didn't anticipate that she'd be unfamiliar with my choice, or how I'd react to surprising her. "It's a county fair for these parts. A local staple for the holiday."

"I'm surprised Knox Creek doesn't host one for the occasion."

"They beat us to it. We didn't want to rain on their parade." I glance at the clock. "Which we missed, unfortunately."

Grace pops her door open. "Eh, we'll catch the next one."

I meet her at the front of the truck. "That's the spirit."

Her zippy pace resembles a pony prancing toward a bucket of apples. "I haven't been to a festival since Swing into Spring."

"Ah, that's where the magic started for us." My brows wag to what I imagine is an irresistible beat.

She slips on a pair of sunglasses, but not before shooting me a glare. "If you're referring to you shamelessly trying to get me in bed, then yes."

"And you let me down not so gently." I clutch at the area above my heart.

"It didn't hurt your ego." She bumps into me with her hip.

I take our proximity as an opportunity to loop an arm around her waist. "Your friendship has softened the blow."

Grace slows her rushed gait to peer up at me. Her eyes are hidden, but there's no mistaking the flush on her cheeks. "I'm glad we reached a compromise. And hey, you're committed to me on some level. Your words, not mine."

My pulse kicks at the term. It would be simple to reject the claim, but I find myself leaning toward the opposite. "I realized this arrangement is in our best interest. We can do all the cool shit together and not worry about getting more involved. It's like we're dating, only platonically. No emotional complications."

"Uh-huh, right." She pulls away, leaving me to question if I fucked up. "So, Wild West Days. It's bigger than I'd expect."

There's a part of me that's wary about her dismissal, but I let it go. I glance at the crowded grounds as if seeing the expansive spread for the first time. Red, white, and blue decorations are displayed far and wide. "We used to come here every year growing up. One of our regular traditions."

"Why'd you stop?"

"Adulting sucks," I offer in explanation. "Owning a bar is fucking awesome, but it doesn't allow for much wiggle room in my schedule."

She kicks at a patch of grass. "You seem to escape often enough."

"With proper motivation." I wrap a stray whisp of her hair around my finger and tug.

"There you go again," she sighs.

"What?"

A noncommittal noise hums from her. "If you're not careful, you could give a girl false hope."

The concern I stifled earlier rebounds with unavoidable force. My pulse hammers as we stride forward onto solid ground that suddenly feels unstable. A sideways glance reveals Grace to appear calm and composed and very much in her element. Her chin is tipped skyward, allowing the sun to soak in after too many days locked indoors. A smile curls the edges of her pouty lips. But there's something simmering just beneath the surface.

I squint into the distance. "Do you believe a girl and guy can actually be just friends? Especially when there's an obvious desire to bang each other."

She angles her head toward me, but the secrets in her gaze are still shielded from view. "Why do you ask?"

"You know why," I croon. "If our relationship goals were aligned, we'd be halfway to the chapel already."

"Assuming I'd have you," she quips.

"Wouldn't you?"

Grace chooses to dodge that sticky spot. "I believe we can put aside our fleeting chemistry for the sake of nurturing a connection that has real substance. As you said, we have a great thing going. Why ruin it?"

"Interesting," I mumble.

"How so?"

"There was a group of girls at Roosters—"

"This can only take a dirty turn," she cuts in.

I swerve to bump into her. "Get your mind outta the gutter, Peaches. They just shared that it's impossible for two single people who share a mutual attraction to remain strictly platonic."

Grace shrugs. "Maybe there's some truth to that."

"Yeah?" Shit, I hadn't expected her to agree.

"The initial interest can be tough to conquer, especially if it becomes one-sided and unrequited. That's just asking for a crack in the system."

My stride falters and I slam to a halt, reaching out to stop her as well. "Is that going to happen to us?"

"Not on my end. I'm aware of the score. It probably helps that you don't plan to date. Will you be able to handle watching me fall in love with another man?" The way her eyebrows move suggests she's fluttering her lashes.

The knot in my gut makes it difficult to form a rational response. I whip off her mirrored aviators. A sea of blue searches mine for answers that are lost in the denial separating us.

"As much as I like staring at my reflection in your lenses, I prefer seeing your eyes. They're very telling."

"And what do they say?"

I ghost my thumb along her upturned jaw. "You're stuck with me."

Grace's exhale is a soft gust coasting along my resistance, tempting me closer. "That doesn't seem like such a bad deal."

The resignation in her voice is an icy blast to sober me. I scrub over my mouth in a pitiful attempt to erase the heat she stoked there. "Damn, I almost crossed another line."

She licks along her bottom lip. "What's a few kisses between besties, right?"

The reminder of my foolish excuse slaps me across the cheek. "If only I could be the guy for you."

"If only," she echoes.

"All right, let's quit spinning our wheels. We're at the fair." I thrust an arm forward to where a variety of booths and stands edge the street. "What should we do first?"

Grace snags her sunglasses from my grip and slides the shield back into place. "This is your non-date idea. You choose."

Sunlight glints off the Ferris wheel, which pulls my focus to the surrounding rides. From experience, I recall rows of carnival games near that area. There's a tent to our left that houses a petting zoo. Motors rev in the distance to announce the go-kart track as an option.

The seemingly endless possibilities trip me up. I'm terrible at this shit. As if I'm not struggling enough, my hunt skids to a stop on Grace's ass. She looks too sexy in those cut-off shorts. Her thighs are another distraction entirely on their own. A visual of her legs caging mine while I thrust deep assaults me. *Fuuuuuuck.*

A breeze carries the aroma of deep-fried sugar and sinful cravings. The scent yanks my concentration over to what's considered the festival cafeteria. From funnel cakes and mini donuts to footlong corn dogs and turkey legs, there's something to satisfy everyone. Picnic tables are arranged in the center of the semi-circle formation.

I spy several available seats, hitching my thumb in that direction. "Hungry?"

She grimaces. "Eh, I probably shouldn't eat greasy stuff. My stomach hasn't fully recovered."

"Good call," I mumble. My attention drifts in an erratic arc across the vast space.

After several stilted beats, Grace must realize I'm floundering. "What was your favorite thing to do here as a kid?"

Fond memories stream in, centering on a particular activity. "Have you ever been in a hay maze?"

chapter fourteen

Grace

PLUCK SOME HAY FROM THE BALE BESIDE ME. "NOT CORN stalks, huh?"

"That's reserved for fall," Garrett explains.

"This is larger than I pictured."

A dimple winks at me from his cheek. "That's what a man likes to hear."

"You're incorrigible," I chide. Too bad there's no malice in my tone. If anything, the giggle that I can't muffle only encourages him.

"Well, duh. It's one of my most flattering character traits." He motions down his body.

"At least you can admit it. Anywho," I verbally pivot before he can send my thoughts spiraling to breathy moans trapped between tangled sheets. "Tell me about the significance behind this maze."

Garrett turns to admire the stacks with a reverence I recognize. "It was a ritual of sorts growing up. This was our first stop and we turned it into a race. Whoever won got to decide what we did next."

"And did you win?"

"Of course," he scoffs. "The rules changed in high school when I'd challenge a pretty girl to beat me."

My eyebrow quirks at his vague description that receives no further explanation. "How so?"

His bottom lip gets tugged between his teeth. "If I caught her before the exit, she had to give me a kiss."

"Why am I not surprised?" Thanks to the fading sunlight, I ditched my shades and can expose my utter lack of shock with an eye roll.

"You shouldn't be."

"How many lucky ladies did you kiss in there?"

"Not important. There's only one target I'm interested in hitting now. What do you say, Peaches?" He steps forward, putting us within touching distance. "Want to give it a go?"

There's already a thrum rushing beneath my skin. "What're the stakes?"

"I'd very much like to kiss you." Garrett's focus dips to my mouth.

"And if I win?" My voice rattles with an uneven exhale.

"That's your choice to wishfully think about."

My gasp is paired with a swat to his chest. "Don't let my plus-size figure fool you. I'm very fast."

He rubs a palm over his hair, properly chastised. "Wouldn't assume you're capable of anything less than bringing me to my knees."

"Is that a surrender?"

"Nah, that's just me recognizing a worthy opponent. But I'll kneel right now if you're offering me something to eat." He smacks his lips.

A flush races up my neck, no doubt painting my skin a rosy hue. "I'll save that as my prize."

"Damn, maybe I should lose this round."

As if I need another incentive to muddy the waters. I

bounce on the balls of my feet to relax the clench in my lower belly. "All right, let's do it. Burn off this excess energy."

Victory shines from his expression. "I'll give you a head start. Consider it a beginner's boost on the course."

"Don't do me any favors." I drop into a squat to prepare my muscles.

Garrett watches me stretch like the simple movements are pornographic. "Trust me, soulmate. The chase is purely for my benefit."

That's what he thinks. But it's not like I'm going to admit that the idea of him hunting me is a major turn-on. Warmth is pumping through me fast enough to provoke a spontaneous combustion. I've never felt this urgency before. There's no harm in exploring this new fantasy.

"Where's the end?" There's no chance of seeing over the wall. Instead, I try to peek through a gap between bales.

"That's for you to find out. I won't leave you stranded for long."

"You're that confident that you'll get me?" A thrill shoots in my veins, fueling me with a heady mixture of desire and motivation.

He stoops until our noses almost bump. "Extremely."

A glance over my shoulder shows that this area is somewhat separated from the fairgrounds. People are mainly congregating around the rides and food, which are barely visible from where I stand. It's almost strange that nobody else is venturing into the maze.

I return my attention to the task straight ahead. "Should I just... take off?"

Garrett's wolfish smile is familiar, a predator in his element. "I'll do a countdown."

He begins at ten—blasting off each digits that follows—while spinning himself in lazy circles. If he wants to make himself dizzy, I'll gladly accept the advantage.

My pulse gallops with each single digit he calls. His voice booms loud enough for the spectators within listening range to hear. But I'm not focused on anyone else.

Garrett tips his head to the sky mid-spin. His Adam's apple vibrates with each number he shouts. Then he straightens to look at me again. Our gazes clash and hold to set off a different timer.

His mouth slants into a crooked smirk that's detrimental to my resolve. "Better run, soulmate."

I giggle and bounce in place, then drop into a ready position. "You'll never catch me."

"Remember what happens when I do." There's a smug edge in his tone that demands to be acknowledged.

He has every intention of winning. I might just let him, but it won't be easy.

Sweat slicks my palms when I rub them together. Just as he's about to strike zero, I sprint forward in what I imagine is an impressive leap. His chuckle hounds my retreating dash into the stacks. Lucky for me, there are several turns and paths that cut off the central strip. It gives me another slight advantage—or just a quicker route to getting lost.

I dart to the left, almost immediately cutting right. This continues until I've convinced myself Garrett will struggle to follow my zigzag pattern. My vision is a blur of rustic yellow and unknown chances at every turn. If he doesn't find me, I can only hope to escape on my own. Or maybe he'll be willing to play a unique spin on Marco Polo.

My sandals slap my soles to the hurried melody of escape. Flip-flops were a bad choice. I'd kick them off altogether, but that would be a bigger crumb to leave behind. Dust rises in thick plumes to reveal my trail. As if I had any chance of actually evading him.

"I'm coming for you," Garrett taunts from somewhere in the distance behind me.

A squeak rips from me at the determination in his voice. It's been twenty seconds at the most. I push myself faster, but I'm just aimlessly barreling forward at this point. A quick backward glance shows no direct sight of him.

My chest tightens in warning. Between the exertion and excitement, I've almost tapped my limit. That's when I notice a shadowed alcove to provide temporary cover. I dodge a rock and squish myself into the narrow corner. Hiding isn't forfeiting so much as altering the game.

Drums hammer in my ears, drowning the stomp of his approaching stride. The thrill gets me hot, and I realize that I want him to catch me. I clench my eyes shut and wait to be captured. The prickle from the hay at my back anchors me. My fingers dig into the bale until a cramp seizes my knuckles.

I release my grip with a long exhale. A calm swoops in to offer a false sense of triumph. When I dare to peek, my heart lurches to the clouds. Garrett is there, inches from my face.

"Gotcha, Grace." He grins and leans forward to cage me between his arms. His crisp woodsy scent is an erotic wave that crashes over me.

I nearly moan from the impact. My lashes flutter when I treat myself to a greedy inhale. "It looks that way."

His chest rapidly rises and falls against mine. "Why'd you stop running?"

"Maybe I wanted to get caught," I relay my previous thoughts.

"Does that mean this reward is as much yours as it is mine?"

"Let's find out." I clutch the front of his shirt in a tight fist and yank.

Our mouths slam together in a burst of feverish need. We moan in unison at the collision. Garrett swipes his tongue out to trace the seam of my lips. I open for him eagerly, rocking my hips into his. There's no mistaking the bulge pressing against my lower belly. The knowledge that he's already hard feeds the flames. Warmth spreads from my core at an alarming rate. This desperation inside of me rages into an inferno when he sucks my bottom lip between his teeth.

I loop my other arm around his shoulder to tug him closer. Heat sparks from every place we touch. Garrett slants his head to weld our mouths in an unbreakable seal. Our tongues slide in an erotic caress. Hay stabs along my bare arms as I arch toward him. The slight sting mingles with the pressure of him on me. His palm grips my ass, hauling our lower halves in a flush embrace, and I groan at that needy bulge throbbing at me.

He tastes like cinnamon and endless pleasure, better than multiple orgasms after depriving myself for too long. A deep yearning spears into the most neglected parts of my body. I want more. Badly.

The frantic desire rushing between us has me grinding against him. Tingles erupt across me in an addictive sizzle. Garrett suddenly breaks our kiss with the snarled ferocity of an alpha male being forced to comply. There's a blaze in his eyes, turning the blue into a metallic liquid. That hungry gleam makes my knees quake. I tremble under the intensity while waiting for him to sever the tension.

"Damn, soulmate. Like holy shit." He rests his forehead against mine. "Didn't expect that much enthusiasm."

"Too much?"

"Fuck no, but what's gotten into you?"

"That was just really good for me," I admit.

Creases appear at the corners of his eyes when he smirks. "The kiss?"

"And you chasing me. It unleashed something… kinky." The slick throb between my legs has me squirming.

"Yeah?"

I'm nodding too fast, jostling our position. "This is a first for me."

A rumble rolls off him. "Wanna go again?"

The idea is tempting, but another thought screams louder. I'm only slightly ashamed to admit that I want to maul him right here and now. The resolve to stay faithful to my resolution wavers. I could blame the lack of physical contact, but it's more than that. It's Garrett. Period.

I gulp at the sudden dryness in my throat. "Do you believe friends can have meaningless sex?"

The seconds he takes to answer might as well be hours. My lungs burn from a lack of oxygen. I never drop my gaze from his, imploring him to leap with me.

He dips until he's sipping the hitched breath from my lips. "Why do you ask?"

"I want to cheat on my diet," I blurt.

"Huh?"

"Just this once." Not sure who I'm trying to convince.

"Gonna need more context, soulmate." He presses into me until his hardness rocks against where I'm aching to be filled.

It's been well over a year since I've felt the weight of a man on top of me while we succumb to pleasure. That can mess with a girl's sound mind, not to mention her confidence. I'm really doing this to reinforce my resistance. Just one night of surrender and I'll be content for as long as it takes to find love. It doesn't make me weak to want a slight indulgence.

"Fuck me like one of your barflies."

He grunts and puts an abrupt end to the friction between us. "Absolutely not."

Hurt smacks me in a punishing blow and it's difficult to breathe for a different reason. I shove at him while fighting the sting in my eyes. "Forget I asked."

Garrett stills my struggles with a solid grip on my upper

arms. "What I meant is that you could never be a quick fuck like that."

I sniff and pin a glare on the dirt path. "Why not?"

He tucks a bent knuckle under my chin and lifts until our gazes clash. "Do you honestly want me to dick you in the nearest bathroom or crammed in my backseat?"

Just the thought has nausea churning in my stomach. "How appealing."

"Exactly." His thumb drifts along my jaw, the touch reverent. "I'm not the man for you."

"You are tonight," I insist.

Garrett shakes his head. "You don't want me, Grace. Not truly."

This conversation suddenly feels very familiar. "It doesn't have to mean anything. Just sex. One and done."

He buries his face in the crook of my shoulder. His tortured groan rattles what remains of my restraint, a foreshadowing of him rattling something else later. "Do you honestly believe I'm not capable of getting attached to you? Sleeping together will complicate things. I don't want to lose you."

"You won't," I vow.

His heavy exhale puffs against the sensitive skin of my neck. Then Garrett traces the shell of my ear with his nose. Static buzzes in my veins. I find myself pushing forward to arch against him. His hardness nudges into me with the shift in position, and I take it as a green light. A soft whimper falls from my lips when he straightens to expose the desperate need tightening his expression.

My mouth brushes his to accentuate what I'm about to boldly voice. "I've thought about having sex with you since the first time I walked into Roosters. You've made it perfectly clear you'd like to fuck me with zero strings attached. We should just do it. Then we can resume our friendship like normal."

He stares at me for several seconds, probably trying to

comprehend the sudden onset of my proposition. "What happened to you refusing to sacrifice your resolution?"

"It's not a sacrifice if you're who I want."

"I won't let you compromise for me."

My finger jabs his chest. "I'm forfeiting for me. Just for tonight. Rules are meant to be bent."

"Not broken?"

My initial response is a casual shrug. "Business as usual tomorrow morning."

"You assume I won't be having breakfast in bed."

A visual of him feasting between my thighs assaults me and I barely suppress a quiver. "The terms can be negotiated."

Garrett towers overs me, a pillar of seduction I'm squirming to climb. "Are you sure about this?"

"Positive."

"Once you ride this bologna pony, you won't wanna stop." He gently thrusts as if I'm not already salivating at the length of his love lure. And that's sight unseen.

Regardless, my eyes roll at his cocky arrogance. "I'll manage to restrain myself."

"This burrito bronco can't be tamed." His scruffy cheek twitches as he fights a grin.

"Not planning to try," I retort.

"All right." The palm still on my ass gives me a squeeze before retreating to my hip. "Don't come crying to me when you're experiencing dick-drawals."

I thump my head against the hay bale, searching the thinning clouds for patience. "I'm beginning to think this was a terrible idea."

Garrett plucks straw from my hair. "Coming to your senses?"

"Something like that." But I don't move a muscle.

His chuckle curls my toes and reveals that he's aware I'm not going anywhere. "That's unfortunate, Peaches. I've already pictured a dozen positions to get you coming in an entirely different capacity. Much more pleasurable too."

"Can't you be serious?"

"That's like asking a prized stallion to only breed one mare."

My brow puckers while trying to compute how that's related to what I said. "What's with all the horse analogies?"

"I'm in a very studly mood thanks to a certain filly stroking my ego." He neighs to accentuate the point, like the ridiculous goof he is.

"Yet you were trying to talk me out of it two minutes ago."

The sinking sun glints across his roguish features. "Changed my mind."

"Why?"

"This way I get to have sex with you. I've been fucking you for months in my imagination. Might as well add some real footage to the spank bank."

Warmth floods me at the image of him alone in bed with just the memory of us to keep him company. That heat spreads to sizzle between us, a fire ready to blaze. I'm prepared to burn with this man. Even if I incinerate our friendship in the process.

I manage to unfurl my tongue from the jumble he's tying me in. "Is that a yes?"

Rather than provide a verbal response, his hand at my waist drifts under my shirt. His movement stalls when he realizes there's no direct contact with my skin. He lifts the hem to inspect the nylon layer stretched over my midsection.

Garrett pinches a section of the stretchy material. "What's this?"

I glance at the garment flattening my belly. "Shapewear."

"What's it for?" He glares at the object in mention like it's personally offended him.

Other than the freedom to take a full breath without worrying about my pooch?

"Smooths out my rolls and bumps." I drift a palm down my abdomen for emphasis.

His gaze searches mine while his fingers wander higher to yank at the elastic band. "I'm a fan of your rolls and bumps."

My pulse sprints in a competitive fifty-yard dash. "That makes one of us."

Once again, I don't need a man to validate how I feel about my body, but the compliment is a confidence booster. The appearance of a slimmer waistline is too.

Garrett's focus dips to the fabric blocking his path. "Looks like a torture device, especially in the heat. Your natural figure is meant to be flaunted. It's a thing of beauty and seduction."

"Plus-size isn't the model standard," I argue.

"Fuck that. It damn well should be. I love that you're generous with the curves."

"Ah, right. You pride yourself on being an equal opportunity *lover* for *all* the ladies." The significance I slide onto those words isn't an accident.

"In that case, you'll recall that twigs aren't my favorite either. It's the person, not the package." He pats my butt like we're celebrating a touchdown.

"Well, this package is enhanced by a spandex exterior." I offer a shimmy to show the tummy support in motion.

His frown scolds me. I expect him to make another swoon-worthy comment that will leave me in a puddle. Instead, he allows a lull to drop in like an uninvited guest. His eyes lift to study my expression, which I try to force into neutral.

Distant voices remind me that we're in a public place. People could stumble upon us at any moment. That signal has me straightening my shirt before I duck under the cage of his arms. A breeze rushes across the space separating us. That slight chill tames my fiendish arousal. My impulsive decision has officially caught up to me.

"We should go," I blurt.

His brows wing upward at my abrupt change in mood. "Where?"

I peek straight ahead where the seemingly unsolvable maze spans in every direction. "It's your choice. You won."

Garrett scrubs over his mouth, but not before I spy a smirk creeping in. "I'd say we're both wieners in this case."

"You're the bigger one." I take a meaningful glance at the denim.

A gruff sound escapes him. "Are you still down to pound?"

I shoot him a look that can only be described as exasperated. "Really?"

He chuckles. "I never claimed to be Prince Charming."

Which severs the last strands of reckless abandon I've been clinging to. "We're better off—"

A fluid motion brings him flush against me and cuts off my moment of clarity. His knuckles stroke along my cheek. Goosebumps erupt along my flesh from the gentle caress. I lean into his touch as if compelled. The softest kiss dusts across my parted lips.

His expression smolders when I flutter my lashes to stare at him. The blatant need in his gaze might as well be a romantic proposal. "Allow me to rephrase. I'd love the opportunity to eat your pussy until you're coming on my tongue. You're gonna ride my face like a champion cowgirl. Once I've guzzled every drop and you've quenched my thirst, I'll thrust my cock deep inside of you until we're joined as one. No beginning or end. Only us. You'll clench around me hard enough to have me begging for relief, but I'll never falter. Not until you're satisfied. After you've had multiple orgasms, I'll finally allow myself to have one. Then I'll take you again and again until we're sated and depleted."

The detailed visual he paints is a vivid scene playing in front of me. My wanton desperation for him rebounds with feverish intensity. I'm flushed and squirming and nearly sway into him from the sudden onslaught. A thick swallow is the extent of my functioning ability, and about all I can manage to accomplish through the lust chasing me.

"O-okay," I wheeze on a choppy exhale. "We should do, um… each other. Just like you described. Right away. Is there an empty building nearby?"

Garrett cradles my chin between his thumb and forefinger. His breath ghosts across my mouth. "If we're only doing this once, I want to take you somewhere I can properly worship you. Then we won't have to worry about anyone hearing you scream my name."

My knees buckle and I slump against him. "Who am I to argue with that?"

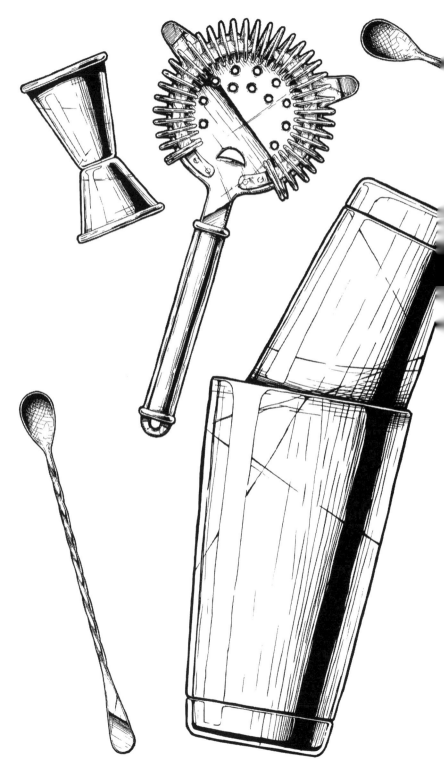

chapter fifteen

Garrett

JUST AS I'M PULLING FROM THE LOT, AN UNUSUAL rambler with a sign posted in the yard catches my eye. Green shutters clash against yellow siding and the purple porch railing to earn a second glance. "How convenient."

Grace leans forward in her seat to squint through the windshield. "Is that a…?"

"Bed and breakfast," I finish for her.

"Those actually exist?"

"Yep. The Butter Bread Inn is right here as proof."

"Just plopped in the middle of a neighborhood like a regular home?" Her arm flails toward the residential area we're approaching at a crawl.

I veer onto the shoulder while we deliberate. "Isn't that the entire point?"

"No clue. I thought they were an urban legend manifested for cheesy romantic comedies."

"Seems appropriate."

She swats my bicep. "We're not cheesy."

"Then why am I pulling over to see if this gouda establishment has any vacancies?"

Her eyes roll to the passenger window, but she doesn't bust my balls about the pun. "Is this the chosen location for our boink-fest?"

My foot slips off the brake and we lurch along the curb. Laughter spews from me while I shift the truck into park. "Did you just say boink?"

"Sure did." She flips down the visor to inspect her reflection, dabbing at the lipstick I thoroughly smeared earlier.

A smirk slants my mouth while I admire her futile efforts. Not sure why she bothers. The rest will be removed soon. Maybe she'll wrap those painted lips around me and leave a stain. My dick twitches to speed this process along. Rather than ravish her in the truck, I swerve back on topic.

"Where did boink come from?"

"I'm leaning into your ridiculous humor." Grace shrugs as if that comment isn't endearing as fuck.

And I'm expected to accept this loophole in our friendship as a one-night thing. The urge to slam my forehead against the steering wheel has me stepping out onto the road. Bodily harm will only guarantee a premature end to our already short-lived affair. A ticking clock taunts me and I round the hood in a hurry. Grace watches while I rush to her side.

Her jaw goes slack when I pop open her door. "Oh, my. Is this the sweetheart treatment?"

My commonly used endearment is a reminder that she isn't just any woman. She refuses to be lumped in with the rest, not that I would ever do so. But her mention of my casual habits solidifies that I do the opposite with her.

I reach for Grace's hand, peppering her knuckles with kisses. "This is the soulmate special."

She allows me to guide her onto the sidewalk. "I'm a sure thing, bartender. You don't have to put in extra effort."

With a palm notched at the base of her spine, I set us in a forward motion. "That's where you're wrong. You're the only one worth trying for."

"Wow," she breathes. Her eyes twinkle while she gazes at me like I've already satisfied her needs. "You're totally getting laid."

I bend to drop a kiss onto her lips. "Pretty sure you already confirmed that."

"Doesn't hurt to repeat the obvious for you."

"What're we waiting for?" I thread my fingers through hers, steering us to the cobbled path leading to our cozy destination.

"This is a nice block." Grace's attention sweeps across the manicured lawns and lush gardens fit for a magazine cover.

Dusk has arrived and delivered a cool reprieve from the summer heat. She snuggles into me to ward off the unexpected chill. I draw her closer without hesitation, a glutton for the warmth only she provides. Crickets chirp to serenade our stroll. The muffled slap from her sandals seems to echo in the stillness.

"It's very quiet," I observe.

"Everyone is across the street." She nods in the direction of Wild West Days. "The fireworks will probably start soon."

"Too bad. They're gonna miss our private show." Which is ideal. This sleepy section of town isn't prepared for what I have planned.

As if listening to my thoughts, Grace giggles. "Aww, shucks. That's probably for the best, though. I'd hate for them to be scandalized by our bang-a-thon."

My shoe catches on a pebble and I stop us just short of the porch stairs. "If you don't quit acting so damn cute, I'm gonna strip you bare on this grass."

Her smile is coy and rimmed with temptation. "Good thing I already landscaped."

"Fuuuuuck," I groan. "Get your ass inside. This place better have an opening for us."

Grace trots ahead, giving me a mouthwatering view of her backside. Her hips sway to a rhythm that throbs in my cock. What remains of the daylight glitters in her dark hair. I pause to collect myself before the scene unravels beyond control.

She twirls to await my approach. "Coming?"

"About to."

I blow out a harsh exhale to douse the flames beneath my skin before climbing the steps. The lobby hours of operation are posted. There's an hour left for us to get checked in, if we're lucky. We pause to search for instructions before entry. Nothing specific is listed aside from when Butter Bread Inn opens and closes.

"Do we just… walk in?" Grace tries to peer through the stained glass.

"Only one way to find out." I turn the knob and usher her over the threshold. "Ladies first."

"Your chivalry is alive and well tonight. Such a gentleman," she teases.

One foot through the door and it seems like we've traveled back in time. My gaze immediately zeroes in on the rainbow lamp dangling from the low ceiling. Colors burst in my vision as I peek around a corner into the reception area. There are too many conflicting patterns. It's almost dizzying. Polka dot drapes frame the large bay window. I stare at the stripped wallpaper and the lines begin to blur. The blue floral upholstery on the couch isn't much better. Fake flowers and fruit clutter every available surface, including a gold table that I'm certain my grandma owns.

Grace spins in a slow circle to marvel at the retro layout. "This is an adorable setting for our—"

"Don't even," I warn.

Her lips purse at my scolding. "You didn't know what I was going to say."

"I can just about imagine, and that's plenty. My restraint is frazzled enough."

An elderly woman appears from behind a swinging door. She ambles to the front desk and plops onto a stool. Her wrinkled fingers fan through a stack of papers. I wait for her to greet us, about ready to twiddle my thumbs.

After what feels like twenty minutes, she peers up at us from her busy work. Her shrewd gaze moves from me to Grace, who's currently fascinated by a brass squirrel. "What brings you to Butter Bread Inn?"

"We're hoping to get a room." I paste on my signature grin that brings in the big bucks. Research has proven that older ladies find me irresistible.

"Mhmm. I saw you two canoodling out front." Her nasally voice packs a scolding punch that makes me want to cower.

Grace sidles up beside me, appearing done with her exploring. Her arm loops through mine in a fluid maneuver meant for established couples. "He's very charming. I allow him to sneak a smooch in public every now and then."

"Can't keep your hands off each other. I remember those days." The woman clutches her palms to her chest and sighs. "Young love is in fresh bloom."

My dick is ready to tuck and cover and become an internal organ. "Uh, okay. Do you have anything available for us, ma'am?"

"Doris," she provides.

"Doris," I repeat automatically. "I'm Garrett and my better half is Grace. We'd love to stay at your lovely bed and breakfast for the night."

She perches a pair of bright red glasses on her nose. "Ah, you're married?"

I balk, seconds away from blasting a Garrett-shaped hole in the door. Beyond the sudden ringing in my ears, I can hear the blame for her assumption. The error is mine for phrasing our introduction in such a way. That doesn't mean her question is easier to choke down.

Grace must catch the sheer panic splashed on my features. She pats my shoulder before smiling at Doris. "Is marriage a requirement?"

"Just a preference." Her wrinkled face pinches. "We're aware that martial norms in society have changed. Respect for the sacred bond between a husband and wife isn't what it used to be. That doesn't mean we can't wish people still honored traditions."

"Well, in that case." I shelf my unnecessary alarm and prop a bent elbow on the counter. "This is our first time together."

"Oh! You're newlyweds. How splendid." That drawn conclusion flips her tune to candy hearts and riding off into the sunset.

Grace makes a strangled noise in her throat. "Um, not—"

"No further explanation needed, dear. I'm sure you're in a rush to experience the physical joining between body and soul." Doris opens a leatherbound ledger and begins writing. "We have somewhat of a honeymoon suite down the hall. It's the only one on this floor. Don't worry about disturbing your neighbors, or me for that matter. I can't hear much these days. Harold might as well be deaf without his aides, which he refuses to wear after dinner. Says he likes the quiet."

"Lucky us." I accept the record book she slides in front of me to jot down the missing details on the page.

She reviews the amenities and price, going into detail about incidental fees if we're careless during our shtupping. Her words, not mine. "Last but not least, there will be freshly baked bread in the morning after you put a bun in her oven."

I choke on my spit. "Bit soon for that."

"That's what you think," she titters. "Your consummation hasn't begun. Remember to be considerate of her needs, champ. The female's orgasm will speed the process along."

Sweat prickles my scalp. I'm suddenly feeling like this is the very last place we should have sex. "Noted."

Doris passes me a skeleton key. "Don't lose that. It's our only copy."

"Looks like it." I study the rusty metal behemoth like the foreign object it is. "Never thought I'd use one to actually open a lock."

She *tsks*. "Such a shame. Those futuristic card readers have ruined the simple joy of entering a room."

"Isn't that the truth," I mutter purely for her benefit and return the ledger to her.

Her narrowed gaze scans the information I provided. "Alrighty, you're all checked in. Enjoy yourselves, love birds."

"We plan to," Grace croons.

Just as we're turning to the hallway, her voice halts our progress. "Hold your horses for a moment."

My gut lurches at the possibility of her discovering our farce. "Problem?"

"I almost forgot it's the Fourth of July weekend. You're not planning to watch the fireworks?" She squints at a cat-shaped clock hanging beside her. "Only twenty more minutes to wait."

"We have our own performance to attend." I wink.

Grace's eyes bug out and she nudges me. "Hush."

The older woman snickers. "Oh, don't censor yourselves for my benefit. I understand the carnal urges. My Harold was a vigorous lover in his prime."

"That's"—I gulp at the bile trying to make a hasty exit—"a pleasant visual."

Doris beams at me in return. "Would you like dinner

before you retire for the evening? Food will boost your energy and stamina."

Grace gasps. "What're you serving?"

Her sparked interest speaks to the modest turkey leg we shared earlier. That's the extent of what our raging hormones allowed us to eat before ditching the fair. I curse my inability to take care of my girl's needs. That gives me pause. *My girl?* Where did that come from?

Doris hums to wrench me from those thoughts. "Tacos and such. There's plenty left if you're hungry."

A chuckle rises from me. "Can she take hers to go? I'll eat it later."

Grace tucks her chin to hide the blush staining her cheeks. "You're so bad."

Our host is none the wiser. "Is that a yes for the tacos?"

"I think we're okay," Grace rushes to say before I can suggest otherwise. "My appetite is craving something sweeter."

"Now who's bad?" I mumble under my breath.

Like the classy lady Doris is, she mistakes Grace's saucy comment for a legitimate request. "Would you like to see our dessert tray?"

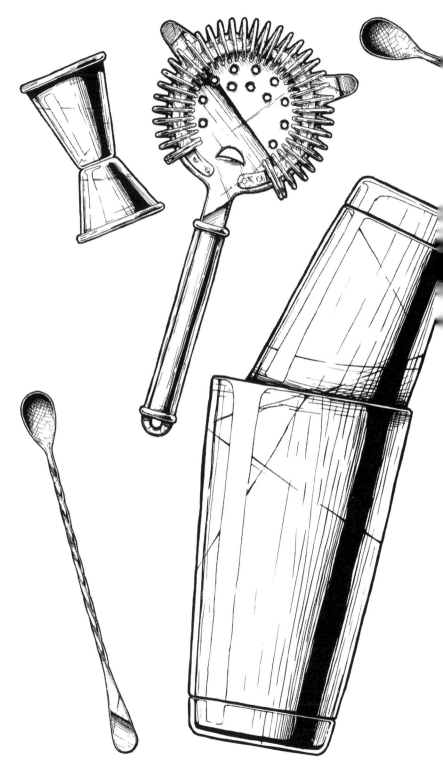

chapter sixteen

Garrett

MY FAST PACE IS MORE APPROPRIATE FOR RUSHING through an airport to catch a flight. The empty hallway mocks me, appearing like a shadowed track that doesn't end. I almost stumble over the desperation burning through me. A curse slips from my pressed lips. The lead pipe in my pants makes the hustle that much more of a challenge.

Visuals from the dining table are chasing me. Who fucking knew watching Grace eat pie would be the worst type of torture. The slow, seductive way she licked chocolate from the fork plays on a loop. The sight was reminiscent of her first time at Roosters when she tongued the cherry I'd plopped in her drink. Something about this woman and food is an extreme aphrodisiac.

Her moans were the tipping point. I hauled her off that chair and toward salvation while she was still chewing. If I don't get relief soon, I'm at risk of a trip to the hospital for this seemingly permanent erection. Those blue pills don't have shit on Grace's potency. I squeeze her hand that's securely clasped in mine and push onward.

"What's the hurry?" Her giggle is a languid stroke to my cock.

"Delayed gratification isn't my preferred foreplay," I grumble.

She hums while sucking whipped cream off her finger. "That French silk was really tasty."

My vision blurs as I fight the urge to fuck her against the wall. "Couldn't tell."

Grace laughs again. "Don't be a grumpy Gus."

"I'll be much happier once my mouth is latched onto your pussy."

She trips over my words and teeters into me. "Oh."

Now I'm the one chuckling. "We're on the same page."

"You, um, actually want to do that?"

I slam on the brakes at the uncertainty in her voice. "Was I not descriptive enough in the maze?"

Her gaze searches mine. "You were, but I figured that might've just been talk to get me agreeable again."

I feed my instincts and press her flat against the wall, towering over her until our lips nearly meet. "Trust me, soulmate. I don't make empty promises, especially to you. I'm gonna eat your pussy until you beg me to stop."

Even in the low lighting, I catch her pupils dilating. "O-okay."

"That's what I thought."

With my palm glued to the base of her spine, I get us moving forward. The door to our suite materializes to finally provide a much-needed end to my suffering. I slide the skeleton key into the lock and a loud click announces a successful entry.

"Doris was right. That's a gratifying sound."

"She's a smart cookie." Grace strides ahead of me. "Don't dawdle. Our honeymoon awaits, bartender."

Any witty response dies in my throat as I step inside. "Holy shit. This is a lot of…"

"Pink," she finishes for me.

That's the only word to describe this monstrosity. A variation of the frilly color stains everything in sight as if we accidentally stumbled onto the Barbie movie set. Even the knickknacks cluttered on the dresser match the theme. My gaze lowers to the blush carpet that's covered with a rug before I sweep the rest of the space. The painted walls, curtains, books on a shelf, a chair and stool in the corner, the bedspread with pillows to match, and a fabric crate at the foot of it. All pink. A strawberry milkshake exploding from a blender comes to mind.

"We've stepped into the bubble gum fortress," I mumble.

"This would be a prime location for Pussy in Paradise." Grace giggles while recalling the fake girls' night at Roosters.

"Got that right."

"You missed the best feature." She points skyward.

I glance at the ceiling and let my jaw go slack. The entire expanse above the bed is mirrored. "Well, damn. Doris might not be that classy after all."

"At least a little freaky," Grace agrees.

"Which reminds me." I strut toward her. "I'm a bit of a freak in the sheets."

She snorts. "Of course, you are."

"Are you ready to find out?"

"This"—she motions to our Pepto-Bismol palace—"isn't a boner killer?"

I prowl into her personal space until our shared body heat simmers. "Just looking at you gets me hard, and my focus is solely on you. Always."

She gasps when I palm her ass and yank to press our hips

flush. There's no mistaking my reaction to her. Her throat works with a thick swallow. Our eyes meet and hold, her blue depths blending with mine.

"Hi," Grace whispers.

My thumb roves along the shape of her jaw. There's so much I want to say but shouldn't. Rules are meant to bend for a reason.

"Have I told you how beautiful you are?"

A flush races up her slender throat. "Feel free to repeat yourself even if you have."

"Your beauty freezes time. I'm caught in a trance whenever you walk into a room or just enter my thoughts. You suspend me, soulmate. My ultimate distraction." The truth spills off my tongue like expensive liquor meant to be savored between us.

She sips at my confessions with a hitched breath. "Must be hard to get anything done."

"It's impossible. You don't steal my attention." I swoop in for a kiss. "You own it, free of charge."

"Good grief." Grace sways into me. "Keep talking like that and my panties will just melt off."

"The better to eat you out."

She fans her face. "And you don't consider yourself romantic."

"I'm making an exception for you."

Her gaze seeks more honesty from me. "Just for tonight?"

"Just for tonight," I confirm.

My fingers unfasten the button of her shorts. I peel the frayed cut-offs down her thighs and toss the denim over my shoulder like a nuisance meant to be thrown out. She's quick to ditch her shirt, blindly adding the cotton bundle to the discard pile. The striptease is stalled by the stretchy layer that confines her natural form. My glare threatens to incinerate the nylon barrier that taunts me.

"Are you attached to this shapewear?" I pluck at the restrictive fabric flattening her softness.

"No—"

Whatever else she planned to say is drowned out by a distinct rip. A solid jerk shreds the insufferable garment in two. I smirk at the ruined scraps and a task completed with fluid efficiency. Her flawless skin is finally on display for me to admire.

Grace blinks in rapid succession. "Um, wow. That was really arousing."

But my focus is latched onto her pussy that I unknowingly exposed. "No panties?"

She wiggles her bare hips. "I warned you that they'd melt off."

"Fuuuuuuck," I groan.

"The Spanx serves multiple purposes." Without prompting, she unclasps her bra and flings the black silk away.

Her breasts spill free. My attention is cleaved in two before I narrow in on her lush tits. Their size overflows my palms while I lightly pinch the stiff peaks. She whimpers and thrusts her chest at me, silently begging for more.

I dip my head to pull a pebbled tip between my teeth. Vanilla and reckless abandon invade my nostrils as I breathe her in. She moans when I gently bite down, then suck to numb the sting. I tweak her left nipple between my knuckles before switching sides to repeat the process.

Grace's fingers spear into my hair, yanking at the roots. Heat floods me from that harsh treatment. A feverish need that wants to be satisfied immediately follows. I refuse to rush. At least not yet. My other palm roams over her supple flesh. She's satin beneath my wandering touch. Every inch is mine to explore. Until pressure at the top of my head demands otherwise. If I'm not mistaken, she's trying to shove me to my knees. Message received.

I pull away to openly stare for a moment. Her body seems to glow in the low lighting, which I realize has a rosy tint. The bulbs must be pink too. A smirk tilts my lips. It creates a dreamy atmosphere that I appreciate. Fantasy and reality merge onto the same screen. Especially with the view of Grace naked in front of me.

"Just gonna stand there or…?" Her teasing voice snaps me from the stupor.

I shake off the haze. "See? I'm suspended in a trance by your beauty."

"Um, that's super flattering, but I'm naked and you're not." She squirms under my blatant ogling.

My shirt and shorts hit the floor to level the field. "Better?"

"Holy shit," she blurts. "You're really hot."

She giggles and slaps a palm over her mouth. I flex like a fool as she checks me out. Grace's eyes widen when she glances at my tented boxers. A blush appears on her cheeks. I almost whip out my dick for further approval. Then her appraisal shifts to my abs. She crosses an arm over her waist and drops her gaze.

"Like what you see?"

"Uh-huh," she mumbles. Her gaze doesn't leave me as she absently backs toward the bed.

"Stop," I command.

That erases the dazed expression. She quirks a brow. "Bossy much?"

"I want you to ride my face."

Her exhale is a wheeze. "And how do you suggest I do that?"

I dive onto the bed, getting myself situated in the center. The mattress creaks like weary joints but I barely notice. Grace hovers near the edge, looking lost and uncertain.

"Come to me, my queen. I've built you a throne." I wipe a palm over my mouth. "Take a seat."

She climbs on, but her movements are stiff. My gaze latches onto her seductive curves as she slinks closer. I grab her hips to offer stability while she swings a leg over me. A shy smile is my reward. Once she's straddling my chest, I fight the urge to yank her into position. Her weight on me is a comfort I secretly crave.

Fuck, I'm unraveling. Control is a fraying rope on its last strand. There's a restless stirring inside of me. If I don't get a taste of her soon, I'm likely to snarl demands like a savage beast.

"Make yourself comfortable," I rasp.

Grace squirms. "You make it sound so simple."

My fingers dig into her sides. "Come closer."

"Working on it," she mumbles.

She's still too rigid astride me. That's when a thought breaks into my lust.

"Are you okay with the lights on?" I'm aware that girls can be fussy about that, and I've never given much of a shit either way. Until now. Grace is different. I want to catch every second in vivid definition.

Grace doesn't shift her gaze from mine. "We can leave them on. You're nice to look at."

I point to the mirrored ceiling. "Don't forget the best feature. Watch me devour you."

She glances up and trembles in my hold. "Oh, shit. That's a sight to see."

"Fucking gorgeous," I add. "Ready for our sex-travaganza?"

Her attention whips to me. "Hey! You're stealing my cheesy thunder."

"That's rich coming from someone who didn't acknowledge our sharp cheddar earlier. Besides, you're the one leaning into my humor."

She inches forward. "What's yours is mine."

Salvia pools when her sweet arousal wafts through the air. Almost there. "I'm about to give you all of me."

A final shift delivers her to where I'm drooling. Her sex is directly above my mouth but out of feasting range. She doesn't budge when I tug.

"Relax," I breathe into her skin.

"Easy for you to say. You're not spread eagle over someone's face."

"Don't make me sound like a random dude. We're better acquainted than that."

Grace taps my nose. "You know what I mean."

"Would you like to change positions?"

"No, I've actually fantasized about doing this."

"After reading it in one of your romance books," I guess.

"Maybe," she hedges.

"Then feed me that pretty pussy."

She lowers, but just slightly. "What makes a pussy pretty?"

"Yours looks juicy, like this peachy bottom." I swat her butt.

She jolts, releasing a yelp with the sharp movement. "I guess that's appealing."

"Very."

"What else?"

"Soft and warm." I stroke a finger along her slit.

"More," she sighs.

"Best fucking dessert tray I've ever seen."

Grace laughs. "You're ridiculous!"

"Nah, no toppings required. Looks good enough to eat plain. Straight from the source." With my hands banded around her upper thighs, I wrench her down to satisfy my insatiable appetite.

"Oh," she squeaks.

I drag my tongue through her center. Any further protest fades into a moan. Her unique flavor is a burst of tangy honey that I'm instantly addicted to. The sugar rush is permanently engrained and seared to memory. She's sweeter than frosting on homemade apple pie.

After that initial swipe, I become ravenous. An animalistic growl rips from me as I indulge in her. Grace squeals and bucks against me. She slaps a palm against the headboard, gripping the wood for support. Our gazes collide in a fiery exchange. The onslaught rocks both of us.

I bury my lips in her slippery heat, buzzing for added sensation. The vibration reminds me of her toys. Beating the effectiveness of those battery-operated dicks is a new goal. A whimpered mewl has me smiling into my next sweep. She grinds down to seek more friction, which only spurs me to work faster.

Grace tosses her head back, thrashing to send her hair flying like a dark halo as my tongue lashes and swirls her clit. I shift my focus to the mirror above. A grin paints her lips when our eyes lock. My cock strains against the confines of my boxers but I ignore the throb. Fuck, the sight of her riding my face might be enough to make me bust.

I suckle her clit in greedy pulls. She claws at my arms in return. Her sugary desire is smeared across my mouth and chin like a badge of honor. It isn't enough. I shove my face deeper, needing to drown in her. Even my nose is buried to drag her scent into me until she's an invasion I'll never escape. Not that I want to. She's intoxicating me with our shared desperation. I'm drunk on her and dizzy with lust. I should pull away for a decent breath, but I'm too far gone.

Her arousal dribbles from my lips and I inwardly curse. I can't swallow fast enough. My motions are getting sloppy. Not a drop should be wasted. I increase my suction to guzzle her down like the priceless brew she is. Grace rewards me with a stream of unintelligible nonsense. Her passion is a chorus of garbled pleas. What I'm able to comprehend is that she's begging for more. Meanwhile, the noises ripping from me are from a man feasting on the best meal of his life.

"You're s-sooo good at this," she cries.

My eyelids droop but I refuse to let them shut. I won't miss a moment of her erotic display. She's gasping, her tits rising and falling with rapid breaths. Red blotches stain her chest. The muscles in her arms bunch as she uses the headboard for leverage. A sheen of sweat brightens her skin. My steady actions falter for a moment. Damn, she's never looked more stunning.

Distant booms crack into our intimate bubble to signal that the fireworks have begun. I couldn't care less. The only explosions I'm concerned about are in this room. On cue, Grace clamps her knees against my ears. The furious beat of my pulse replaces her siren song. That won't do. I wrench her tighter against me, reinforcing the seal between our lips, which allows her serenading to spill free.

"There," she pants. "Yes, yes."

Grace rocks against me to the tempo of my lashings along her pussy. A quake ripples from her into me. The cue that she's close doubles my efforts. I stiffen my tongue to plunge inside her. A drawn-out whimper slips from her parted lips as I fuck her with my mouth. Ecstasy splashes across her features. Jaw slack and eyes drowsy, she surrenders to the release I'm providing. Her climax strikes with a scream that she belatedly muffles behind a palm.

Watching Grace unravel feels like a gift meant solely for me. Each shudder and quiver is a bonus I earned. The pressure deflates and I slow my pace. Tension melts from her as well. She slumps forward until her forehead rests against the wall.

"That's one," I murmur against her folds.

Clarity returns in a lazy wave, but I'm no less crazed. Before she can recover or attempt a response, I flip her onto her back in a fluid motion. She bounces on the mattress while

I get situated in the next position. I roll until I'm flat on my stomach with a direct view of heaven. Her legs are hooked over my shoulders while she's still trying to catch her breath. Then my mouth lowers to her slick pussy.

"Ready for another?" I exhale into her wet slit.

Aftershocks still twitch her muscles. "S-sure."

"Coming right up."

chapter seventeen

Grace

"O-okay, that's enough." My voice is a hoarse plea when I'm able to speak.

Garrett's tongue takes a leisurely swipe through my sex. "I've heard that before."

The tease is wholly at my expense. I made the mistake of begging for a reprieve, only to change my tune minutes later once the afterglow faded. His smirk taunted me as he dove in and fulfilled my request. Twice or thrice. The man loves to eat. And as predicted, he leaves zero crumbs.

"This time is for real," I insist.

The limit has presented itself with indisputable certainty. Shocks zap me from the overwhelming onslaught. Cramps radiate from places I didn't know could seize. Sweat slicks my skin as I struggle to prop myself upright. My body rebels and I collapse flat on the bed. I'm a soggy lump after too many orgasms. I've lost track of the number he's blessed me with, but another might just wreck me beyond repair.

"Did I fulfill my oral requirements for the evening?" Garrett sweeps across my sensitive clit.

I jerk in his hold. "Yes! Please have mercy on my lady bits."

"But you're so delicious." He withdraws the two fingers plunged into my core.

I whimper as he sucks the glistening evidence of me from his digits. "Yes, you've made that clear."

"Better than pie," he groans.

A fire blazes along my cheeks. "I'll take your word for it."

"Wanna taste?" He puckers his lips but doesn't move from between my splayed thighs.

I try to force my limbs to cooperate and meet him in the middle. The effort barely grants me an inch. "Maybe later."

He peppers kisses to my inner thigh. "Are you too tired for more?"

"That depends on your definition. If you're finally going to let your rooster out of the barn, I'm here for it." Or I could just lie here and stare at him.

The view is impossible to beat. Blue eyes captivate me the longer he refuses to look away. His full lips have a glossy sheen that reveals how he's spent the last however many minutes. Chafed patches decorate my skin thanks to his thick stubble. I'm not mad about it. Quite the opposite as a zing spreads from my tender nipples. That has me focusing on his hair. The dark strands are mussed from my constant pulling. As if that's not enough, he pushes himself onto his knees and puts his chiseled abs on display. I'm certain he flexes on purpose. A pleased exhale whispers from me.

Garrett catches my perusal. His chuckle is an erotic tune that manages to spark my arousal back to life. The mattress creaks in protest when he rises to his feet. Then he strips off his boxers like an extra on *Magic Mike*. I don't get a spare moment to appreciate his slick moves.

"You're pierced?" Shock pitches my tone to the stars. I bat sticky hair from my face to get a better look.

"For your pleasure."

He nods at his dick, which has a barbell vertically through the tip. One steel ball sits at the top, nestled at the center of his flared head. A peek underneath shows the other end rests directly below. It's a straight shot.

After I gawk shamelessly for several seconds and regain control of my slacked jaw, I'm able to comprehend what he said. "My pleasure? Let's not pretend you did this for me."

"You're the one about to enjoy the benefits."

No lies detected. The full frontal I'm currently receiving already has my kitty purring. "Why didn't you tell me sooner?"

"Would my pierced cock have made a difference somehow?"

"Um, yeah. I would've agreed to let you do me dirty weeks ago." And I have no shame admitting that thanks to my crusty dry spell. The climaxes he provided are probably to blame for my slacking filter as well.

Garrett blanches. "What?"

"What?"

"Are you serious?"

"Hmm?"

He cups himself, stealing the object of my infatuation from view. "Are you listening to me?"

"I'm distracted by your magical penis," I freely admit.

"Wanna touch it?"

"Yes, very badly."

A sweeping motion grants me permission. I palm him eagerly in a firm grip. His length is harder than concrete but sheathed in velvet. A roll from my wrist offers a lazy stroke. My thumb toys with the barbell. He doesn't react other than a muscle twitching in his jaw.

"What's it feel like?"

He grunts when I fiddle with the metal balls. "A slight tugging sensation."

"Doesn't hurt?"

"Nah, your hands on me could never be anything except pure ecstasy." The throaty groan he emits confirms his confession.

I continue caressing him absently. He strains in my grip as if seeking more. Our legs brush when I scoot closer. It's only then I remember we're having this conversation stark naked. Strangely enough, though, I'm completely at ease. That's my only excuse for the word vomit.

"I bet the ladies you shtup appreciate the enhancement to your pleasure wand."

He laughs at the term I borrowed from Doris. "I've never had any complaints."

I gulp at the sheer size of him in my grasp. "No wonder you have to swat the barflies off with a fake girlfriend rouse. They must hound you relentlessly."

Garrett scratches his chin like this is a normal exchange. "My reputation is somewhat legendary. I'm actually surprised you didn't hear any rumors around town."

"Oh, I did. I just assumed they were full of shit."

The low lighting plays off his irresistible smirk. "For once, they spoke the truth."

"And I didn't listen." I lightly scrape my nails along a vein on the underside of his cock.

He pumps into my hand. "You're under the influence now."

I admire his dick as if a flying unicorn just landed in a field to graze on rainbow clover inches from my face. "Is this a Prince Albert? Or what's it called?"

"Fuck, you're too cute," he chuckles. "This is an apadravya."

"That's a mouthful."

"You're welcome."

"I can't believe you didn't tell me."

His fingers drift idly along my sides while I leisurely stroke him. "The topic never came up."

"It's hard to believe you wouldn't find an excuse to mention your bedazzled dick."

"I honestly didn't think about it. This is just a regular part of me."

"There's nothing regular about this." I tap the barbell.

"Are you impressed?"

My head bobs in earnest. "Never have I ever seen a pierced penis, not to mention felt one inside of me."

"Better not," he growls. "Mine is the only one for you."

For tonight, I silently remind myself.

Rather than let that storm cloud sour the mood, I find myself bending forward to lick him like a lollipop. The impulse is a natural response beyond my control. His blinged tip is practically leaking, begging to be sucked. A hand on my shoulder halts my blowjob attempt.

"Save that generous act for later."

I pout. "Just a quick sample? You're like a mythical creature. I need to confirm you're not a figment of my filthy imagination."

"All right, as you were."

I don't hesitate to latch my lips around him. A moan tumbles from me as his salty flavor bathes my tongue. The metal adornment is cool compared to his steely flesh. He fists my hair, wrenching hard enough to sting.

"Fuuuuuuck, soulmate. You gotta stop."

I pop off his dick, wiping at the corner of my mouth. "Yummy, and definitely not a dream. That's an authentic slab of man meat."

"Organic and homegrown," he agrees.

The smile I offer in reply is woozy. "You totally get me."

Garrett squeezes my hip. "I think you got me first."

"I'm yours to catch, bartender. Come get me." I shuffle backward toward the pillows.

He fetches a condom from his jeans and rips the foil packet with his teeth. I'm dick-notized as he rolls the rubber down his length with the practiced efficiency of a professional sexpert. A desperation to be filled gnaws at me.

Drool puddles in my mouth when he finishes the task. "I'm gonna need that inside of me. Pronto."

"Someone recovered quickly."

"Have you seen your penis? It's like a majestical monument erected from my depraved fantasies."

The bed dips and squeaks as he returns to me. Amusement gleams in his fixed stare. "You're something else. A pierced dick isn't that uncommon."

"It is to me. Now"—I resume my previous reclined position, but spread my legs wider—"show me what I've been missing."

He moves into the gap I've created. The tops of his thighs bump the backs of mine as he shifts into the desired position. This entanglement gives him a clear shot of my pussy while I sprawl on my back. Meanwhile, I'm blindly waiting for the dicking to commence.

"I should warn you, Peaches." Blue flames blaze from his unwavering focus. "Rough and hard is my preference. But I'll go easy this first time."

"Don't go soft and slow for me. I don't need special treatment."

"You do," he insists. "The apadravya makes me wider. You'll need to adjust."

That gives me pause. "What if you won't fit?"

His expression flashes with a fiery possession that

spikes my pulse. "We'll fit. You'll take every inch of me like you can't survive without it."

I'm already nodding, an obedient deviant for him to mold. "Give it to me."

"You want to be stretched to the brink?"

"Yes," I whimper.

Garrett shifts forward on his knees until his dick bumps my slit. "This is all for you, soulmate."

My gaze flicks to our reflection above where he grips himself to angle downward. He enters me at a slight diagonal. I immediately understand why when his barbell prods at my sensitive flesh. His pierced tip teases me, barely pushing in before withdrawing. These preparations alone leave me gasping.

Our eyes meet on his next nudge. Trust blooms from our stare to spread warmth through me. Garrett must determine I'm ready for more. An unmistakable burn strikes a match to my core as he pushes inside. I wriggle against the sheets, shoving him deeper. We share a mutual groan when he pauses at the halfway point.

Even with my body primed from several orgasms, his thick length is a snug fit. The hollow ache is replaced with a fullness that can't be replicated. My neglected muscles twinge from the intrusion, stretching to accommodate his girth. A wiggle and shift from my hips allows me to accept more of him. He's gentle and careful with his motions. The slow glide is almost a tease from his shallow thrusts.

I suck in a sharp breath once he's fully seated. "Ohhhh."

He tips forward until his body is blanketing mine. "Fuck, you're tight."

It's such a cliché phrase, but I preen all the same. The compliment rolling off his tongue sounds like erotic poetry. Or I'm already mindless from this introduction.

He retreats until his piercing tickles my opening. Just

as I'm about to protest, he punches forward to fill me again. I arch into him, my sensitive nipples rubbing against his chest. The sensation zaps me. My pussy clenches from the shock, earning a rumble from him. We smile in unison as if practiced.

"See?" He slams forward until we're joined to the hilt again. "You're made for me, soulmate."

A content sigh breezes from me. "We're a perfect fit."

"So. Fucking. Perfect." He punctuates each word with a thrust.

I'm too blissed out to overanalyze. My concentration is consumed by our flow. It's just so natural, sweeping comfort over me. Each push and pull lulls me into a heady space. This man is hypnotic. I loop an arm around his neck and get lost in his steady motions.

A greedy part of me begins to demand more. The sluggish delay in his movements suggests he's holding back. I wait for him to gain momentum, but the tempo remains relaxed.

"Give me the regular." I bump my hips into his. "C'mon."

"What I'm giving you is better." Garrett swoops down to suck on my nipple.

I clutch his head to my breast, but the surge of pleasure won't deter me. "It's okay. I can handle it. Do me the way you want to."

His rhythm hitches as he studies my expression. The strain in his form reveals that he's fighting a silent battle with himself. "What if this is what I want with you?"

"But you just said—"

"You're different for me. Let me spoil you." His lips press to mine. "My good lover girl."

I swallow the armored retort that rises. Too many thoughts swirl to the surface as he resumes the madness. Garrett props himself on a bent elbow. His other hand sweeps the hair from my face. I cup his cheek, petting the scruff on his jaw. For whatever reason, a painful knot clogs my throat. The urge to cry multiples when he nuzzles my nose with his. I'm afraid to ruin the moment, but my heart can't handle this tenderness from him.

The friction between us builds with every measured drive. My bent knees lift higher to settle into the notch at his hipbones. The slight change sends him impossibly deeper. A breathy moan rips from me. There's a blistering hunger sprouting roots and flourishes from where we're connected. His piercing tempts my fantasies, but the impact is stifled. A sultry tune whispers that I need more.

If we're doing this, we might as well raze the boundaries.

"Wait," I blurt. "Stop."

"What's wrong?" He rears back. His wide eyes scour my face for evidence of upset. "Am I hurting you?"

"No, it feels good." I lick my lips, seeking courage. "But I think it could be better."

Garrett scoffs. "Excuse you?"

"What do you think about taking off the condom? Then I could really feel you. Bare."

"Fuck." He dips until our foreheads touch. "That's the hottest thing I've ever heard."

"Is that a yes?"

His eyes bore into mine. "Are you on birth control?"

I nod, the motion bumping our chins together. "Have been for years."

He doesn't take his gaze off me. "I've never gone without."

"Me either."

"Damn, you're bad for my resolve." There's a rough edge to his tone.

I avert my stare. "We don't have to."

He silences my protest with a searing kiss. "Yes, we do.

195

I want to experience this with you. Only you. Nothing between us."

That's exactly how I wanted him to respond. A whimper escapes me when he pulls out to tear off the rubber. When he enters me again, pleasure swells in my core and heat flushes my face. I'm stunned and immobile for several beats. The barbell studs drag along my sensitive flesh in a provocative caress. I'm too warm, yet I cling to Garrett. I couldn't have anticipated how much closer this brings us.

Tingles skitter across my skin as I take every inch of him without a barrier blocking us. It becomes clear that I was wrong earlier. The continuous climaxes won't be what ruins me. His fancy penis will do the honors.

"Wow," I breathe.

Garrett grunts in response. "Best idea ever."

For a brief moment, my gaze lifts to the mirrors overhead. His ass clenches with each powerful thrust. I move my legs, crossing my ankles against those sculpted globes. My teeth gnash to take a bite.

"You're incredible," I whisper.

"Me?" He chuckles. "This is all you, soulmate. I'm just the cock."

"Who is very talented."

Rather than respond, he tucks his face into the crook of my shoulder. I can hear him take a deep inhale of me. I feel joy curling his mouth against my throat. He plants a garden of kisses there. A shiver racks me from the onslaught. This man intoxicates me. He's more inebriating than a dozen margaritas. I'm drunk off him and his well-oiled motions.

Garrett's palms drift over my arms, lifting them above my head and interlocking our fingers. The mood shifts in a turbulent tide. What began as a carefree—albeit impulsive—hookup is gaining complications. His gaze never strays from mine. There's an underlying yearning in his expression. The sight has me reaching for nonexistent restraint. It's too intimate, but I can't deny this is exactly what I want. Even if it's just for tonight. Regret can scold me tomorrow.

Affection brims in his eyes as he watches me. "We should've done this from the start."

I'm quick to agree with a nod. My voice is trapped behind the lust clouding reasonable logic. His thrusts become more potent. Each motion is electric. I quiver from the current zapping me.

His focus never wavers while he pumps into me. This isn't meaningless sex. It's the opposite, which terrifies me. How will our friendship survive after this? I hurl caution against the pink door, forcing those concerns to flee. Denial becomes an accomplice to this charade, but I can't overlook his thoughtful actions. His thumb rubs along my knuckles. He's being too gentle and caring. The concern crinkling his brow is when I crack.

"Are you okay?" He kisses away the stray tear that escapes.

I choke down the emotion in my throat. "Yes, this is just different from what I was expecting."

Garrett's smirk lacks its usual smugness. "It's the same for me."

Our passion blends into a synchronized routine. My toes curl against his calves. His mouth seeks mine. Our tongues tangle along with our desire. A swarm of hummingbirds race in my lower belly. He smiles into our kiss before pulling away.

"You're so fucking beautiful. My ultimate distraction," he murmurs.

My smile wobbles. "You've already charmed my panties off, overachiever."

Garrett's stoic expression breaks into a grin. "Damn, soulmate. You annihilate me."

I swat his ass. "Finish us off before you perish."

"Don't worry. I'd never leave you unsatisfied."

His smooth pace stumbles into a rush. The headboard knocks into the wall at a steady thump. Shivers skate down my spine as the edge nears. I press my nose to his throat and breathe deep. My lashes flutter shut. Even his scent wrecks me. Fresh pine, raw strength, and obliterated restraint consume me while he chases our tipping point.

He's a pillar of seduction towering over me. Sex appeal oozes from his pores while he grinds his pelvis into mine. Each slap from him bottoming out strikes my clit just right. The consistent friction sends me spiraling. His consideration for my pleasure borders on obsessiveness. Not that I'm complaining. Just the opposite as another keen wail trips from me.

"What the lady wants"—he increases his speed—"she better hold on tight for."

Before I can question the warning, his hands abandon mine to palm my ass. He lifts until he finds the desired tilt, then begins swiveling his hips. The elevated position allows his piercing to rub against a secret spot I was beginning to believe didn't exist.

"Oh, shit," I squeal.

"That's right, baby. Let's visit the stars."

Static fills my ears like white noise. My pulse is a hammer, slamming in my veins for release. Convulsions spasm my entire body. A coil unwinds, spreading tingles in an outward rush. Bright light bursts from behind my clenched eyelids.

There's a flicker of indecision where Garrett questions whether or not to pull out. At the last second, he thrusts deep and stills. Warmth spills inside of me.

I can't determine where his peak ends and mine begins. There's no separation. We become one in our simultaneous orgasms. I'm floating with only Garrett as a tether to reality. Or maybe he's soaring in this dimension with me. We launch into the abyss where only his body jerking against mine exists.

The tension in his body deflates and he slumps over, tipping to the side to avoid crushing me. Loud creaks from the bed accompany his heavy movements. Garrett's sated gaze latches onto mine, crinkling at the corners. That smile will be my downfall.

"We made an awful racket," he rasps.

My grin matches his. "Good thing we're alone on this floor."

Garrett reaches for my hand and laces our fingers into an intricate knot that I'll never escape from. "You might've ruined me, Grace. That was unforgettable."

Which is what scares me the most.

chapter eighteen

Grace

"Fuuuuuuck," Garrett bellows.

My stretched lips curl at the corners while he jerks in the euphoric decline. After a parting lick, I crawl out from my spot under the covers and snuggle into his side. I pat his toned pec before using the muscular slab as a pillow.

"You're right. Breakfast in bed is delicious. Very refreshing," I croon.

He's quiet for several rapid beats tracked by his racing heart. It's apparent he needs a moment to recover from that spontaneous blowjob. The triggered climax seems to have shocked him into oblivion. His harsh breathing sounds like he did all the work. Finally, he blinks from the stupor and his hooded eyes meet mine.

"Best way to wake up is with your mouth around my cock," he rasps.

"Your morning wood pitched one helluva tent. Looked painful. Besides, it's polite to reciprocate." I dab at my lips.

"And you swallow? It's official. You're my dream girl, soul-mate." Garrett tugs me tighter into his cozy nook.

"Shouldn't say things like that," I chide.

"But things are going so well." He drops a kiss on the tip of my nose.

"Be that as it may, the clock is ticking on our screw shack." That reminder is for my sake more than his.

The easy smile he flashes confirms as much. "There's still time for a final round."

A cramp seizes my chest. "Or we could talk."

His carefree expression slips into a frown. "About what?"

"Whatever comes to mind." I snap my fingers. "Oh, I have something to ask."

"That was quick." His tone is a lazy drawl steeped in hesitation.

This idle chatter is necessary to resurrect our walls and protect my heart. "What possessed you to pierce your dick? Is it just a service to women in general?"

"There isn't a heroic reason. The apadravya was a gift to myself after Hillary cheated on me."

I wince. "That's one way to cope."

"My thoughts exactly. A buddy of mine agreed to pierce me for free, as a symbol of my eternal single status. He did these too." He rotates his left arm to show off the tattoos inked there. That's another area to explore at a later date.

"How selfless." I focus on the underlying meaning and flutter my lashes at him. "All the floozies you bang benefit from your bedazzled cock."

His shrug jostles my position. "That's one way of looking at it."

Speaking of, I whip off the blanket to shamelessly gawk at his dick. The decorated pleasure baton is still semi-hard. "How long did it take to heal?"

"Six months maybe?"

My jaw drops. "You didn't have sex for six months?"

He chuckles. "Didn't say that. Just had to be cautious."

"Awww, the energizer sex machine couldn't go rough and hard?"

"Worth it."

"I agree."

Garrett stares at me for a solid minute without speaking. There are too many unknown possibilities swirling in those blue depths. I squirm under such blatant scrutiny. If this re-action is any indication, it's going to be impossible to pretend that sex didn't ruin our friendship. His gaze drops to my lips, releasing me from the captivating hold.

"What do you think about amending our pact?" He grabs my hand that's still resting on his chest.

"Do we actually have one? I thought you agreed to find Mr. Monogamy for me out of the goodness of your heart."

His thumb rubs over my knuckles. "Are you really talking about another man while in bed with me?"

Sharp laughter is my initial response. "Let's be honest, he's a figment of my imagination."

"You'll find him." His voice carries a flat detachment I could learn from.

"Um, okay. Tell me about this amendment."

He toys with my fingers that are interlocked between his. "If you're not married by thirty-five, I'll do the honors."

"Oh, please. Don't do me any favors." My dry tone is brit-tle at the edges.

"You'd be doing me one." That soul-aching yearning is back in his gaze.

I avert my eyes, landing on our reflection above. That's an instant mistake. The sight of us tangled together steals my breath. It's too intimate. We're not a couple. Repeating the truth doesn't erase the lie we're putting on display. I don't want to believe this was a mistake, but the ache splitting me in half suggests otherwise.

The knot in my throat doubles in size. "I guess we'll see what Cupid has planned."

"Should we make this a regular thing in the meantime?" Garrett squeezes my ass to accentuate the point.

There's a pit growing in my belly. "A no-strings-fling?"

He flinches. "Would it be more acceptable if I don't sleep with anyone else while we're hooking up?"

I recoil. My entire face stings, as if slapped with heat. "Seriously?"

"Nah, I'm shitty for even voicing that as an option."

"Maybe it's best if we just pretend nothing happened." I slam down my guard with a painful disconnect. My body breaks from his embrace with an innocent stretch that blesses me with personal space.

"I can assure you that's not going to happen." He taps his temple. "Constant replay."

"Fine, I'll block it out for both of us."

Garrett tucks a bent arm under his head. The position puts his bicep on bulging display. "I should warn you that I'm impossible to forget."

"Not to mention extremely full of yourself," I mutter.

His head rolls on the pillow to catch my gaze. "You were full of me all night."

I whip the blanket over my head and groan. "Don't need to remind me."

He tugs the sheet down until I'm forced to face him. His handsome features glow in the early sunlight streaking through the window. "Hey, why are you hiding?"

"No reason."

But the urge to duck and cover makes me twitchy. If pressed, I'll admit this internal struggle was my prediction. The way I felt about Garrett before we slept together was already muddled. Now I'm screwed, and not in the way I wanted to be.

He reads my grimace like the clue it is. "Are things going to be weird between us?"

"Nope. We'll figure it out," I vow. Fake it or break it. "I'm still looking for love and you, most certainly, are not."

"That's right." His clipped response doesn't believe me.

"Uh-huh," I continue. "I'm in my happily ever after era. Completely and hopelessly."

He sweeps hair off my forehead, drifting a gentle caress along my cheek. "Whoever you deem worthy as Prince Charming is a lucky bastard."

"Now who's talking about other men?"

"Consider me a hypocrite."

Garrett's smirk is relaxed and oblivious. That signature expression slams a boulder into my stomach with punishing force. He's just fine with this arrangement, as he should be. Those are the terms we set. I can't be upset about him sticking to them.

That doesn't mean I don't want to scream and cry and rage. It could be him. *Should* be, based on the warmth his touch fills me with. But I respect his restrictions and refuse to push. He provided me with a temporary glimpse at what it feels like to be worshipped. However superficial he might claim it to be. The phantom sensations will be useful motivation while I search for a replacement that will never measure up.

Until then, I'll wallow in my bad decisions and poor judgment for a few more minutes.

"The pink palace will always be ours." I wave an arm at our vibrant surroundings.

Garrett's exhale is loud in the quiet space. "Back to business as usual once we leave?"

"That's what we agreed on."

He squints at me. "Second thoughts?"

"Not at all. The dozen orgasms are much appreciated. Just try not to picture me naked. That would be inappropriate." I begin to scoot off the mattress, very aware that I'm stripped bare and exposed. "And on that note, we should probably get moving."

He turns onto his side, propping himself on an elbow. A frown pinches his casual expression. "What just happened?"

"Nothing." Other than me whacking myself with a dose of harsh reality. An icy blast snuffs the heat I've been blissfully basking in. "I've been out of commission for two weeks. There's a lot I need to catch up on. Plus, Doris promised freshly baked bread. We don't want to miss that."

Garrett accepts my answer with a nod. "Sure, I guess that makes sense. But we're good?"

I paste on a smile that's weaker than my confidence in this sham. "Couldn't be better, bestie."

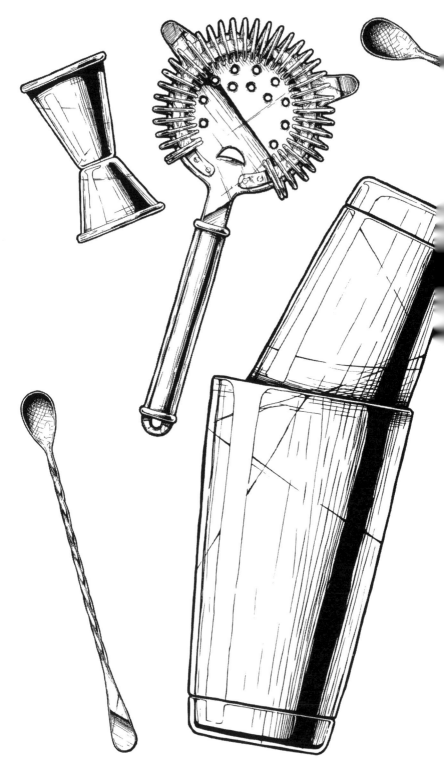

chapter nineteen

Garrett

"YOU'RE AN IDIOT, FOSTER." RIDGE'S GLOWER could make a hardened criminal quake in his orange jumpsuit.

I mirror his irritation, but mine lacks the threat of bodily harm. "Takes one to know."

"Real mature," he grunts.

"How do you expect me to respond to yet another unexpected gang bang?"

Drake slings an arm around my neck. "As if you didn't see us coming."

I shove him off before he can knock on my skull. "Are we making this a regular thing? Pretty sure I've already asked Ridge for lube, but he has yet to deliver."

The ex-hockey star manages to darken his expression. "Why are you sulking like a bully stole your toy? Call Grace and confess your undying devotion to her. Either that or yank the soggy coaster from your ass. Customers are complaining."

My nostrils flare at his false claim. Even that small action is forced. "Why don't you take your own advice and actually talk to Callie?"

Harper gasps at the mention of her friend in relation to the stoic grump. "Oh, you should. She would love that."

Ridge's glare softens, most likely picturing his long-standing obsession. The dreamy glint on this brute's face is comical. "Soon."

"You two could be super cute together." The bubbly blonde shakes off the interruption. "But we're not there yet. Excellent diversion attempt, boss."

I shrug. "Worth a shot."

She wags her finger at me. "The topic at hand is *your* grumpy mood. No one else's."

"I'm fine."

Her eyes narrow. "But you could be better."

"Couldn't we all?

"Of course," she scoffs. "There just so happens to be a simple solution for you."

My captive audience hums in agreement. I face the group that's gathered to review my mistakes under the guise that they care. It's still a mystery as to why my love life is so damn interesting. Roosters might as well be the stage for a reality show. Although to be fair, nobody busted my balls until Grace entered the scene.

"I'm allergic to romance, remember? Committed relationships give me hives." I scratch at my arm for emphasis.

"You don't think people already assume you're blissfully shackled to Grace? They can't stop talking about the girl who tamed our beloved bachelor."

"That's a bit extreme," I mutter.

Harper flings a rag over her shoulder. "Is it? You kissed Grace in public."

"That was actually for my benefit to chase off Jasmine."

"What about her wearing your clothes?"

"She didn't want to recycle her dress from the night before," I explain.

"Might as well pee on her," Cole laughs.

"At least I didn't find out she was pregnant with my baby six months later." I glare at the guy who was my friend until he knocked up my sister.

"Low blow," he snarls.

"What do you call this?" I thrust my arms out to indicate the current pressure cooker.

"Okay, okay. We don't need to get heated," Joy chides. The warning in her eyes moves from her fiancé to me. "You're not a jerk, Garrett. Quit acting like one."

The knot that's been festering in my gut triples in size. It's bad enough that Grace hasn't responded to my texts for days. I don't need those I rely on for support to come at me from all angles.

My irritation burns a path across the meddlesome bunch. "This is beginning to feel like an intervention."

"That's because it is one. Mom and Dad should arrive shortly." Joy beams at me while bouncing Belle in her arms.

"You have a baby in my bar." Not that I mind seeing my niece, but I'm grasping at flimsy defenses.

"Wouldn't be the first time. How's that changing station coming along?"

I silently fume at her for several beats before swerving to avoid that losing battle. The newest addition to our staff seems as good a target as any. "How about earning that paycheck, Harps?"

The blonde snaps her gum but doesn't move otherwise. "Do you have an issue with my productivity?"

"The ice could probably use…" But my suggestion meets an abrupt end at the sight of the full bin.

"Nice try." She leans against the counter in a show of parking her ass for the foreseeable future.

"How about that couple? Maybe they need a refill." I motion toward a pair cuddled in the corner booth.

"For the record, everyone is in tip-top shape. We're very entertained by this conversation. Please continue." She beckons to her fellow meddlers.

My skin begins to crawl under their intense scrutiny. "I'd rather you didn't."

"Grace isn't a random girl you'll forget tomorrow," Drake chimes in.

Shame prickles the back of my neck. "I'm aware."

Joy spins her wrist, waiting for something I can't give. "And that's all you're going to say?"

"Yeah?"

She thumps her forehead. "As previously stated, you're already devoted to your situationship. Might as well make it official."

"Or we can stay friends." Which sounds like a stale alternative even to my own ears.

Joy mutters a string of unintelligible nonsense that repeats my name too many times to be a coincidence. "When are you going to quit sabotaging your happiness? Hilary is a cheating twat waffle. It's super unfortunate that she broke your heart and trust. I hate her for that. Trust me. But you shouldn't let what she did dictate your faith in love."

"I'm not. This is my choice." The waver in my voice isn't doing me any favors.

"It's hard to believe you, bro. Should we take a vote?" She draws a checkmark in the air.

"My relationship preferences aren't up for debate. This isn't a democracy."

"Would you prefer to be overruled? That can be arranged. Otherwise, you can admit the decision is unanimous." My sister motions around our rectangular formation, saving me for last.

"Don't let Grace get away, Foster. You'll never forgive yourself." That slice of wisdom rumbles from Jake as he sits on his favorite stool, mostly cast in shadows.

I gawk at Knox Creek's favorite asshole. "You're giving me dating advice, Evans? Shit, am I that bad?"

"Yes," the group answers in unison.

"Well, fuck. Didn't expect that." I drag both palms down my face.

Talk about a knee to the groin. It's tough to breathe while I muddle through this revelation. Not long ago the roles were reversed. I strongly encouraged him to get over himself to win Harper back. It's not fun being on the receiving end. Especially from this jackass. I'd never expect Jake be the voice of reason.

That's when I catch Joy wincing. "What's wrong?"

"I know you're struggling, but can you keep the cursing to a minimum. There's a baby present." She nods toward Belle who's snoozing in her mama's cradled embrace.

My jaw hangs slack. "She can't understand me."

"That's not the point."

"Fine. Whatever. Sorry," I mumble in choppy segments.

Joy rests her palm over the fist I have clenched on the bar. "Our pestering comes from a genuine place. We're looking out for you."

"Sure about that?" I have to admit that their collaborative efforts are encouraging.

My sister nods. "This is a pivotal moment, Gare-bear. If you don't make a move, she's a goner. Don't do that to yourself."

"Grace won't talk to me," I grumble. Even the one-word replies have stopped.

"I wonder why." Ridge's sarcasm isn't appreciated.

My middle finger is a raging bull ready to charge. I flip him both to get the message across. "It's not my fault. Not completely at least. We made the decision together."

"But you alone are letting the best thing that's happened

to you slip away in the aftermath." Joy's grin is kind. "She's your soulmate. Deep down, beyond the hurt and resentment, you gave her that nickname for a reason."

Harper clutches a palm to her chest. "It's true. When you look at her, it's like reading a romance novel. It makes me swoon. And also curse your name for being such a nincompoop. You're the clueless hero who insists on remaining 'just friends' for whatever seemingly noble reason. I want to shake you a lotta bit."

My mind whirls while trying to process her underlying meanings. I almost forgot they share a passion for those books. "Is this where I apologize for something I don't remember doing? I recall some extreme groveling."

She rolls her eyes. "Let's skip ahead, shall we?"

"To what? "

"Want to hear a spoiler alert?" She leans closer to whisper, "Grace is just as smitten with you."

Drake grips my shoulder. "She's worth changing the game, man."

A game I'm not equipped to play. Misery strikes hard and I nearly stagger under the force. My gaze bounces to the table where I first saw her. The empty chair taunts me. She should be here. Always. It's a bitter reminder of why she isn't.

"Grace can do better than me," I mutter absently.

My sister pats the hand she's still covering. "Why don't you let her make that decision?"

She might compromise, but that doesn't sit well with me. In truth, I want to be with Grace in whatever capacity will make her smile at me again. That's equal parts thrilling and terrifying. It's a line I've been straddling since we met. I just need to try. For her.

Joy huffs at my lengthy silence. "Do you like her?"

"Obviously."

"Do you love her?" She wiggles her brows.

My chest tightens. I avert my eyes in fear that the truth bleeds through. "No."

She squints at me. "Liar."

"Even if I did, which I don't, you wouldn't be the first to know."

"Hmmm, that's fair." The twinkle in her eye is too smug.

"You're a pain in my ass. All of you," I add.

"Admit you'd be lost without us."

"Dammit, I would be." I groan and immediately prepare to get reprimanded.

Instead, my sister is gawking at me. Her arm that isn't clutching Belle blindly swats at Cole. "Holy shiitake mushrooms. We're finally getting through to him."

"Let's not count our chickens before they hatch," Cole murmurs from the corner of his mouth.

"It's not that simple. I'm permanently stuck in my no-strings era, and she knows it." Not to mention stubbornness is my most toxic trait. "Grace isn't going to believe I've suddenly had a change of heart."

Harper pouts. "Why not?"

"Because that's our thing. She's searching for her happily ever after. I'm not the type to even consider the risk."

"But you could ride off into the sunset." Drake pretends to snap a fake pair of reins.

I sigh. "With her? Maybe."

Joy and Harper squeal, their combined excitement sharp enough to shatter glass. My sister is the first to recover from her victory. "I'm super proud of you, brother."

"I said maybe."

Harper bats my response away like a pest. "That's just a delayed yes."

"Grace is probably gonna think I'm full of crap."

"Ask her on a date and find out." She says that like it's so obvious.

"Or offer to eat her pussy," Jake suggests from the shadows.

"That'll do the trick and grant you more sexual favors," Harper agrees. Her voice holds a wistful edge that suggests she's speaking from experiences that will traumatize me.

Joy gasps and clasps her palms over Belle's baby ears. "Language, dirty birds."

Harper's laugh is a mockery. "Oh, puh-lease. Cole was talking about the shaggin' wagon earlier. You're the last person who can censor us."

My sister scowls and nudges her fiancé, who doesn't appear slighted in the least. "It's the principle and we're trying to form better habits early."

"Fine, whatever. Going down under never hurt anyone."

Joy purses her lips. "I can't argue with that."

The door bursts open and Abbie rushes toward us. "Phew, sorry I'm late."

"More reinforcements?" I glare at those already in attendance.

My sister avoids eye contact. "It doesn't hurt to be prepared. There's power in numbers."

I press against the throbbing in my temples. At least this new arrival is good about sharing intel. "What's the latest?"

Abbie settles onto a stool, parking a bent elbow on the rail. "Pour me a drink and I'll tell you."

chapter twenty

Grace

A BEAD OF CONDENSATION TRICKLES DOWN MY GLASS to land on the cocktail napkin. My gaze tracks the descent with too much interest. What I'm really manifesting is a similar exit strategy for the chatterbox who's plopped himself beside me.

"I've pushed her to one-twenty, but she's got more to give." Wade's nasally voice takes another stab at my indifferent attitude.

My focus stays on the sweaty drink in front of me. I'd scrounge up more tolerance for his passionate presentation if he wasn't having the majority of this conversation with my boobs. "Uh-huh, that's really something."

The clueless car enthusiast launches into more detail about his precious Mustang. I get the impression this is his version of bragging about a favorite child. The apple of his eye is a sight to see. He swipes through no less than a dozen pictures on his phone.

Laughter bubbles from me when I envision Garrett in Wade's spot. He'd be boasting about boozy recipes instead of turbo engines. My mood sours like milk left out in the sun. I'd been doing well for all of two seconds. Feigned interest returns to the photoshoot.

"GRNPONY, huh?" I comment on the custom license plate just to humor him.

Wade beams at my interest. Such a proud papa. "It cost a pretty penny, but I decided to splurge. We only live once, right?"

The sentiment leads me to the erotic marathon I ran with Garrett last weekend. My thighs still ache from being spread wide for hours. Damn, that man can eat.

But this isn't the ideal place to reminisce about the chafe left behind.

"Exactly," I mumble as a noncommittal response if he's even expecting one.

"Would you like to take a ride sometime?"

"Where?"

"In my green pony." Wade tilts his screen to share another image with me.

"Umm," I stall.

I'm honestly at a loss for words. Not because he's fixated on his car or ogling my breasts. He's just not who I want to be sitting next to.

My wheels are spinning again. It physically pains me to ignore Garrett's texts, but I'm too weak. The distance I've shoved between us is necessary to restore my resolve. At this stage, I'll gladly surrender and volunteer to be his fuck buddy. Indefinitely.

The entire point of forcing myself to this bar was to forget Garrett for an hour. Even ten minutes would be acceptable. But no. The unattainable bachelor plagues my thoughts non-stop on a daily basis. He was correct that I'd be suffering from dick-drawals.

It has to stop. I'm fooling myself but I have to try.

Otherwise, I'll be stuck in a miserable pattern, pining after a guy who doesn't want me.

A pathetic groan escapes me. My rationale is a frazzled mess. This disaster is of my own making, but that doesn't calm the chaos currently wreaking havoc. The emotional turmoil is taking its toll.

Might as well go for broke and let the freak flag fly.

"Is your penis pierced?"

Wade blanches, beer dribbling from his lips. "What?"

What's left of my modesty demands that I change the subject, but I'm too far gone. "Do you have a pierced penis?"

His blush is a neon sign, even in the dim lighting. "Um, no."

"That's too bad." I can't even muster the tact to let him down gently.

And with that, I've added an awkward component to this already stilted exchange. My cringe is aimed at the chipped counter. Maybe he'll leave me to lick my wounds in peace.

"My dick is bedazzled. Most recently, a chick called it a mythical creature. It's like a majestical monument erected from her depraved fantasies."

I gasp and swivel to confront the voice that's been haunting me. "What're you doing here?"

"Looking for you." He sends Wade a dismissive glance. "You're in my seat."

The other man bumbles over a retort. "I didn't know this spot was reserved."

"Well, you do now. Take a hike." He hitches a thumb over his shoulder.

Wade straightens his shoulders. "Excuse me?"

Garrett expels a harsh breath as if this interaction is expending too much energy. "All right, listen. I'm gonna level with you. She doesn't want your pokey pony. I'm the only mount for her."

I choke on my saliva. "Someone's cocky."

"Thanks to you." He boops my nose before addressing Wade again. "She's not gonna twist your crankshaft. This classy lady has finer tastes. Try your luck elsewhere."

Wade ambles off, muttering under his breath about the lack of appreciation for true American muscle. I watch him go for no other reason than to gather my scattered wits. Nerves somersault in my belly at a gold medal pace. Garrett's unexpected appearance sprouts questions in all directions.

A gentle grip on my chin has me facing the one I've been missing. "Hey, soulmate."

"Hi," I breathe.

"Thanks for saving me a seat." He slides onto the freshly vacated stool.

The shift in position snaps me from my stupor. "That was rude."

Garrett scoffs. "Were you actually interested in him?"

"Maybe."

He bends until his exhale breezes across my neck. "Your pants are on fire, liar."

A shiver rolls down my spine. "What're you doing here, bartender?"

Our eyes lock when he leans on the rail. "Already told you."

"Let me guess." I tap my chin. "Abbie told you where I was."

"Led me straight to you."

"She's such a traitor," I grumble.

"Is she? I'm glad she switched teams." He rotates on the stool until our knees bump. "I wouldn't have found you otherwise."

Heat rises from where we touch. "You're far from home. I believe you called the drive to my neck of the woods a long haul. It's an hour round trip."

A reflection from the television hanging nearby plays across his features. "Eh, you're worth the trip to Timbuktu. I wouldn't be upset if you moved closer to Knox Creek, though."

"And why would I do that?"

"So we can slot more activities into our regularly scheduled traditions."

"I'll consider it." But my tone flatlines at the notion.

Garrett's smile drops. "Why are you avoiding me?"

"I'm not," I hedge.

His finger wags to scold me. "Be honest."

I toss my hands in the air, almost smacking him in the agitated process. "You were right. Sex complicates things. It's a total joke to assume otherwise. Although to be fair, I knew this would happen. On almost every level. You did too. Obviously. We can't sleep together and pretend nothing has changed. Things are going to be weird between us now. I needed space to figure out how to handle our friendship."

He calmly watches me rant. "And you came to someone else's bar to get hit on by men who don't deserve you?"

"It would be awkward meeting guys at Roosters," I deflect.

His stare is too intense. "Why is that?"

I avert my gaze to a stain on the counter. "You're going to make me say it?"

"Absolutely."

My throat is suddenly very parched. I sip at my drink to soothe the burn. It takes several gulps to gain the liquid courage to look at him again. "I might've developed romantic feelings for you that seem to be even stronger since we had sex."

There's a fire in his eyes that smolders into blue flames. "You're telling me this while suckling on a cocktail that another bartender made for you?"

"That's what you're choosing to focus on?"

"Hard not to." Garrett whips something from his pocket, holding up the pink object for me to see.

"You brought me a straw?" On closer inspection, the plastic is molded in an unmistakable shape. "It's a penis."

"For your sucking pleasure. Wrap your lips around this little guy. Pretend it's a smaller version of mine."

"Umm." I find myself stumbling for words again, but for a completely different reason.

"Your mouth belongs on the peen I provide." He rips the standard straw from my glass and tosses it in the trash. Then the tiny dick slides in as an apparent upgrade. "Try that pecker hole on for size."

I quirk a brow at his antics. "How very territorial of you."

"Call me a caveman if you'd like, just so long as I'm yours."

"Now you're being charming. My panties are in trouble." I fan myself and add an eye roll for extra impact.

"Funny you should mention that." Garrett digs his phone from his pocket, quickly tapping at the screen.

Mine buzzes from its place on the bar. I swing my gaze from the vibrating device to him. "What're you doing?"

His smirk is crooked. "See who it's from."

I flip my cell over to see the notification. Nobody is shocked that the message is from Garrett. What has my pulse spiking is the picture that's attached. I blink at the image of him for several seconds. "Why did you send this to me?"

"As a potential candidate. I can vouch that he's the real deal."

"Are you making fun of my system?" I poke him in the pec, my finger bouncing off the chiseled muscle. "Which, by the way, you invented."

His inhale is long and loud. Those broad shoulders roll back. He looks like he's ramping up for a big reveal. "I want to be considered for the role of Mr. Monogamy."

My blank stare shifts to his earnest expression. "Huh?"

"We should date."

I laugh, nearly doubling over from the powerful punch of amusement. My humor sobers into a choppy tune at the sight of his lips formed in a firm line. "Wait. You're serious?"

Garrett scoops my hand off my thigh to lace our fingers together. "I've always been serious about you. It just took a hot second to realize what I was missing."

"Am I hallucinating?" I glance from left to right, but the posh atmosphere remains the same.

He waits until my gaze returns to his. "Can I eat your pussy?"

The air gets sucked from my lungs and I gasp. "Now that better be a joke."

His head hangs low. "I knew Evans was full of shit."

"Jake?"

He peeks at me from his sullen slouch. "Uh, yeah. The entire group bombarded me earlier. It was somewhat of an intervention."

My stomach sinks along with the temperature. I shiver as understanding dawns on me. "That's why you're here."

"No!" He flings forward to grip my arms as if I'm about to take off. Once he realizes I haven't budged, his posture returns to a more relaxed state. "I mean, sure. They shoved me in the right direction faster than I was crawling. But I was planning to make a move on my own."

"Uh-huh." There's a numbness to my tone.

"Grace, I wouldn't be here if I didn't want to be. They didn't influence what wasn't already set in motion." Garrett reclaims my palm, giving me a gentle squeeze. "I'm an ignorant mule who needs several spanks to his ass before he considers behaving. Probably a few swift kicks too. Be patient with me."

My mouth twitches. "You're a fixer-upper."

"Does that mean you're gonna do me at home to renovate my manwhore-ish habits?"

That gets my cogs grinding. "Do you actually sleep with a lot of women? I haven't noticed."

He scrubs the back of his neck. "Not since I first saw you at Roosters. You were sitting at that table, tonguing a cherry, and taking possession of my attention without even realizing it. Once I laid eyes on you, nothing else existed. You suspend me, soulmate. That's not going to change."

Warmth blazes my cheeks at the reminder. "I saw you that night."

"You might've mentioned that before."

"But I didn't admit that I had a tough time focusing on anything else either."

Garrett jolts. "Really?"

"I guess we've never talked about this."

"Nope, you're holding out on me."

A squirmy sensation tickles my belly. "I planned to order another drink. This time directly from you. Tie Me to the Bedpost to be specific."

His chuckle is filthy rich. "That would've knocked you on your ass."

"Yeah, well, I never made it to your section of the rail to find out. Your adoring fans were flocked too thick. I chickened out and tucked tail back to my table."

"Damn, I fucked that up."

I shrug. "Not really. You were appeasing the masses. I watched you shamelessly flirt with every other woman in the bar. It was a captivating performance. Abbie burst my bubble and confirmed you weren't relationship resolution material."

"She wasn't wrong," he chuckles.

"Yes, I recall our countless conversations on the subject." How could I not? It's the main reason we're stuck in the friend-zone.

He's quiet for a few beats. His gaze implores mine, delving

deep enough that I feel him searching. "You have no damn clue."

"About what?" My voice is breathy from the impact of his stare.

"How much I want to prove I can be the man for you."

"Then why don't you?"

"I don't trust it."

Hurt slashes my chest. "You mean me?"

"Just this"—he motions between us—"in general."

"You won't know if you're not willing to try," I murmur.

"Which circles back to us dating."

I shake my head to clear the haze. "Where is this coming from all of a sudden?"

"It's not out of nowhere." Garrett cups my jaw, his thumb brushing over the tipped angle. "You have to know I'm crazy about you. I just…"

"Don't trust it," I repeat his earlier phrase."

"But I want to try. Maybe we can do a trial phase. If I suck after a week or two you have my permission to dump me."

Bullish laughter snorts from me. "And where will that leave me?"

"Right back here." He waves a dismissive hand at our surroundings. "Consider it a slight detour that might lead to happily ever after."

"Your faith in yourself is extremely reassuring." But I can't lie. This test phase holds appeal. Mostly because I get to be with Garrett.

"I'm rusty. Cut me some slack."

"You want strings attached?"

"With you? Absolutely. Until we're a knotted mess that can't be separated."

"That sounds very entangled," I muse.

"I'm already committed to you, Peaches. I was just being

a coward. Afraid to define the depth of that term where we're concerned."

Am I foolish for stumbling into his admission? I can't find a single reason to not trust him. Garrett has only been honest with me, even when the truth was painful to hear. The comfort he provides just sitting beside me is telling.

I could drag this out and play hard to get, but that would just delay the inevitable. It's no secret I want Garrett Foster in a more than friendly manner. The fact that I already slept with him should reveal as much. Might as well make it official.

Rather than leave him hanging, I lean into his touch that's still cradling my face. "This is beginning to feel like I'm getting everything I want."

He flinches. "Maybe not everything. I can't promise that I'll ever want to get married. But I'm willing to consider the possibility for you. Only you. But—"

My finger presses against his lips. "I don't need more conditions on yet another amendment to our agreement."

"Listen," he mumbles around my flimsy gag. "I can't let you compromise for me. You want the fairytale ending with a bow attached. That's what you deserve. I'll understand if you don't accept my cautionary stride into the dating pool as significant enough."

"Who's to say we need to get married?"

"Other than Doris?" He cracks a smirk.

"I'm aware that I've referred to marriage as the token at the end of this resolution, but maybe my preferences are shifting too. You're who I want to be with. Period. That's not a sacrifice. It could never be anything less than complete satisfaction." My heart is suddenly galloping. I take a moment to breathe deep. "A committed relationship, even on a trial basis, is a happy medium. I'm more than willing to meet you there. To be honest, it's not a compromise if I get you in the deal."

The strain in his shoulders doesn't deflate. "Are you sure?"

"Are you?"

"Without a shred of doubt."

Relief floods in and I divert my focus to the ink decorating his forearm. "I've been meaning to ask you about this."

He rotates to put more of the design on display. "What about it?"

I admire the half sleeve for at least a minute. Near his wrist is a football field that blends into a street view of Roosters. The tattoo ends at his elbow with a replica of the bar's interior.

"Well, now that I've had a good look, the meaning is self-explanatory. It's very sexy."

"Adds to my bad boy image."

I snort. "That's you in a nutshell."

Garrett's posture loses the tense corners, his smile relaxed and carefree. "Can I kiss you?"

"I'd be disappointed if you didn't."

We lean toward each other in the next instant. Our lips meet in the middle. I sigh into him, my mouth curving into a grin. His arm snakes around my waist to tug me closer. Static sparks along my skin as his tongue glides across mine. Just as I'm about to climb onto his lap, someone clears their throat. Loud enough to crack through my lust.

I break the kiss, not bothering to glance at our interruption. "We're busted."

He bends until our foreheads touch. "Barely noticed thanks to my ultimate distraction. Already off to a stellar start. I'm gonna fulfill your every need." His lips brush mine. "Make you blissfully happy on a daily basis." Another soft peck. "Be the best version of myself for you." One more for good measure. "Trick you into thinking I actually deserve you."

My nose drifts along his. "You already do."

"That's only because you inspire me."

Which reminds me of his little gift. "I can't believe you brought me a penis straw."

"And I can't believe you're drinking another man's cocktail."

"Who said the bartender was a guy? Ruby actually made me this tasty refreshment. Although, I've always had a thing for redheads. Delish." My tongue fondles the tip of the micro-peen.

She wiggles her fingers at him. "Hello."

He waves in return. "Thanks for taking care of my girl."

"You're welcome," Ruby replies.

She doesn't sound all that accommodating. It's only then I notice she's hovering. I wait for her to wander off. An awkward lull settles between us. Another glance proves she isn't moving. She's most likely the one who intruded on our public display of affection.

An unwelcome itch has me squirming on the stool. "Should I pay my tab?"

"It's already been covered."

Garrett winks when I gape at him. "Wasn't about to let some other shmuck buy you that drink."

I giggle at his sneaky methods, but the humor tappers off when Ruby still doesn't leave. "Do you want us to go?"

"That depends." She pauses for dramatic effect. "Are you done groping each other?"

"Probably not," Garrett spouts without hesitation.

Her focus is particularly trained on him. "This is an elegant establishment. Take your humping elsewhere."

Garrett knocks on the bar. "You got it."

After a parting glare, she walks away while I stifle a laugh. "Wow, you certainly have a way with women. What do I have to gain from this trial period again?"

"Other than nine inches of pierced penis perfection erected in your honor?" He points to the bulge in his jeans.

I groan. "You're incorrigible."

He drifts a bent knuckle down my arm. "I want to hear more about these depraved fantasies concerning my bedazzled cock."

"I'm looking at him."

Garrett emits a low rumble that sounds tortured. "Should we get outta here?"

"Either that or Ruby is gonna show us the door." I scoot off my seat.

"Don't forget your tiny dick!" His voice carries across the room as he plucks the straw from my glass.

"His name is Bruce." I swipe the pink addition for my collection from his grasp. "This bad boy is gonna come in handy later."

Garrett rushes after me, slinging an arm around my shoulders. "Can I watch?"

I peer at him from under my lowered lashes. "We'll see where our first date takes us."

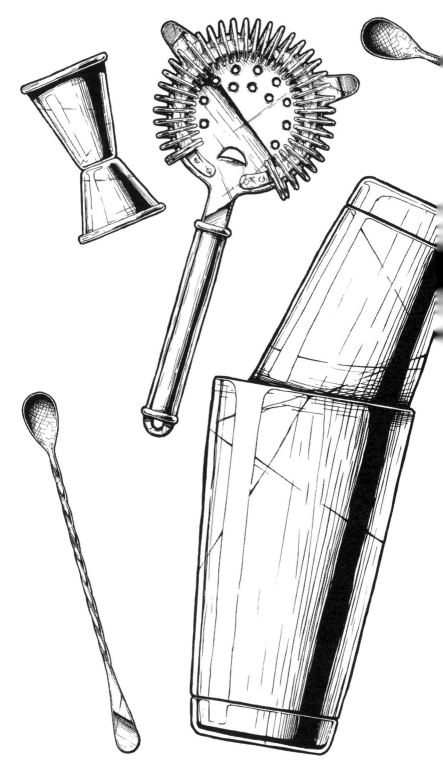

chapter twenty-one

Garrett

GRACE GAWKS AT THE BRICK BUILDING LIKE SHE'S A kid at the entrance to Disneyland. "You brought me to Bound by Love?"

"I sure did." My chest puffs out as I bask in her reaction.

Her chin quivers a bit and there's a glassy sheen in her eyes. "This is my favorite bookstore."

"Lucky guess. I saw it on my way to Sunsets." I spit the name like the upscale expletive it is.

A coy smile curls the edges of her lips as she peeks over at me. "You're really offended I went to a different bar, huh?"

"Extremely." That's why I hauled her ass out of there and insisted on driving to a better location.

"Behave yourself and I won't be tempted to repeat the crime against your pride."

My arm flings forward at the shop. "What do you call this?"

"A very good start. Well done." Grace pats my cheek.

I tuck my chin and press a kiss to her inner wrist. "Thanks for giving me a chance."

Her sigh is a bowl of candy hearts dipped in chocolate and sprinkles with a cherry on top. "I missed you."

"Likewise, soulmate. Times infinity."

She rolls her eyes at my exaggerated efforts to up the ante. Almost immediately, she begins bouncing in her sandals. "Can we go inside?"

I guide her toward the entrance. "Otherwise we're just loitering on the curb."

A chime greets us as I usher her through the door. Grace rubs against me with sultry purpose. I gnash my teeth and follow her like the loyal hound she's trained.

Artificial brightness envelops us as we venture into Bound by Love. Rows of organized shelves fill the large room. Display cases holding random items like stationary, art supplies, and totes are arranged in the center. There's a café of some sort off to the right, but it's closed.

"This place stays open kinda late, huh?" I was surprised to discover we could still make it in plenty of time tonight.

"They want to make sure everyone gets their fix."

I glance at the darkened coffee shop again. "Of books?"

"Mhmm. You smell that?" She wafts the air to her nose. "It's so complex and unique. Boosted energy. Uplifted spirits. Hours getting lost between the pages. Fantasies explored. Imaginations running wild and free."

The papery aroma reminds me of a library, but I'm not about to dull her enthusiasm. "I can understand the appeal."

Grace whirls to face me, a wide grin stretching her mouth to comical proportions. "This is a great surprise."

The sight of her pure joy almost has me crashing to my knees. Fuck, she's beautiful. An ache spears through me from just being in her presence. I can't believe she deems me worthy of the privilege. It's too much, but not nearly enough.

"You're staring," she whispers.

A smirk tilts my mouth. "You're captivating."

She tucks some hair behind her ear. "Aren't you going to look at books?"

"I'd rather look at you."

Red splotches bloom on her skin. "A girl could get used to this flattery, bartender."

"Good." My hand clasps hers as I steer us in the direction marked for romance. "I plan to keep you around."

"And I might just let you." But the sparkle in her gaze tells me that our paths are already weaving into a complicated tangle.

I squeeze her fingers that are threaded in mine. "Did you see this coming for us?"

Grace shrugs. "The friends almost always become lovers. It's my preferred trope for a reason. But I wasn't sure if you felt the same. That's why I forced a lid on my emotions. Unless intoxicated or chased through a hay maze. The last thing I want is for you to feel pressured."

"Well, I want to spend every spare moment with you." And there's no sign of unease after admitting that. Not even a pinch.

"I happen to have lots of free time in my schedule. That's why I've considered getting another part-time gig. Maybe on the weekends, when your sister doesn't need me to watch Belle."

The off-handed comment tastes like she's baiting me. Might as well take a bite.

"How about Roosters?"

"Absolutely not," she blurts.

I stumble to the side while clutching my chest. "Damn, you could've at least hesitated."

"Oh, my bad." She clears her throat and blinks at me. "What I meant to say was that's never going to happen."

I scowl while she cackles like a hyena. "What's wrong with getting a job at my bar?"

"Other than the fact that I see you enough already?"

"There's nothing wrong with that."

Grace crinkles her brow. "I'd hate for you to get sick of me."

"Now there's something that's never going to happen."

"We've been dating on a trial basis for"—she glances at an invisible watch on her wrist—"less than two hours. Let's simmer in this stage for a bit before you hire me to do your dirty work." Her gaze wanders to the shelves surrounding us. "I thought about getting a job here once upon a time."

"Why didn't you?"

She drifts her open palm across a colorful arrangement of journals. Her other remains securely tucked in mine. "The nanny position fell in my lap."

"Probably meant to be. Those kiddos love you."

Her gaze shifts to mine. "How would you know?"

"I've seen you with them on occasion. Harper and Joy sing your praises like I'm going to be struck with the urge to knock you up."

Grace chokes on her breath, mirroring my thoughts exactly. "Um, that's… frightening."

"Which is precisely why they say it. My sister has a sick fascination for watching me squirm. Any woman who catches my eye for longer than common courtesy gets the third degree."

"No wonder you swore off relationships," she laughs.

"I did. Past tense." A wink solidifies my point.

She fans herself. "There you go spoiling me with too much credit again."

"It's the soulmate special," I correct. "And I'll gladly gobble any free time you have to spare. Just like how I'll meet the three of you for lunch sometime."

"I'd like that. Bradley will be especially pleased to meet you."

"Why's that?"

She waves it off. "Not important."

"All right. Just let me know where and when. I'll be there."

"It's a date. In the meantime, how should we spend the rest of tonight?"

"Pick a book for us to read." I gesture at the options piled high in every direction.

A glint enters her gaze. "Should we visit the raunchy erotica section?"

My stride falters on the potential alone. "This innocent-looking establishment houses such racy material?"

Her brows twerk. "Some call it a sex dungeon."

I gasp for her benefit. The laugh I earn is a rich reward. "Those actually exist in public places?"

"It's hidden along the far wall, and it's monitored. No funny business in the stacks." She sends me a pointed look that's well deserved.

"Is that where your stash comes from?"

"Most aren't that explicit. There's plenty of plot. The smut gets blended in. But tonight… I'm in the mood for the opposite."

"You've been saving the extra filthy stuff for me." I hum as a specific title comes to mind. "Like the Kama Sutra."

"We can get creative. Let's see what's available." She bumps her hip into me at a scheming tempo.

I let her drag me down the aisles to our destination. "Someone's in a hurry."

Grace twirls and peeks over her shoulder with a flirty grin. "Well, duh. Several of my most beloved things in one spot gets me antsy."

My smile in response can only be described as cheesy. "Maybe we'll get inspired and stop at a different type of shop before getting freaky between the sheets."

"Now that's an idea," she murmurs. Her blush rebounds

with fiery intensity. "Don't forget about my other boyfriends in the drawer."

"Couldn't if I tried."

"Maybe I'll use Bruce to slurp cherry syrup off you." She taps the penis straw that's poking out of her purse.

That visual punches me into the nearest rack. A few books tumble to the floor. "Shit."

A kinky giggle escapes her as she scoops up the fallen titles and returns them where they belong. Then she skips away. My cock points straight ahead, desperate to catch her. She drags her fingers along the spines in a lover's caress. I want her hands on me. The demand is about to spew from my lips when she comes to an abrupt halt.

"Oooh, what's this?" Grace snags a silver box off the shelf.

I tilt my head while inspecting her choice. "A board game?"

"It's called Lust!" Her seductive voice purrs the title boldly scrawled in red.

"You've caught my attention."

She prattles off the description. My selective hearing snags on certain words such as 'intimacy', 'provocative', 'sexual indulgences', 'risqué positions', and 'endless pleasure'. 'Explore fantasies' and 'push boundaries' aren't bad either. The most enticing might be 'thirty-thousand different combinations'.

"Then we can write our own scene rather than recreating one." Her eyes burn into mine with that final note.

"Toss cash on the counter and let's go." My voice is a croak.

She bites her bottom lip. "Just like that?"

I'm moving before she's done talking. Her back bumps into the shelf, rattling more than the novels. She sputters and arches into me. My palms clamp onto the cool metal while caging her in. Our gazes feast on each other, heavy breaths accompanying the trance.

"Or we can play here," I whisper against her lips.

Grace presses her mouth to mine for a brief kiss. "Management won't approve."

Fire blazes under my skin. "I need to be inside you."

"That can be arranged, but not in the store. They take security very seriously."

"I thought this place was supposed to bind love," I mutter.

"Not that literal." Her body sinks against mine. "Damn, I missed you."

A content rumble rises from me. "How much?"

"Want me to show you?" She toys with the button on my waistband.

My vision blurs with demanding hunger. "That's not even a question."

Grace ducks under my arm and begins retreating down the aisle. "C'mon, bartender. We've got a bet to make and rules to bend. Winner chooses the position."

chapter twenty-two

Grace

GARRETT LAUNCHES HIMSELF ONTO MY BED IN A familiar maneuver. Only a stretchy pair of boxer briefs corral his trouser snake. The material does little to contain what he's packing. He's hard. Very much so. A glint of silver peeks out from the elastic waistband to tease me. Drool puddles in my mouth as I watch him test the springs for our sexcapades.

"Not bad, soulmate. We won't make much racket with your squeak-free mattress. The frame doesn't creak either. Very cooperative for what's to come." The smirk that slants his full lips is devastating.

A quake trembles through me. "My neighbors will appreciate that."

He does a few more pelvic thrusts for good measure. "Excellent craftsmanship. You've got quite the screw shack for us to nail each other. All. Night. Long. The carnival acrobatics are about to flip the tent over."

The thrashing in my ears makes it difficult to laugh at his ridiculous lingo. "Uh-huh."

"Even the posts are sturdy. We can take turns tying each other up." He stretches his arms to demonstrate.

"Apparently, I've been lying on wasted potential. Good thing I have a friend to fix that."

"Boyfriend," he corrects. "At your service."

I squirm on the sidelines, the hive in my belly too busy to ignore. Garrett notices and pauses his pillow fluffing. His palm pats the empty space beside him.

"Whatcha doing so far away?"

"Just enjoying the view." My feet carry me forward without permission.

"Aren't you forgetting something?"

I freeze as my mind whirls. "Um...?"

"The game," he laughs.

"Oh! Right." I scramble to grab the box off the floor, then resume my snail's pace toward the bed.

Garrett's unwavering focus tracks me with a predator's precision. "Nervous?"

"If you must know, I don't usually put out on the first date."

As in never have I ever. But this man goes against the norm like pinstripes at a black-tie affair. Or maybe using crude humor to entertain a prestigious crowd is appropriate in this situation.

"You're giving me the soulmate special." His fingers clutch at the sheets as if reeling me in.

"And then some," I promise while inching closer.

His expression smolders. "You're still forgetting something."

"What?" I glance behind me.

"Ditch the threads. Undies only." He motions to the tank top I still have on.

"That better include my bra 'cause I'm not letting the ladies swing free."

"Probably for the best. I wouldn't be able to keep my hands to myself."

I slowly strip the shirt over my head. Losing that barrier feels personal. My arm itches to slink across my stomach. Dammit, it's a tough habit to break. A shy glance at him stalls my breath. The heat in his gaze is enough to melt away those cruel insecurities.

"You're the most stunning sight I've ever seen." The grit in his tone is a coarse graze along my bared flesh.

I shiver from the phantom touch. "Thank you. But honestly, I'm still shocked you want to sleep with me. Again, I might add. And on a semi-regular basis."

Garrett lunges at me before I can process that he's moving. In the next beat, he's wrapped around my waist and hauling me onto the mattress. The wind is knocked out of me for a moment as I comprehend what just happened. It doesn't seem possible, but he lifted me like a feather. That sends a giddy thrill to boost my confidence.

"I want to do much more than sleep with you, soulmate. This is real for me. The whole deal. Whatever you're willing to give me. No matter what anybody else says, including the toxic whispers in your brain, you're my dream girl." His gentle caress against my cheek is at odds with how he just manhandled me. "If it's not too much to ask, I'd like that to include sex on a *very* regular basis. Nothing semi about it."

"That can be arranged," I breathe.

"Then we understand each other."

"You're like cover model hot," I blurt.

His eyes narrow as if he's remembering something. "If I send you another selfie, would you believe I'm a legit candidate? Or would you accuse me of being fake?"

"I'm not sure. Maybe? You'll have to try again. The first might've been a fluke." I roll my lips between my teeth to trap a goofy smile.

"Believe it, beauty. You're mine, and this is yours." He palms himself, a tortured groan spilling from his lips. "I could burst just looking at you."

"Keep it together, bartender. We have a game to play." I nudge the box that's wedged between us.

"Can we skip it? I'll take you straight to the eggplant patch. No need to stop for cucumbers."

My cackle is shrill and borders on embarrassing. I wipe at the amused tears leaking from my eyes. "You're relentless. We can do a speed round."

"Better be fast. Delayed gratification isn't my preferred foreplay."

"Yes, I recall. But it builds anticipation, Mr. Rushy Pants."

"I already erected a stone pole in your honor. What more do you want?"

"To discover how and where I'll take that girthy rod." I roll my wrist to mimic a hand job, then poke my tongue into my cheek. The lower region clenches at being left out.

"You drive a hard bargain, but the thirty-thousand possibilities are tempting."

I whip off the lid and spread out the board. Garrett shuffles the cards. The hunger in his gaze spikes to starvation status whenever he peeks at the pictures. I review the rules, which are fairly straightforward.

"The object is to build an ultimate fantasy with your lover. We take turns, collect cards, keep only one of each color, and reach the bed space."

"That's too complicated," Garrett complains.

I huff and shoot him a frown. His body shifts at constant intervals. He's beginning to resemble an impatient boy who's within feet of Lego Land.

"It's easy," I retort.

"But it could be more efficient. How about we each draw once. Keep it hidden. Don't show me even if I try to peek.

Then we'll do rock, paper, scissors to see whose position comes out victorious."

"Okay," I concede.

His grin suggests that he's already beat me. "Pick a card."

I swipe the top one from the deck and put it face down. Garrett does the same. We don't look at what lies ahead. The unknown has me fidgeting. He gets his hands set for the next step. I'm quick to mirror his actions.

"Rock, paper, scissors." We recite the command in unison while slamming a fist on an open palm.

My mind screams paper, but I choose scissors. Garrett smirks while crushing me with his rock. I blink at him before lowering my gaze to his card.

"What could it be?" He taps the center, still not revealing the face.

"Should I show you mine?"

"Please do."

I flip the card to reveal a red border, which is the steamiest. "Sex toys."

Garrett scrubs over his mouth, likely masking his urge to forfeit. "Shit, that's tough to beat."

We did, in fact, stop at an adult store on the way to my apartment. The brown bag on my nightstand taunts me. Maybe we'll use the kinky purchase later. That is if he plays his card right and the twist we created calls for it.

Garrett rubs his palms together. "It's time for me to collect. Are you prepared to discover your fuckery fate, soulmate?"

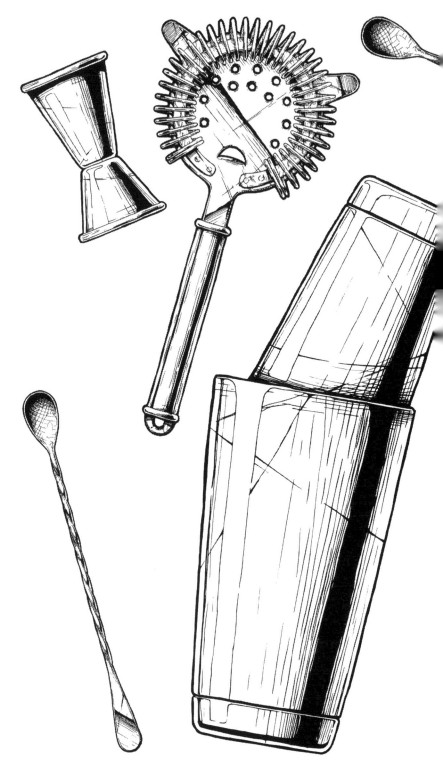

chapter twenty-three

Garrett

GRACE WOBBLES A BIT AS SHE GETS SITUATED ON HER hands and knees. Her ass sways in front of me like a sacrificial offering. Control becomes a foreign concept. I'm operating on instinct from this moment forward. She's mine. That's what matters.

My palms drift upward and curl around her inner thighs. With a firm grip, I lift until my face is smothered by her pussy. The crotch of her panties is soaked, and I greedily suck the fabric into my mouth.

Tangy sweetness coats my tongue, spurring me for another taste. My eyelids slide shut while I groan from the intoxicating flavor. Her sugar is my addiction. A noticeable strain spreads across my groin as my cock tests the limits of these boxers. At this rate, I'm going to come before we have sex.

"Holy shit," she wheezes.

I pull away from her honey scent. "Is that a good curse?"

"Very. You're just dirty."

"The better to fuck you," I rasp.

Grace's knees quake. "Sweet jeezus, you're going to turn me into a puddle."

"You're already very wet." I bury my nose in her center and inhale.

"Please." Her whine is accompanied by labored breaths.

"What can I do to you?"

"Fuck me, bartender." But her body language suddenly changes.

That swift flip strikes me as strange. I study her rigid movements for a moment. My palm roves over her lower back, but she doesn't react. The demands roaring at me pivot to focus solely on what she needs.

"Is doggie style okay with you? I can choose a different card."

This position isn't new for us. I took her from behind at the bed and breakfast. It's the game we're playing that adds an obscure element. The fact we're still learning each other's preferences is another layer. Not to mention the potential pressure of what's in the bag. I feel compelled to ensure she's comfortable.

Grace glances at me through the curtain of her dark hair. "Yeah? Why wouldn't it be?"

"You're acting weird. Almost stiff. Am I being too aggressive?"

A flush races along her throat, highlighting her thick swallow. "No, you're sexy as fuck. Keep going. I'm just really excited, but don't want to come off as desperate."

"Soulmate," I growl. The control I managed to rein in begins to wrench free.

A coy gleam sparkles in her eyes. "Problem?"

"Let me see how badly you want me. Nothing could be hotter."

She whimpers and lowers onto her elbows. The mattress dips as she spreads her legs wider. This angle puts her on full display. Well, almost. That damp strip hides where I'm aiming to go.

Before my clouded lust consumes me, I steer my focus to the nightstand. Grace watches while I grab the paper sack from Fantasy Gifts. The so-called concealed packaging might as well be a neon sign for something explicit. The contents have already been opened and sterilized. That was somewhat of a bonding experience. Her blush had me harder than the silver pierced through my tip. I drop the bag on the bed for later—or sooner if she's interested. Her enthusiasm at the sex shop was encouraging.

A snarky brow quirks at me. "Someone is getting ahead of himself."

"Doesn't hurt to be optimistic." My palms roam the soft flesh of her ass.

She's pliable under my touch, arching and molding into me. "We didn't say the cards would be combined."

"Consider it a creative liberty on the rules. It's a tie. We both win."

"I'm beginning to believe this game is rigged in your favor."

"Only to enhance your pleasure," I assure. "Trust me. You're gonna thoroughly enjoy the DP."

"Should I be concerned that I don't know what that is?"

"Double penetration," I chuckle.

"Kinky," she croons like a siren song.

"That's why the card was red, right?"

"A very explicit suggestion," she recites.

"You're in charge. I won't go there until you beg for it."

"Noted, and appreciated. Please continue." She wiggles her juicy curves.

My attention returns to where she's mostly bared to me. Only her thong restricts my view. I bend to snag the skimpy lace between my teeth. The elastic snaps against her sensitive skin when I let go.

Grace hisses in a sharp breath. "I like you rough with me."

"Just getting warmed up." Conviction is branded on that statement.

My fingers hook under the stretchy band and begin lowering the scrap, but I quickly realize her splayed position won't allow for easy removal. I bunch the black material in my fist and yank. The flimsy fabric rips like tissue.

She jolts from the motion. "What—?"

I treat myself to a whiff before tossing the ruined garment on the floor. "I'll buy you a new pair."

She doesn't get a chance to protest further before I sink two fingers into her slick heat. A long sigh spills from her while she accepts my onslaught. The glide is slippery as I pump my digits to a feverish pace. I stretch my thumb to circle her clit. She trembles and clamps around me.

My other hand travels across her supple flesh. "Have I ever told you that I'm an ass man?"

"Must've slipped your mind." She sinks down on where I'm fingering her.

I groan while stroking her cheek. "This peach bottom looks good enough to eat."

"Please don't put your mouth where I think you're about to."

"How about just a bite?" I nip at her before she can object.

"Smack my ass and call me Peaches," she blurts.

"The fuck?" I pause until Grace erupts in giggles.

"Just testing you."

I give her a light spank. The jiggle that follows has my eyes crossing. "Fuuuuuuck, soulmate. Your ass will be the end of me."

She grinds into my hand, seeking more. My hungry girl.

The sight of her wanton kicks me into action. I lick my fingers clean while simultaneously dropping trow.

Grace squirms impatiently. "What're you gonna do now that you have me naked, spread, and near the edge?"

I fist my entire length, squeezing at the base, while creeping forward until we're aligned. "I'm gonna watch you take my cock."

She whimpers when I nudge her opening. I push in slowly, focused on where my tip enters her. Fuck, it's a snug fit. Her inner muscles clench at the intrusion. The steel balls of my apadravya stretch her, but she's wet enough to take me. My shallow thrusts barely penetrate. It's just a tease to prepare her. Based on the quiver in her splayed form, she's getting needy.

I'm fixated on where my pierced head fucks her. My dick is drenched from her arousal after a few pumps. Grace tries to scoot back to take more of me, but I still her efforts with a grip on her ass.

"Quit tormenting me," she whines.

"You love it."

Which is proven by the noises her eager pussy makes for me. The squelch is obscene and delivers me straight to madness. I feed her another inch, captivated as my dick disappears inside of her. Grace claws at the sheets while bucking against my restraint. Our tolerance meets at zero. I hold onto her waist for leverage and thrust until my cock is buried to the root.

"Ohhhhhh," she sighs. "I missed your bedazzled unicorn penis."

"How about the rest of me?"

"Sure," she mumbles absently.

I bottom out again, immediately withdrawing for another plunge. She has to whack her palm against the headboard to stop herself from hitting the wood. Rather than complain, she begs for more.

"Harder," she pants.

Her command is the fuel for my determination. The bed shakes as I plow forward to do her bidding. My tempo resembles a fluid cycle as I piston in and out. Sweat prickles my scalp while I get lost in the motions. I fondle her curves like the precious gifts they are. Endless dips and angles for me to worship. She slams her ass backward to greet my next lunge. The slap echoes around the room to serenade our passion.

"I need…" Her request fades prematurely.

"Do you wanna play your card?"

"Yes, yes, yes," she chants.

"That's not begging," I chide while sliding deep.

Grace stammers on her pleasure. "Please, please, please."

"That's my girl." I blindly grab for the bag. "My soulmate has a kinky spot."

Grace swivels into me when I pause balls-deep to gather the supplies. "You bring this side out of me. I want to try things I've never considered before."

"It's the biggest fucking turn-on hearing that we're going to spread our horizons together." A quiet click announces the bottle of lube opening. I squirt a generous blob on my finger. "Have you ever experimented with anal play?"

"No."

"Allow me to introduce you to the act." I trace her puckered rim with my slippery digit. A slight prod sinks the tip into her untried hole. She shudders and releases a low moan.

"Okay?"

"Uh-huh."

"More?"

"Please."

I push to the first knuckle before sliding out and repeating the process. "How does that feel?"

"Odd, but not bad. There's some pressure. I like it." She wiggles to test the foreign breach.

That shift has me resuming the practiced motions where we're already joined. She mewls while I work my finger into her ass. My steady pace fills both of her holes. I maintain a measured rhythm to build her pleasure. A minute later, Grace is rolling against me.

"Want another?" I swirl my digit in her tight hole to confirm my meaning.

"Yes, I'm ready."

After more lube, I slide two fingers into her snug ring. The resistance makes my entry a struggle. "Relax for me, soulmate."

Grace exhales and her muscles loosen to accept me. The actions are still a fight. It takes several rounds until I'm able to move comfortably. I pump into her, swirling my joined digits for heightened sensation. Her breathy cries push me faster. My fingers spread to make more room.

"Fuck, that's sexy. You're full of me."

"How it should be," she pants.

I push in, my cock gliding along her slick walls. "Just one more reason you're my dream girl."

She's quiet for a beat, but I can hear her mind spinning. "Can we try the toy?"

"Whatever you want. This is your win." I snatch the plug, more than grateful that we already took care of the pre-cleaning process.

"Thought it was for both of us? A tie," she hums.

"But you make the rules. We stop whenever you want."

"That won't be anytime soon. Give me more." Grace grinds into me for emphasis.

"So damn greedy and all mine." I tap her upturned bottom.

Once the rubber shaft is slick, I press the blunt tip to her pucker. The girth is slightly larger than my combined fingers. I'm gentle, carefully sliding in and out as her hole adjusts. She's prepared and there isn't much friction. A low groan wheezes from her parted lip. My gaze bounces between where I'm fucking her to where she's babbling in bliss.

Her head hangs limp between her shoulders. "Ohhh, that's bigger."

"Too much?"

"No!" She clenches as if I'm going to remove it.

I chuckle at her reaction, pushing the toy deep. "You'll get used to it."

"Have you ever done anal?" Her tone borders on meek.

"Nah. I think that involves a lot of trust between partners which I've never had."

"Maybe we could"—she moans as I plunge the plug all the way in—"try it sometime."

"Fuck yes. I'll do anything you want." Although, it's difficult to imagine my cock ever squeezing inside such a narrow opening.

Grace rocks against me. "Like make me come?"

"Already?"

"I'm about to either way."

"Well, shit. I better catch up."

Not that I'm too far off. I sink the plug in until the notch at the end catches at her rim to lock the length in place. My fingers dig into her hips as I chase our mutual release. Her motions assist in getting us there faster.

"So full," she whispers.

"So. Fucking. Tight." I punctuate each word with a thrust.

She thrashes her head, sending black hair flying. "Why does that feel so good?"

"Because you're with me."

"Yessssss," she groans. "More."

My hips snap forward and back in a frantic tempo. I pry her cheeks apart for a better view. Her back hole is stretched around the plug while I stuff her cunt with my cock. Warmth races down my spine and collects in my balls. A noticeable tightening warns me that the end is near.

Grace smacks the mattress with both hands. "This is going to make me come."

"Thank fuck. I'm close too."

"Almost there," she wails.

A final plunge tips us over. She clamps around my cock with the force of an iron vise. Stars burst in my vision while I surrender to the pleasure spurting from me. Her body jerks along with mine. It feels like I'm suspended in relief for seconds or minutes. Time ceases to exist. Tingles spread across my body in a numbing wave. Even my lips seem to have lost sensation.

Grace collapses onto the bed. Uneven breaths tremble her slumped form. I remove the plug and wipe her with the towel I'd stashed in the bag. Then I gather her in my arms.

"You're incredible, soulmate."

"Not so bad yourself." She pats my chest with a sloppy palm.

"It's never been like that for me. I'm in awe of you."

"Yeah, that wasn't just sex. It was something else entirely." Her voice is a hoarse wisp.

"It's us. Thanks for trusting me." I press a kiss on her forehead.

Grace grins at me, her expression dazed. The post-coital glow shines in her eyes. "Should we play again?"

chapter twenty-four

Grace

THE BIGGEST PARK IN KNOX CREEK IS JUST OFF THE south end of Main Street. Castle Pointe sprawls far and wide and offers a variety of spaces for recreation. A large playground stretches across one side. There's a sandy beach that edges a section of Twin Lakes. A dozen or more tables sit on top of a slope that overlooks a grassy field. Violet chose one in the middle for us to occupy.

Sunshine kisses my cheeks and I tilt my face skyward for another dose. This spot was Bradley's idea after I mentioned a friend wanted to join us for lunch. We packed a picnic and several activities to keep us occupied for the afternoon. I think he's been itching to get more male interaction.

On cue, the impatient boy groans. "When is Garrett gonna get here? I'm bored."

I pause in distributing their food. "Um, ouch. Do you see me?"

He shoots me a scowl that only kids and Jake Evans can pull off without repercussions. "Yeahhhhh? You're always here."

"Rude, dude. You'll miss me when you start school next month."

"Loves you." Violet cuddles into me.

"And I love you, cutie pie." I give her a quick hug before glancing at Bradley. "At least someone likes having me around."

Bradley's mean mug flips into a megawatt grin that I foolishly believe is for me. "Garrett!"

"Hey, everyone. Am I late?" He rounds the table to sit beside the little guy.

Bradley has stars in his eyes as he stares at him. "Nuh-uh, you're super on time. But I've been waiting for you."

Garrett laughs at the contradiction and ruffles the kid's unruly hair. "I'm known for my prompt arrival."

His attention shifts to me, and a heatwave spikes my temperature. It's almost difficult to look at him without blushing. The things I've let him do to me—along with more that I hope to explore—aren't appropriate to reflect on in public. Tingles burst across my cheeks as an unmentionable recap from the other night streams live, regardless of where we are.

"Hi," I breathe.

He winks and I almost fall off the bench. "Thanks for inviting me."

Bradley tugs on Garrett's shirt. "Wanna share my ham and cheese?"

He studies the half-eaten sandwich as if debating internally. "Nah, buddy. That's all yours. How else will you grow to be big and strong?"

Bradley eyes him while absorbing that nugget. "I wanna get muscles like you."

"Keep eating."

"M'kay." He shoves the rest of his sandwich in his mouth and chews with gusto.

"I tink tis yummy." Violet is happily munching on hers in much smaller bites.

Meanwhile, I pass Garrett a pre-packaged meal. "And one for you."

He removes the lid and takes a peek. "What did you make me?"

"Ham and cheese. We keep it uniform so nobody gets upset." I nod to the toddler diva next to me.

"Looks delicious." The hunger in his gaze appears to be craving more than cold cuts.

I gulp at the tightness in my throat. "Hope you like it."

"You gotsta eat it all gone," Bradley interjects to douse the flames. "Then you get an Oreo. It's double stuffed. My favorite."

Garrett holds up his palm for a high-five. "Solid choice, buddy. If I'm gonna stuff something, it's gonna be double."

I choke on the next bite, my mouth too full. "Good grief."

The amusement dancing in his eyes skips to me. "Something on your mind?"

"No." I dip my chin to hide the fire blazing across my face. "You're just a stinker."

"And you're flushed," he murmurs.

I press my palm to a fiery cheek. "Stop it."

Bradley is tuned into our interaction with too much perception. His attention lands on the instigator beside him. "Are you gonna marry Grace?"

The question hits Garrett just as he's about to take a sip of soda. His can pauses in midair. "Um, what?"

"She doesn't have a husband 'cause she's waiting for Prince Charming. Is that you?" His nose scrunches at the idea.

Violet gasps, as if putting the pieces together. "Pwetty pwinshess."

"Oh, no," I mumble under my breath.

Talk about putting a barely reformed bachelor under pressure. But Garrett flashes that signature grin that puts everyone at ease. "She's my soulmate, buddy."

The troublemaker in training screws up his features while

trying to decide if those two terms align. "Does that mean she's not gonna do boring adult stuff on the weekends anymore?"

"She probably still will, but we're gonna do it together. As a team." Garrett points from me to himself.

My eyes roll to the clouds above. "Jeez, thanks a lot."

Bradley's expression brightens as he focuses on me. "Super awesome. You're gonna have lotsa babies. Then you won't miss me so much when I'm at school."

"Okay, whoa. Let's press pause. We aren't getting married and having lots of babies," I interrupt.

Garrett whispers something that sounds like, "We'll see."

Before I can delve into that contradiction, Bradley bounces on his seat. "I wanna marry Sydney."

Garrett spits out his recent swig of Sprite. "Jake's daughter?"

"The one and only," I sing.

He snorts and pats the love-struck kid on his back. "Good luck with that bold move."

Bradley isn't dissuaded. If anything, he gains confidence while rolling his skinny shoulders. "She's gonna be my girlfriend once I start kindergarten. I'm gonna get dripped out for her."

I gape at him. "Dripped out?"

He tugs at the thin silver chain around his neck. "Uh-huh."

Garrett laughs at my dumbstruck expression. "Like super fresh and cool. Get with the times, soulmate."

"You're older than me," I jest in return.

"Doesn't mean I can't stay relevant."

The last bit of sandwich gets popped into my mouth. "I'll study the latest trends when I get home."

Bradley nudges his bench partner. "See? She does lame things like *study*."

My seemingly considerate boyfriend puts on a brave face. "I'll try to fix that."

"You two shouldn't be sitting next to each other. Bad influence," I grumble.

"Too late. We're already bonded." Garrett lifts his hand to the little boy for another celebratory slap.

"You're like, really fun." Bradley stares at him as if he's responsible for inventing ice cream.

"Same to you, buddy. Your sister and Grace are nice to have around too." Garrett blows me a kiss, which I pretend to catch on cheesy instinct.

"Gonna have soooooo many babies," Bradley teases.

All I can do is hang my head to conceal a wide smile. I wouldn't want to encourage him. Garrett doesn't hide his amusement. Instead, he gives the kid a thumbs-up.

We manage to complete our lunch without further incident or embarrassment on my behalf. After we toss the trash, Bradley looks ready to suggest something that will scare me. Violet snags my focus before he can get the words out of his parted lips.

She whimpers and rubs her stomach. It seems the tiny peanut ate too fast. I lean toward her to offer assistance. Right when I'm in range, she lets a loud one rip.

I straighten with a jolt. "Oh, my. Do you feel better?"

The size of her grin is unmatched. "Yep."

Garrett is howling, nearly doubled over in laughter. "You should know better than to enter the danger zone after a meal."

"Real funny." But a giggle escapes me nonetheless.

"I wanna cwolor." Violet grabs her assortment of art supplies from the bag.

My eyes follow her methodical prep like the professional she is. "Oooooh, are you going to make me a pretty picture?"

She shakes her head, pointing a red marker at a certain someone. "For him."

I cluck my tongue at Garrett. "Gosh, you just waltz in and steal the show."

"What can I say? I'm irresistible."

"Alphabet Go Fish!" Bradley whips out the small container that's easily identifiable.

"Good call, buddy. Grace likes to play games." Garrett wags his brows.

I kick at him under the table. "Hush."

"Why? You're really good at coming out on top." He rubs my shin, hooking his shoe around my calf until we're connected.

Bradley is oblivious while attempting to shuffle the cards. That is until his leg bumps into ours. His eyes widen and he glances down.

"Are you playing footsie? Mommy and Daddy do that all the time."

"Just getting in the mood for our game," Garrett explains the innuendos in the same manner he would about grass being green. Equal parts impressive and sneaky.

"It's ready! We're gonna practice our letters." Bradley proudly waves to the pile spread out. "Take five cards, but don't show us. It's a secret."

"Sounds familiar," Garrett mumbles while making his selection.

"Good grief." If I survive one round, I'll be shocked.

"I'll go first. Listen carefully 'cause we don't do repeats." The kiddo sends us a stern expression as if we're the ones about to enter kindergarten. Then his eyes stay on me. "Grace, do you have a H?"

"Sure do. Here you go." I pass him the card.

"Yay!" He pumps a fist into the air.

"Is it my turn now?" Garrett looks too eager.

"Nope, I go 'til I don't get a match. So, I'll ask you. Do

you have a dabo-yoo?" Bradley makes a pinching motion as if anticipating success.

"Aww, shucks. I don't." He frowns for the boy's benefit but immediately perks up when focusing on me. "I'm pretty sure Bradley doesn't have this one. Grace, do you have an O?"

I quirk a brow. "How do you know? Nobody has asked for an O except you."

"How about your V? I'd like to take your V and lie it down with my P."

Bradley twists his lips. "Those letters don't match."

My head bobs in agreement. "That's not how you'll win. You won't beat us that way."

Garrett shrugs. "I don't mind coming last."

And he proves that to be true, double meaning aside. Although, to be fair, I threw the game in Bradley's favor. Call me a softie but I love seeing him cheer for victory. Garrett catches on quickly and becomes my partner in the task. That's precisely why Bradley is the first to run out of cards for the third time in a row. His stack of matches towers over ours too.

"Woohoo! I'm the master. Nobody can beat me." He leaps off the bench and begins to dance.

"You're way too good at Go Fish, buddy. I'm not sure I can compete in your league. Do you have a ball in that bottomless bundle of fun?" Garrett nods to the oversized tote I meticulously packed.

Bradley digs inside. "Uh-huh."

His gaze sparkles at what the little boy whips out. "Ah, a pigskin. Even better. Wanna play catch?"

In response, the boy's eyes light up like Christmas morning. "Yes! Yes, yes, yes."

"Is that all right with you, boss?" Garrett is thoughtful to ask me, but there's not a chance I'll deny Bradley, who has his palms folded in a pleading gesture.

"Have at it. I've got this cutie pie to keep me company." I

peek over at Violet, but she's still preoccupied with her drawing. That just means I can share my attention.

"This is really great, by the way." He makes a circular motion around our group, then spreads the loop to the park in general.

"Worth ditching your other responsibilities?"

"And then some," he assures.

"C'mon." Bradley loses his patience and begins yanking on Garrett's arm.

I bite my bottom lip to trap a content sigh. The picture they create is just too adorable. "You're good with this?"

Lunch is one thing. Entertaining a kid is another. Especially when he has zero obligation to do so.

"Couldn't be better." His eyes are on me when he drops that conviction.

As Garrett trots off with the football spinning on his palm, I get an idea for our next date. A smile curls my lips just picturing his reaction.

Game on, bartender.

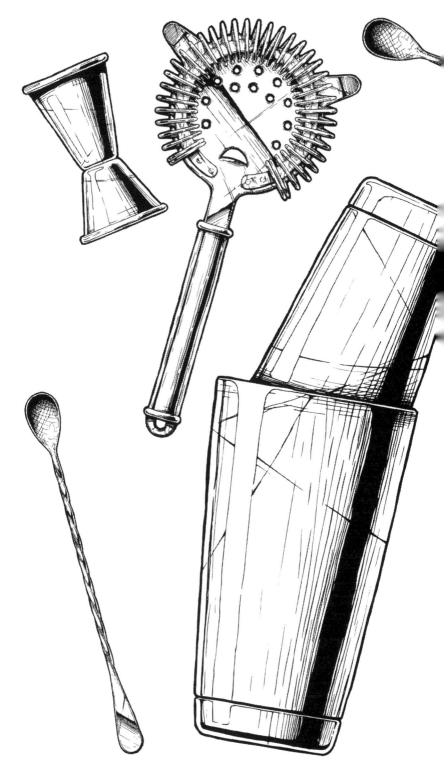

chapter twenty-five

Garrett

GRACE'S KNUCKLES TURN WHITE AROUND THE steering wheel. "I can feel you watching me."

My stare doesn't waver from her. "Can you blame me?"

"Not comfortable in the passenger seat?" Her lips twitch with the assumption.

"Wrong." I make the sound of a buzzer. "The view from over here is exquisite."

"Exquisite?"

I bite my fist and growl like the rabid beast she's created. "Have you looked in the mirror? There better not be other men around wherever you're carting me off to. I won't promise to be civil when you're wearing that."

Grace in athletic gear is a next-level test of my restraint. I've been trying to sneak a hand under her black leggings since she arrived at my door fifteen minutes ago. Now we're pulling into an unfamiliar lot of an equally unrecognizable park.

Her hand trembles as she shifts the car into park. "We're here."

"Care to be more specific?"

"I'd rather show you." She slinks out before I can respond.

A breeze fondles me when I step into the elements to meet her. The evening sun dips lower as we walk along a paved path. My stride falters when an unmistakable field appears in front of us. I attempt to process the scene, but fumble over nostalgia. Grace must misinterpret my awe for discomfort. Her features collapse into a wounded slump. That launches me from the stupor.

"This is… shit. I don't even know what to say."

"It's flag football. Is that okay?" Nerves hitch her voice while she wrings her hands.

"Abso-fucking-lutely. Why wouldn't it be?"

"I wasn't sure if college or… whoever else… ruined the game for you." Her slight hesitation lands on a certain guilty party.

Hilary left a stain that I avoided scrubbing clean for years. Just hearing her name would make me cringe. But that's ancient history with Grace beside me. The bitterness has been replaced by a constant flow of sweet relief.

I drift a bent knuckle along her jaw. "Nah, my ex wishes she had the sway to taint my passion. She knew my love for the turf ran too deep. It's not the sport's fault that I wasn't good enough to go pro. That's why she chose to strike at an easier target."

Grace's upper lip curls. "I've never met her, but I despise her for hurting you."

"I'm beginning to believe she did me a favor."

"How so?"

"Those jaded edges needed the right girl to restore my faith." With a downward swoop, my mouth brands hers with a searing kiss. "I found her."

"You're such a romantic."

"Only for you, soulmate." I cup her nape and tug until our foreheads touch. "You're already the best girlfriend I've had."

"That's just a line to get into my panties. Spoiler alert," she whispers. "I'm not wearing any."

My eyes slam shut. "Again? Dammit, woman. I'm only so strong."

"Had to really prove I was the best." She winks like the saucy seductress she is.

"Totally unnecessary. My ex never would've planned something thoughtful like this."

"Why not?"

Acid churns in my gut at the reminder. "She was into appearances and social status. That's probably why she cheated on me with a guy on my team who was guaranteed to get called up. A total shoo-in to get drafted and go pro."

"Got it," Grace mutters. "That's shitty."

"Like I said, it was a blessing in disguise. Dodged a bullet." I whistle as if that close shot just whizzed past my ear.

"Are they still together?"

"Fuck if I know. Probably not since he got injured during training and had to retire before his rookie season even started."

"Karma."

"Yep. He was no true friend of mine. Good riddance." I shake off the past with a shudder and focus on what lies ahead. "Another game, huh? We're developing habits at a rapid pace."

"Can you blame me? You were a huge player back in the day." She tips her head back and laughs.

I tickle her until she squeals and begs for mercy. "Yep, that's me. I'm ready to get on the field. How did you come up with this idea?"

"Watching you toss the ball around with Bradley

reminded me of a flyer I saw. I went back to the board and got the details. They organize games that anyone can join."

I scoop her hand into mine. "This is really badass. Thanks, soulmate."

"It's nothing."

My fingers squeeze hers. "To me, it's everything."

Her eyes search mine. Blue clashing into blue. Whatever she finds in those depths must give her the reassurance I'll gladly provide on a regular basis.

Grace melts into me with a long exhale. "Okay."

"See? That wasn't so hard."

"Hmm, not yet. Maybe later." Her hips nudge mine. "Is that a penis straw in your pocket or are you only marginally excited to see me?"

I swat her ass. "Dirty girl. Quit trying to distract me."

"It's part of my ploy to beat you at your own game." She tugs me forward.

"Hey there!" A blonde woman motions to us from the sidelines. "Welcome to Chicken Catchers."

I sputter on the league name. "Well, shit. That goes great with Roosters."

Grace elbows me. "Figured you'd get a kick out of that."

"The cock den approves."

The blonde eyes us. "First timers?"

My girlfriend bounces on her sneakers. "Are we that obvious?"

"Just a bit." Her smile is friendly. "I'm Nancy."

"Grace and Garrett." I gesture between us for the introduction.

Her expression turns gooey. "Aw, that's adorable. You're a cute couple."

The compliment would've sent me running before I hitched my wagon to Grace. Instead of an icy chill invading my system, a pleasurable warmth spreads through me. "Thanks.

It was a tough battle, but I finally wore her down. Now she's stuck with me. Forever."

Grace hums, which drags into a sigh. She looks at me like I hung the moon and stars in her honor. The shimmer in her gaze suggests I'm totally getting laid later. That has me feasting on her curves in preparation. Heat wafts over me when her thighs clench. I meet her stare to expose the hunger rapidly overtaking my composure.

"Okay, wow. Cool off before you set the ground on fire." Nancy fans her face.

"Sorry about that." I clear my throat, widening my stance to hide any evidence not appropriate for the public. "She just really gets me going."

"Ditto," Grace murmurs.

"No problem. Use that enthusiasm for the game. Don't get rough, though. It's just fun. We don't take the game too seriously. Well, most of us." Her eyes shift to a guy several yards away. "Anywho, just take a belt. One of you will be red and the other is blue. Are you okay being on opposite teams?"

Grace shrugs. "Doesn't make a difference to me."

That's what she thinks. A competitive thrum pumps into my bloodstream. Fallen leaves and memories swirl with the wind. This is going to be even better than I thought.

I smirk. "This isn't going to end well for you, soulmate."

"Show me what you've got, bartender." She crooks a finger and I nearly trip over my own feet to follow.

After we grab our equipment and join the others, Nancy reviews the rules. "No physical contact. Period. Grab a person's flag rather than touch them. Only direct handoffs are allowed. The quarterback gets seven seconds to ditch the ball before he or she becomes a target. Try to score. Be safe. Enjoy yourself. Does anyone need further instructions or clarification?"

The group waves away the offer in unison. Then we break apart into teams. I strut onto the field like this is the Super

Bowl. Flashbacks hit me when the floodlights illuminate the striped turf. Plays and formations from years past filter through my mind. Fuck, I've missed this. My soles sink into the earth, anchoring me to this moment.

Comfort washes over me while I stretch. Time ceases to exist when Grace bends and puts her ass on display. Those stretchy pants might be the end of me. A smack to my shoulder reminds me that I'm needed in the huddle.

Our captain, who also happens to be the quarterback, is the leader. "Okay, newbie. Do you have a preferred position?"

"Near her." I blatantly point to my ultimate distraction.

He narrows his eyes but doesn't argue. "Gonna hand you the ball. Try to score and don't lose a flag. Can you handle that?"

The urge to boast about my forgotten talent is tough to silence, but this is Grace's thoughtful gesture. I'm not going to blow it. My teeth grind as I force a grin. "You got it."

Both teams face off at the line of scrimmage. The ball is snapped, and everyone dashes into action. They're a blur that instantly fades. My eyes track Grace as she scampers across the field. There's no logic to her aimless movements. She spins and dips and appears lost. Out of her element is more like it.

A fresh memory slams into the present with startling clarity. We're back in the maze and she's telling me how much it turned her on to be chased. My feet pound in her direction. I'm blinded to all else. The game doesn't exist. My teammate's shouts are static buzz.

I catch her around the waist. Grace thrashes in my hold but I'm able to get her on the ground using gentle force. My palm cradles the back of her head while I settle my weight on top of her. I'm breathing hard, our chests pressing together with each heavy exhale. Her smile is blinding. This is the most successful formation I've ever participated in.

"Hi," I breathe.

Her pinned hips shift beneath mine. "You got me."

"I think that was your plan."

She strains upward for a kiss. "I'm yours to catch."

"Not sure what I did to earn the honor, but I'll never give you a reason to regret it."

Mist shines in her eyes. "You make me forget everyone else and the pain they caused."

"Damn straight, soulmate. That's part of my job."

A heavy tread bursts our intimate embrace. I glance up to see the quarterback glaring at our illegal tackle. Steam might spew from his ears.

"Dude, you know the rules. If you wanna fuck, do it off the field." He hitches his thumb toward Grace's car.

"You heard the man." I rise to my feet, lifting Grace onto hers in a fluid motion.

She giggles and nudges me as we head off into the night. "You're always getting us booted from places."

"It's your fault. I can't keep my hands off you."

Grace's fingers walk up my arm. "How about a snack? I'm famished after exerting so much energy."

There's a tent in my shorts from the purr in her tone. "I know somewhere we won't be disturbed."

chapter twenty-six

Grace

GARRETT UNLOCKS THE DOOR AND SWEEPS HIS ARM forward to usher me inside. I cross the threshold, but my steps are measured. Almost hesitant. The only other time I entered his domain, I was in an altered frame of mind. Drunk on booze and horny off Garrett's intoxicating fumes. Both had a sudden onset that was staggering. The potential of getting a peek at his penis had me salivating.

That gives me pause. There's a noticeable amount of drool collecting in my mouth. Maybe tonight isn't that different.

I do a twirl to appraise his home under the scope of sobriety. "Ah, the bachelor pad. Nice to see the place is still accommodating."

He props himself on the jamb with a bent elbow, putting his body at a mouth-watering angle. "You gave my loft new meaning that night."

"I find that difficult to believe since we didn't sleep together."

"That's precisely why, soulmate. You shifted the balance."

"As I recall, you had to fight off my inebriated advances." The memory makes me blush, even weeks later.

Garrett's thumb traces the heat blooming in my cheeks. "Warmth fills the space. Can't you feel it?"

"It's very toasty," I confirm.

"Would you like to get reacquainted with my bed? I'll strip your clothes off myself this time."

"Who am I to refuse an offer like that?" I trace the bumpy texture on the walls.

A low growl rumbles from him. My pulse skips before leaping into a sprint. I stride further into his apartment under the guise of needing to cool off, or maybe I'm just nosy.

"I hope you did some pelvic stretches on the field. You're about to get a solid dicking."

The floorboards creak seconds later. He prowls toward me in what I'm beginning to predict as a practiced move. That doesn't make the pounce less thrilling.

A cool surface touches my back seconds before Garrett's solid strength blankets my front. I mold to his warmth, a wall of muscle and orgasmic bliss. Our mouths crash together in a turbulent wave. Teeth clack and noses bump as we surrender to the frenzied need. His tongue slips along mine, a smooth glide to stir my arousal. I moan and open wider. He takes advantage, tilting his head to connect us deeper.

His taste mingles with mine to create a heady mix. Our combination is stronger than a tall shot of Everclear. I'm dizzy off us after a small sip.

I feel him seeking what I'm more than happy to give. A hand travels down my side to palm my ass. A determined push delivers friction between us. He's hard against me, grinding his need into mine. My fingers drift along his covered chest, clutching the material at the center for leverage. If I'm succumbing to lust, he's joining me. Then my stomach rumbles to act as an impenetrable twat swat.

Garrett wrenches away as if the sound offends him. "Shit, I need to feed you."

My hand remains fisted in his shirt. "Maybe just a quick bite."

"I'll see what I have." He begins to move backward but stops when the slack in my arm pulls taut.

"It seems we're attached."

"Would you like to join me in the kitchen?"

I laugh and drop my grip. "Can't be too clingy."

"Did you hear me complaining?" He's the one to dive in for a parting peck.

Giddiness gives my sigh the consistency of syrup, stretching and spreading until he opens the freezer. He rummages in the contents while I lean against the archway. Plastic crinkles on his hunt for sustenance. The muffled grunt he expels doesn't sound promising.

"I don't have much," he mumbles.

"That's okay. Don't worry about it." My appetite can easily be persuaded to him instead.

His sheepish expression is endearing and would have me agreeing to eat whatever he finds. "How do you feel about onion rings?"

"Is that a serious question?" A growl from my belly eliminates any confusion.

He chuckles. "Okay, I'll drop some in the air fryer. They'll be done in seven to nine minutes."

"That's a tight window," I muse.

"I'm sure we'll find a way to occupy ourselves."

Garrett doesn't wait for me to list the options. Instead, he becomes a blur of productivity. Deft fingers press buttons faster than I can track. The bag of onion rings is ripped open with a brute force that my panties are intimately acquainted with. A hefty portion gets tossed in the metal basket. Oil is drizzled on top. My gaze devours every subtle movement.

There's something very sexy about a barefoot man preparing food. Or maybe it's just him. Definitely the latter.

His eyes find mine already latched onto him. "Would you like something to drink?"

I'm rather parched after watching that mouthwatering display. "Sure."

Garrett goes to the fridge and disappears from view. I hear the distinct pop of a can opening. While he handles that, I treat myself to a tour of the area that serves as his living room. It doesn't occupy me for more than a minute.

Other than a couch and two chairs with a coffee table arranged in the middle, there isn't much to see. It almost resembles a model unit that's left purposefully bare. There aren't any decorations. No pictures or unique touches to reflect his personality. Not even a speck of dust. I didn't notice before, too focused on what he had below the belt to pay attention to much else.

"You're very tidy," I comment.

His chuckle reaches me from where he remains out of sight. "Is that the polite method of asking where my shit is?"

"I feel like I'm not the first to notice."

"My mom and sister nag me relentlessly." He sidles up next to me with two mason jars in his hands. "Hope you like it."

The words etched into the side of mine deserves to be read aloud. "I love to wrap my hands around it, suck hard, and swallow."

That sneaky dimple carves into his cheek as he smirks. "Bought that special for you."

"Very fitting." A thought sprouts and grows roots as I clutch my gift. "Can we take a selfie?"

"As if I'd ever deny you."

I whip out my phone and lift the screen to the optimal angle. Garrett wraps himself around me, his cheek plastered against mine. The jostling almost has me spilling my beverage. Laughter spews from me as I capture the moment.

My thumb swipes to inspect the evidence of our couple-dom. "Perfect."

"Only because you're in it."

"Nope, you light up the view. Our future is bright thanks to you." Damn, that's poetic.

He's quiet for a beat, then several more. His gaze volleys from me to the plain walls like a tennis ball. I almost wonder if he's merged into my lane of planning. The lull trickles onward. I sip my drink to stop myself from filling the void. The fruity beer catches me by surprise.

"Oh, that's different."

"Juicy Peach shandy," he absently replies. His cogs are still grinding over whatever scheme he's concocting.

Rather than interrupt by prying, I stay on track. "Is this a local—?"

"You should move in."

Liquid dribbles from my lips while I mentally repeat his impulsive suggestion. "Aren't we still in the trial phase of our relationship?"

"Are we? I kinda figured you'd agreed to be mine in a permanent sense. We can flip this sparse wasteland into a real home."

I rack my brain for that conversation. It doesn't add up. Not that I'm bothered in the least. This just feels like we've switched roles. He isn't supposed to be the one taking giant leaps. The fryer beeps to release me from this wonky situation.

"We'll discuss relocating you later. My woman is hungry." Garrett backs into the kitchen to fetch my food.

A rich aroma fills the air and I moan. In the next instant, an overflowing plate appears on a wooden cart that's probably used as a dining table. I move on autopilot, steered by cravings.

My mind is still reeling, too preoccupied to notice the steam rising off the crispy goodness.

I snatch one and take a huge bite. Regret immediately singes me. "Owwww, crap. It's hot."

He parks himself on a stool while I fan my tongue. "A quick blow can go a long way."

"Speaking from experience?" But I listen to the advice before chomping down again.

There's no response from him. Most likely due to his attention feasting on my mouth. A pleased mumble compliments the chef as I ingest the greasy delight. I lick my fingers before snagging the next one.

"Damn, Peaches. Want some protein in your diet?" He shifts on the seat, a noticeable bulge tenting his shorts.

"Is someone jealous?" My grin spreads around a third onion ring.

"Watching you eat something I cooked—regardless of the preparation—is causing a very primal reaction. You're extremely arousing." His palm grips the hard ridge, squeezing tight enough to earn a hiss.

"Are you hungry?"

"Not for food."

Another idea hatches and takes form. "Want to play a game?"

"At this hour?" His strained muscles appear ready to shred fabric.

I nibble my bottom lip. "It won't take long. Then I'll give you relief."

"Whatever you want. Just tell me what to do."

"Take out your cock." I collect four rings in my hands and move in front of him.

He stares at me for a pregnant pause but yanks down the waistband of his shorts to free himself as directed. His dick stands tall and proud. The silver balls from his apadravya shine under the overhead lights.

"Hold the base," I order next.

"Am I allowed to ask why?"

"If you want to spoil the surprise." I squint while imagining the throw.

He catches on when I mimic an arc for practice. "You're going to toss those on my cock?"

"That's the plan, but my aim is shit." As proven when my first try smacks his shoulder.

Garrett laughs, sliding the missed shot onto his length. "You're my favorite."

"Right back at you."

He licks his lips. "Whip your tits out for me."

A cackle explodes from me. "No shame, huh?"

"Not when I could get a front-row seat to your breasts bouncing in my face."

"That's fair." I yank off my shirt, making sure to jiggle for him.

"Fuck yeah," he groans.

"Okay, back to business." I spin the next attempt on my finger pre-launch. "The holes on these are very generous."

"The easier to capture my cock. C'mon, soulmate." He thrusts his hips. "Put a ring on it."

"I'm trying." But the second throw goes wide.

He snatches the stray snack from midair and adds it to his shaft stack. "Gonna have to do better than that."

"Okay, baller. I see you." A heavy exhale streams from my pressed lips. "I feel like your piercing is a toll booth that requires a fee to pass."

He grunts and crosses his arms. "Yeah, that's the problem."

"This is harder than it looks."

"So am I." His palm lifts toward my bare breast, but I swat him away.

"Just two more and I'll accept defeat." I bend my elbow and prepare to release the third try.

"Do what you need to do." Garrett catches the wayward toss and adds it to the discard pile on his cock.

"I just want to make one," I whine.

"Move closer."

"But that's too easy."

"Baby," he chuckles. "We're going to be here all night at this rate."

"Good point." I shuffle forward until hitting the target should be a breeze.

"Use this big guy." He passes me an oversized onion ring. "It'll be like sliding a hotdog down a hallway or hooking a hat on a nail. Unless you prefer lassoing a sleeping bull. Maybe landing a plane in a flat prairie?"

"Yeah, yeah. I get the picture." Only two feet separate us as I line up the shot. My arms fling upward when the Hail Mary toss lands in the direct center of the end zone to score. "I did it!"

Garrett claps, appearing thoroughly impressed. "Didn't doubt you for a minute."

My celebration continues with a squealed cheer. "I totally delayed winning on purpose to build anticipation."

His cocked eyebrow isn't convinced. "Now that I'm loaded for your pleasure, what are you going to do with me?"

"Allow me to remove these." I lower to my knees and munch on the top tier. "Yummy."

He grips onto the stool with white knuckles. "Fuuuuck. This is equal parts satisfying and excruciating."

"Victory tastes like fried onions and delayed gratification." I gobble another off the tower.

"Woman," he growls. "My patience is reaching extinction."

"Just in time." I polish off the last one and wipe the crumbs from my hands. "I'm ready for my dessert."

Without warning, I slide his entire length into my mouth. His girth stretches my lips to obscene limits. I retreat until only his bedazzled tip fondles my tongue. The barbell is cool compared to his feverish arousal. I clamp the metal between my teeth and tug gently.

"Ohhhhhh, fuck." The stool rattles underneath him.

My groan is stifled around his dick. "You're very big."

He plants his feet on the floor to give me better access. "I know I'm a handful, but that's why you have two hands."

"That sounds familiar."

The cocky phrase encourages me to flaunt. After swirling my tongue around his tip, I push him deep until my mouth touches his root. Pressure prods my tonsils and I gulp at the slight burn. Garrett mutters a curse, his entire body rigid. I stay locked in that position until my lungs protest for a full breath. The withdrawal is lazy while I lick a vein that snakes along his shaft. My lips apply more suction to his head, and then I swallow him whole again.

"Fuuuuuuck, my girl can deepthroat."

"I would've spoiled you sooner, but I didn't want to reveal all of my hidden talents. No gag reflex." My wink is exaggerated.

"Marry me," he blurts.

"That's not something you joke about with a hopeless romantic," I chide.

"Who said I was joking?"

"Knock it off."

I shove him in my mouth before he can spout more outrageous requests in the throes of passion. His gulp is audible when I tongue his piercing again. My lips glide up and down his dick with ease. Warmth pools in my belly as I set a steady rhythm.

Garrett's fingers tunnel into my hair. "Do you trust me?"

My nod is immediate.

A rumble rolls from him, approval dipped in seduction. "Can I take control?"

I'm quick to give my consent again. My palms rest flat on my thighs. Garrett mutters a curse. A peek at him from my heavy lids exposes the approval gleaming in his stare.

Without removing his cock from my mouth, he rises from the stool and widens his stance. He cradles my chin in the curve between his thumb and forefinger. I let my jaw go slack as he feeds me his length. The pace is slow and timid, as if he's unsure. That hesitation clenches my heart. This man always puts my needs at the highest priority.

To prove that I'm comfortable, I relax into his motions. The bottom ball of his piercing glides along my slick tongue. When I swallow, the metal on top brushes the roof of my mouth. That slippery friction is stimulating. Heat wafts from me like a finely tuned radiator. My nipples stiffen into pebbled peaks. The urge to tweak the tips twitches my fingers, but I stay still. Instead, a sultry purr quivers from me on his next pump. I need more.

Garrett must comprehend my wanton plea. His timed strokes begin to increase in frequency. Each thrust is more confident, but still restrained. His control is an iron band refusing to let him take too much. He's not rough or forceful. I could reclaim the reins if I tried.

That entices me to participate. It's important to me that he's getting what he desires. He can push farther. I lean forward into his flowing movements. On the following plunge, his tip strikes the back of my throat. A garbled sigh praises him. Garrett drives deeper on the next strike. My eyes roll at the sensation. I'm slick and needy from him fucking my mouth. It's such a power position, but I feel in charge. That's a thrill on its own.

Then I see his balls tighten, which is a compliment of erotic proportions.

"Just like that." A tremble quakes his knees. "Shit, I'm gonna come."

He stills and for a split second, I think he's going to pull out. How easily he forgets I want all of him. Every drop. My fingers curl around his legs to keep him locked in place. He spills down my throat with a long groan. My entire body sighs, a ripple of contentment flooding me.

Silence swaddles us in the wake of his climax. I gently kiss his dick as he floats in bliss. Garrett shudders and releases himself from the afterglow. My lips press to the underside of his shaft in farewell.

With a sturdy grip, he gathers me into his arms for a tender embrace. "Not sure what I did to deserve you, but I'll never take you for granted."

I snuggle into his hug. "Just keep my faith in good guys alive. You're a rare breed, but you've restored my belief and revived my broken heart."

And earned my love. But it might be too soon to admit that.

He hooks a knuckle under my chin and lifts until our mouths meet. "I'm gonna take such good care of you, soulmate."

I smile into the next chaste peck. "Does that include the solid dicking you mentioned earlier?"

In a fluid motion, Garrett hauls me over his shoulder and smacks my butt. "What the lady wants, she better hold on tight for."

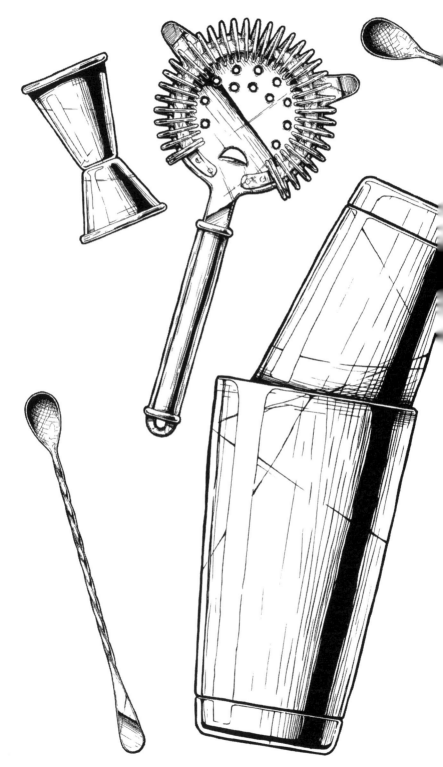

chapter twenty-seven

Garrett

I ATTACH A PINEAPPLE SLICE ONTO THE RIM OF GRACE'S cocktail as a final touch. In the six months I've known her, it's become blatantly apparent that she prefers her drinks fruity. This one is extra tart. That punchy kick better bust its own ass in my favor.

Grace's eyes sparkle when I lift the fishbowl onto the bar. Pride stretches my chest as she admires the finished product. At the last second, I remember the most important element. I slip the special straw into the rainbow-layered liquid.

She coos at the sight. "Is that a heart?"

My throat cinches into a tight knot. "I have a question."

A collective gasp sounds from those surrounding us. The pounding in my ears drowns them out. All I see is my soulmate, the beauty who took a chance on me.

Grace releases a thick exhale and stretches her fingers. "Okay, I'm ready."

I cradle her palm between both of mine. "Will you be my date for the Summer Sizzler?"

"Yes!" Her ass flies off the stool as she bounces for joy. "I'd love to go with you."

"What. The. Fuck. Excuse you?" Ridge is suddenly beside me. "Your ass is working behind the bar for the festival."

"Bossy much?"

His scowl threatens to dismember me. "I'm not dealing with those rowdy customers."

"What about Drake?"

My co-owner makes a production out of searching for our third leg. "Good question."

I suck air between my teeth. "Shit, someone needs to get laid."

Harper scoffs from her section of the rail. "Ridge is just grumpy because Callie hasn't been around."

"Haven't seen her in days," he mutters.

My irritation deflates for the broody brute. "I totally understand. Grace ghosted me for weeks when she was sick."

My girlfriend groans to the rafters above. "Oh, my gosh. You're still bitter?"

"I just missed you."

She leans over the counter to kiss me. "We can sixty-nine later to settle this upset once and for all."

A wistful sigh breezes past my parted lips. I glance at our captive audience. "She gets me."

My focus whips straight ahead to the front door when it opens with a bang. Tension immediately flexes my muscles at the sight of the traitor who dares to step foot into my bar. The fucking audacity is almost comical. When his beady gaze narrows in on Grace, I vault over the bar to stand beside her.

She swivels on her stool to see who captured my attention. Her mouth pops open. "Dale?"

I choke on my disbelief. "You know him?"

"He's my brother. Well, half. But we're fully estranged."

"Not a fucking chance."

She turns back to face me. "What's wrong?"

"Hilary cheated on me with him." I fling an arm his way, pointing with my middle finger.

Her jaw drops with a sputtered breath. "No."

"Yes," I grate. "He was my teammate. I thought he was my friend. So much for allegiance. They betrayed me together."

Dale shrugs. "The grass was greener."

"Past tense," Grace mutters.

The jackass has the balls to smirk while lifting his nose at Roosters as if it's a city dumpster hours before trash collection. Not that his opinion holds any weight. The dude looks worse than shit scraped off the concrete.

His upper lip curls. "This is what you're doing for a living?"

My fists clench. "Cut the shit. What do you want?"

His eyes rove over the sports memorabilia before latching onto his sister again. "Is this your pathetic attempt at revenge? Nice try, buddy. I don't give a fuck about her."

Grace is off her seat, primed to launch herself at him. "Then why are you here, huh? We haven't seen each other in a decade, and this is how you want to stage a reunion? Stay gone, *brother*." Her sigh is steeped in disappointment. "And I use that term very loosely."

"I couldn't believe it was true. Had to see it with my own eyes."

"Why? Because he's the greatest guy I've ever met? His pinky finger has more compassion than most hold in their entire body. He's responsible and successful and honest. Did I mention loyal? Toss in kind and patient too. The list is endless, really. But you?" She stabs a finger in his direction. "I can't even comment on your character other than you stole another man's girlfriend."

"Can't steal what wants to be taken," he boasts.

Grace does a slow clap. "Wow, that's commendable."

"You're one to talk, shacking up with that clown. The guy is a loser. He's just going to drag you down."

Her gaze swings to me, finding my eyes already on her. There's so much warmth and understanding reaching out. The storm raging inside of me calms as I allow the comfort to sink in.

She lifts a palm to cup my jaw. "He's not, but even if he did, that's my choice. Garrett is my choice."

"Fucking pathetic," Dale spits.

Grace drags in a slow breath before confronting him again. "I hope you find peace. I hope you catch whatever haunts you and put the pain to rest. But most of all, I hope you reach a point where you no longer need to put others down to make yourself feel better."

He looks stricken for a brief moment. Almost as fast, the slack in his features pinches into a glower. "I'm fine. It's you who needs a reality check. An athlete like him isn't going to settle for a chunky—"

"Get. Out." My voice is a drawn bow with a notched arrow aimed at him.

Dale would be wise to follow my command. But of course, his feet remain planted and begin to grow roots. The idiot is more stubborn than a pack of mules.

Ridge slinks through the shadows undetected. The sneak attack sends my condolences to those who suffered his wrath on the ice. This douche he's currently targeting? Not so much.

Dale's wide gaze takes inventory of his size. "Holy shit, are you—?"

"Two seconds away from knocking you out? Yeah, that's me. I suggest you take Foster's advice and get the fuck out."

The dumbass is still starstruck but begins to backpedal. "All right, man. No need for a fight. She ain't worth it."

The empty stool beside me clatters to the floor. I'm lunging forward when Ridge grips Dale by the collar.

"Take care of your girl. I've got this pesky shit handled." My true friend shakes the imposter like a rag doll. "We're going outside."

The door slams with their hasty exit. An eerie lull blankets the room as the scene struggles to get back on track. But the static doesn't bother me. My focus is trained elsewhere. Always.

I have Grace tucked flush against me before she can notice the dynamic shift. "Fuck, I love you."

Cheers and applause erupt from those surrounding us to acknowledge that I'm crazy about this girl.

Her gasp glues our chests together. "What?"

"I probably have for a while now but that"—stabs a finger in the direction where Ridge dragged Dale—"brings my feelings to the surface."

"My estranged half-brother, who was supposed to be your friend but stole your girlfriend instead?"

"This isn't really about him. He didn't take anything worth keeping. But what you did just now?" I pause to gather my composure. "Damn, soulmate. You're the one meant to breathe life into me. I've been trudging through muted gray until you arrived. You bring the definition and detail and devotion."

Grace's bottom lip trembles. "Yeah?"

I clutch her face between my palms. My thumbs smooth over her cheeks. "You make me forget that I'm scared to fall in love. Mostly because I already have. Fallen, that is. I've been yours since you first walked into this bar. Yours to catch and keep."

"And love." She pushes up onto the balls of her feet to kiss me. "I love you, bartender. You've shown me the true meaning. It's better than any romance novel. Bright and vibrant and ours. We're real."

"A match made from the start." I cup her nape and tug until our foreheads meet. "Thanks for defending me."

"Well, yeah. Why wouldn't I?"

"My last girlfriend slept with him."

"I'm aware." She gags. "I hope that doesn't reflect poorly on me."

My grip on her tightens. "How could you even think that?"

Grace shrugs. "We're related."

"But you couldn't be more different." I brush my mouth against hers. "You've fixed what was broken."

"And you've healed wounds that I kept hidden."

"We're quite a pair." The ugliness that Dale flung at me wafts into our moment. "You don't believe him, right?"

"No." Period. She didn't even ask for specifics.

But I still want to clarify. "I didn't know he was your brother. And even if I did, that wouldn't matter."

A sly grin teases me. "And why is that?"

I stoop until my lips touch her ear. "You're mine."

She sways into me while fanning her face. "If you insist."

"Thirsty?" My bent knuckle traces the flush covering her slender throat.

"More like parched after all that swooning."

"Don't let your drink go to waste." I boost her onto the stool and drag the glass closer. "Bottoms up."

"What's this one called?" She stirs the contents with her heart straw.

"Love of My Life."

Grace flutters her lashes. "You're so ridiculously romantic."

I flatten a palm to one side of my mouth and stage-whisper, "Don't tell the others."

chapter twenty-eight

Grace

MY STRIDE STUMBLES TO AN ABRUPT HALT AT THE patio that's built in front of Roosters during the festival. The Summer Sizzler is in full swing and then some. Sweat gleams along Garrett's forehead as he mixes drinks under the August heat. Six or seven people wait in front of his station for their turn to order. More clump in the center while sipping their specialty cocktails.

I glance at Dad and Layla. "Looks like he's busy. We can circle back."

But before we exit the temporary space, a panty-melting voice stops us. "Oh, look! It's my soulmate and her family."

The crowd turns to us, where Garrett is pointing. Warmth blazes across my cheeks while I wave at him. I should've known he'd spot me.

He clutches a clenched fist to his chest. "Don't leave me."

My sister whistles. "Wow, he's super hot."

"Layla," I scold.

She picks at her black nail polish. "What? I'm just being honest."

Garrett trots over to where we've stalled. "Were you seriously about to sneak off before I could say hello?"

"You're working. I didn't mean to distract you."

He scoffs. "As if I could carry on like normal while you're nearby. Ridge can cover for me. I'm due for a break."

I didn't even see him at the cart in the corner, too preoccupied by my favorite bartender. "Are you sure he won't mind?"

"Didn't say that, but I'll return the favor when he's ready." His attention shifts to the two individuals I dragged along for the event. "Hey, I'm Garrett. This lady deems me worthy enough to date her. At least until she comes to her senses."

My previous blush reappears in a blaze. I thump my forehead. "Whoops, sorry. This is Paul, my dad. Layla is my younger sister. I might've mentioned them a time or two."

My father chuckles at my delayed introductions. "Don't worry, kiddo. Love has a way of scrambling our minds."

"That it does. Great to meet you, sir." Garrett stretches his arm forward in offering.

Dad clasps his palm, giving him a sturdy shake. Something passes between them. The silence that follows would make me nervous if my dad didn't crack a grin seconds later.

"Likewise. I've heard a lot about you. Looking forward to getting acquainted."

"Same, I guess." Layla purses her lips while eyeing my boyfriend like the prized stallion he is.

I swat her arm. "Don't worry about this one. She's bold and brazen and lacks a decent filter."

Layla shrugs. "Guilty."

"Well, well, well. Fancy seeing you here."

I whirl to greet the chipper voice. Joy wiggles her fingers at me while approaching our group. Cole is beside her with Belle cradled in his capable arms. An older couple flanks her on the other side.

Garrett hoots and rubs his hands together. "Mom and Dad, this is Grace. She's my soulmate."

"Glad you finally admit she's more than a friend," Joy mutters.

Meanwhile, his mother beams at me. "You can call me Mary, for now. This is my husband."

"Kent," he provides and extends his palm.

I accept his proffered greeting. "Pleasure to meet you both."

Without warning, Mary lunges forward to wrap me in a hug. "Thank you."

I lift my arms around her, although my movements are a tad wooden. "You're welcome?"

She pulls away and there are tears shimmering in her eyes. "I'm grateful that you found him. He needed you."

"We found each other," I whisper.

Her sniffles tug at my heartstrings. "Yes, of course. It's a miracle."

After another tight squeeze, Mary releases me. I handle the remaining introductions. Dad and Layla seamlessly blend with Garrett's family. My pulse thumps to a giddy beat at the sight.

My father scrubs over his beard. "I heard you had the misfortune of bumping into Dale. That kid has always been a punk. A huge chip gouged his shoulder after his parents split. It didn't help when I married his mom."

Garrett's sigh is thick. "He's definitely dealing with something. Your daughter put him in his place. We probably won't see him again."

"Or if we do, Ridge will take him out back." I nod to where the protective grump is slinging drinks.

"I wouldn't mess with him," Cole mutters.

That draws Garrett's focus to him and who he's holding. "Gimme that baby."

Our bunch coos as a whole when Belle is transferred onto him. He peppers her tiny face with kisses. My ovaries whimper while preparing for overtime shifts. Mary dabs at her wet eyes when he begins rocking to a natural rhythm.

"Is it too early for me to ask for grandbabies?"

"Yes," Garrett blurts.

I just giggle. "It wasn't long ago that he refused to be in a relationship. We're making a lot of progress."

My boyfriend hums. "See? She gets me."

Mary squints at us. "I give it three months before there's a bun in the oven."

"Mother," Joy chides.

"There's no denying fate," she quips.

"Don't I know it. Doris would be delighted." I wink at Garrett.

My father juts his chin at Belle and her smitten uncle. "If you haven't already decided, those two will have you moving to Knox Creek tomorrow."

I haven't made an official decision, but Garrett makes it a point to ask me at least once a day. It's becoming a habit, which we're equally fond of. "My lease ends in September."

He nudges me. "Good answer."

"So," Joy scoots in beside me. "All is going well and according to the fairytale script?"

"Your brother makes an adequate Prince Charming."

"Always knew he had it in him."

That's when I notice Garrett has handed off Belle to his mother and pulled my dad to a secluded patch several feet away. Their heads are tipped close together. There's an uncharacteristic tension radiating from his stiff posture. If that's not enough, he's fidgeting. The combination sets off an alarm in my brain.

"What do you think they're talking about?"

"The weather," Joy recites automatically.

I balk. "Huh?"

She laughs in return. "How am I supposed to know?"

"Seems suspicious."

"Or proactive."

Before I can question her further, Garrett breaks from the

huddle and struts toward me. I narrow my eyes at his cocky demeanor. "What was that about?"

"Just a little chat."

I study his expression. Glee might as well be leaking from his pores. "Are you plotting?"

"A man is allowed to have his secrets, soulmate." He ducks down to rub my nose with his. "You'll like this one."

"I almost forgot." After reaching into my purse, I pass him the button that matches mine. "Our original number was taken. I settled for sixty-nine."

"What a coincidence." He digs in his pocket and whips out a pin. "Here's that fifty-three that brought us together."

I attach both numbers to my strap, much like I did months ago. A soft breeze ruffles my hair. Idle chatter swirls from all directions. Everything feels as it's meant to be.

"How unexpected." I breathe.

"The buttons?" He glances at where they gleam on his collar.

"Our family gathering in general."

Garrett loops an arm around my waist. "But it's very on-brand for us."

"Wouldn't have it any other way." I release an exhale that reveals my contented mood. "This is really nice, bartender."

"Worth the bumps in the road?" He mimics hitting several potholes on our trip to happily ever after.

"Those detours were necessary to renovate your man-whore-ish habits."

"Good thing you were up to the task." He wags his brows.

"Are you up for something else?"

Garrett sweeps stray hair off my forehead. "For you? Always. Just name it, soulmate."

"The rest of our lives." I fist the front of his shirt and pull him in for a kiss. "Together. Forever."

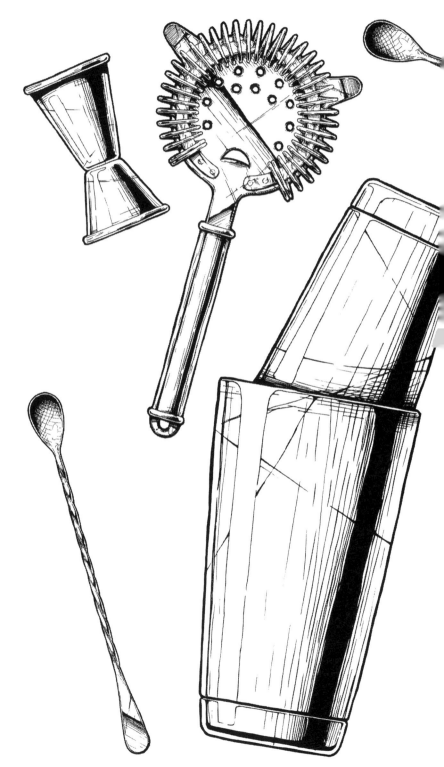

epilogue

Garrett

"ISN'T THIS CONVENIENT?" I SWING OUR JOINED HANDS between us. "We can walk to the farmer's market from our home."

Grace's ruby-stained mouth twitches. "Yes, the commute to our weekend tradition was the main selling point. Not to mention you had nothing but empty space for my book collection."

I yank her toward me to kiss the snark off her lips. "Don't tease me, woman. You love being rocked awake from my morning wood grinding into your ass."

She sighs and I greedily sip her breath. "I choose to be the little spoon for a reason. My eager beaver approves of your chipper dipper."

A fresh memory from two hours ago surfaces. Waves of black hair tickled my thighs. Perky tits were thrust out for me to suckle. Cries of passion as Grace rode me to completion.

And now I'm walking into a family establishment with a boner.

"Sure do complement each other," I rasp.

My girlfriend is completely oblivious to the havoc she wreaks just from walking beside me. She smiles at fellow shoppers that we pass, whether they're recognizable or not. They return the gesture. That's just her effect on folks. I even find myself smirking for no reason other than watching her interact. It's involuntary and infectious.

"Let's be honest," Grace murmurs. "You didn't have to twist my arm. I'm extremely infatuated with you."

My palm finds her ass, giving her a gentle squeeze. "That's good, seeing as I love you to infinity plus one."

"You know that doesn't really make sense."

"Just go with it." I lean in, nibbling on her upturned jaw.

A disgruntled scoff disapproves of my public affection. "You didn't dump him yet?"

I straighten to find Jasmine glowering at us. "Thanks for the boost to my pride."

"Oh, poop. Did I wound your fragile ego?" She snorts, resembling an angry mare that the stud rejected. "Aww, so sad for you."

A weary exhale whizzes from me. "I'm a changed man."

Grace nods. "He's stuck with me."

"More like stuck on you."

"Permanently," she coos and nuzzles my nose with hers.

"Gross," Jasmine mutters. She trudges off without another unkind word.

Grace shrugs at her retreating form. "Bet she wishes there was a thick piece of morning wood rocking her awake every morning."

I hum while rubbing my chin. "That would probably improve her mood."

Three familiar faces appear in the crowd. The little girl sprints toward us, spreading her arms wide. We're both going down in a messy collision if I don't catch her. She launches herself at me in a graceful lunge. I spin her around until the landscape blurs, then for a precise collision with the ground.

"Hi, Garrett!" Sydney's expression brightens the already sunny sky.

I tug on one of her pigtails. "Hey, kiddo. What's new?"

"Umm…" She scrunches her entire face in extreme concentration. "Oh! I'm a first grader now."

My hand hangs in midair for her to slap. "Excellent. Your brain is going to grow super big."

She bobs her head in rapid succession. "My teacher says I'm the smartest."

"It's the truth." I point at the love of my life. "Do you remember Grace?"

"Uh-huh. She's the nanny for that cute boy who's in kindergarten."

Grace chokes on a laugh. "That's me. Have you seen Bradley at school?"

"Yep," Sydney chirps. "He pushes me on the swings at recess and makes me origami balloons."

"How romantic," the expert on the subject breathes.

"He wants to get married, but my daddy told me to keep my options open."

"Solid advice," I commend.

Jake and Harper arrive at the next moment. Their lazy pace proves they're not at all surprised by their daughter's burst of energy. The bubbly blonde waves while the grumpy mechanic appears to be barely tolerating this outing. His scowl could rival Ridge's on the worst day.

That prompts me to give him shit. "Come here often, Evans?"

If possible, his expression becomes more sour. "Very funny."

"We like farm fresh produce," Harper explains. "Plus, it's nice to spend quality time together."

He makes a noncommittal noise. "Can do that in our backyard."

"Did you get married?" Sydney points from me to Grace. "Is Garrett the husband you've been searching for?"

My girlfriend hangs her head. "Not this again."

I chuckle. "We're dating. Does that count?"

The little girl wrinkles her nose. She edges closer to Grace and whispers, "If you need me to show him the light, just give me a thumbs-up. Mom says I'm really good at that. Whatever it means."

Harper sputters, which morphs into an awkward laugh. "And on that note, we better get moving along before Jake's tolerance for people expires."

He grunts. "Only here for you and Syd."

She pats his chest. "That's why we love you."

Sydney must see an opportunity sprout from thin air. She clasps onto her dad's thigh and gazes at him with devotion. "Can I have a pony?"

The grouch almost cracks a smile. "If you find one for twenty bucks or less."

Her gasp is immediately followed by a yank on his arm. "Let's go!"

"That's our cue," Harper says. "Tootles."

"Buh-bye," we respond in unison.

"Jinx," I tease as we resume browsing.

"Adorable. Have I mentioned that you're really good with children?"

"Don't get any ideas, soulmate. I'm not getting you pregnant. We can practice all you want, though."

Grace rolls her eyes. "Are you ever not thinking about sex?"

"When you're nearby? It's a constant livestream of porn up here." I tap my temple.

"You're something else."

"I'm yours." A particular stand catches my attention. "Ah, what do we have here?"

She buries her blush behind a flat palm. "Oh, jeez. I won't look at onion rings the same ever again."

"Doesn't mean you can't eat them." I guide her to the counter and order a basket for us to share.

Grace cradles the paper boat while blowing on the hot food. "Learned my lesson."

"I can always offer you something to drink." My brows wag at the direction this conversation should go based on previous accounts.

"Like a lemonade?" She bites into an onion ring and moans. "Yummy."

"Better than those stacked on my—"

"Nope," she interrupts. "Missing that extra spice, but still delicious."

"Look at this tiny one." I grab the mini version that's no wider than the rim of a shot glass.

"That would never fit over your bedazzled unicorn."

"Not unless you pay the toll."

The flow of our banter spreads warmth through my chest. I glance at the scenery while a plan takes shape. We've made the seasonal market our summer tradition. There isn't a better place other than Roosters or the spring festival. I'll be damned if we wait that long.

Grace freezes on the spot as I get down on one knee. I snag her left hand and hover the makeshift token of my devotion in front of her third finger. "It's not a secret that I'm in love with you."

Her wide stare scans the crowd already gathered around us. "Are you about to propose with an onion ring?"

"Is that not enough bling?"

"I'm not sure how to respond to that," she whispers.

That has me digging in my front pocket. "How about this?"

"Is that a"—she squints at the object pinched between my thumb and forefinger—"straw?"

"Bent into a circle for the occasion, and your approval."

She rolls her lips between her teeth, amusement lifting her cheeks. "It's really difficult to take you seriously right now."

"What do you say, soulmate?" I lift the plastic creation higher.

"Yes?"

"You don't sound very confident." My stomach cramps from the effort of containing a laugh.

Grace appraises my kneeled position. "I'm still trying to figure out if you're just messing with me."

"What if I use this?" I whip out the velvet box from my back pocket. With a flip of the lid, diamonds sparkle under the sunshine.

She claps her right hand over her gaping mouth. "Holy shit, you're serious."

"About you? Always. Now, I'll ask you again. Maybe you'll be a bit more agreeable." I wink. "Grace, will you do me the honor of becoming my wife?"

"Yes!" Tears streak down her face as she nods wildly. "Yes, yes, yes."

I slip the small fortune over her knuckle and rise to my feet. Grace flings herself at me. With a grip around her upper thighs, I hoist her off the ground. Her ankles cross at the small of my back as our lips smash together. Cheers erupt from those bearing witness to our engagement. We smile into our kiss, exchanging joy forevermore.

Grace pulls away and thrusts her hand into the air. The orange solitaire surrounded by a halo of diamonds reflects her awe. "This ring is… just wow."

"Fit for my Peachy Bottom Grace," I reply. "Better than an onion ring or straw?"

"I would've said yes to any of the above."

My thumb traces the pure delight shining on her features. "You had me from the start. One glance and I was yours."

Her smile steals the oxygen from my lungs. "Took you long enough to admit it."

"What can I say? Somehow, I knew you'd appreciate the chase."

"I've also grown quite fond of the catch," Grace exhales against my lips.

"Damn straight, soulmate. I've always been yours to catch."

That's technically the end, but I do have a little extra something for you. If you'd like more from Garrett and Grace, grab the bonus scenes here!

what to read next?

Jake and Harper have their own story in *Wrong for You*, which is available now. Here's the prologue to get you in the mood for this grumpy single dad, second chance romance.

prologue

Harper

GOSSIP IN A SMALL TOWN SHOULD BE IGNORED MORE often than not. I learned that lesson after my fifth-grade teacher almost quit her job based solely on spiteful hearsay. That doesn't stop the rumor I heard earlier from playing on repeat.

I whirl on my heel and pace to the tall oak that marks the hiking trail's entrance. Dust kicks up from my frantic stride as I turn to retrace my path for the ninth time. My skin is slick and balmy, which has little to do with the nerves eating at me. The July heat hasn't relented even as dusk casts shadows across the woods.

A twig snaps to my left and I pivot to see Jacob Evans— the one I've been waiting for in more ways than one. I rush forward to fling myself at him. Fresh pine blended with lingering traces of motor oil and fraying patience welcomes me.

My arms struggle to encircle his torso as I soak in his sturdy warmth. Jake is already broad and muscular, far larger than the boys I just graduated with. His steady pulse drums beneath my ear and soothes me. I breathe him in again while trying to silence the doubt pestering me. Everything is going to be okay.

"You came." Stark relief raises my voice to an embarrassing pitch.

"Said I would." Meanwhile, his tone is flat and stiff.

The brittle response sets off an alarm in my brain. Denial and desperation have me clinging tighter to him. It's only then I realize he isn't returning my embrace. Toned arms that rarely hesitate to haul me in stay glued to his sides.

I step back from the false comfort of his presence to do a quick assessment. Only three years separate us, but Jake appears older than twenty-one right now. There's an underlying tension thrumming from him. His rigid posture matches the stony expression avoiding my gaze. The dark features I could trace from memory are purposely guarded.

Only his eyes reveal emotion. A barely contained storm swirls in those blue depths. Jake must feel my imploring scrutiny and bites off a curse from his clenched jaw.

"Please tell me it's not true." I lift trembling fingers to my lips.

He averts his stare further from mine. "Afraid I can't do that."

Fire blasts under my skin as understanding dawns. I lunge at him, bunching his shirt in my fist. "You cheated on me?"

No wonder he was willing to wait until I was ready to lose my virginity. The good guy act was just for show. He's really an asshole in disguise, getting action elsewhere.

"Didn't fucking cheat." The icy retort might as well be frozen shards stabbing at my flesh.

I scoff to hide the pain. "How else do you explain getting Morgan pregnant when you're dating me?"

Jake pins me with a glare, but his face remains an impassive mask otherwise. "It happened before we started seeing each other."

"And she just found out about the baby?" Disbelief drips from my snarky reply.

"Guess so," he drawls.

"That would make her four or five months along. She should've noticed her missing period much sooner."

He shrugs. The motion is jerky, much like the rest of him. "Don't ask me."

My fingers clench the fabric still in my hold. "Are you sure the baby is yours?"

"I'll get the test done, but there's no reason for me to assume she's lying."

None of this makes sense. Heat begins to collect in my eyes. His indifference is worse than this unpleasant detour. He's already shutting me out, minutes after confirming what I swore was fake news. Too many thoughts and emotions pummel me at once. I'm more confused than anything. Answers would be appreciated.

"But when…? How…?" It seems that I can't form a proper sentence. "You told me this is exclusive between us. That you'd wait until I was ready."

Jake dips his head in acknowledgment. "Already said we are, or were. I slept with her in March. It was just once. Hadn't talked to her since until she texted yesterday."

That's a lot to digest, but my mind snags on a single word. "Were? As in, past tense?"

The defeated grimace pinching his expression is telling. Then he's withdrawing further behind the blank walls he thinks I can't see through. "This is over between us, Harper. I have to do what's right for Morgan and the baby."

It feels like my chest is caving in with that declaration. I could gasp or scream or wail, but that won't accomplish a damn thing. It's not as if I expected him to stay with me while another woman has his child. I did think he'd be more upset about it, though. For my benefit if nothing else.

That's precisely why I pound my fist against his sternum. If only I could break through and shatter his hardened resolve. Just for a moment to prove he gives a shit about me. A sob rips from my tight throat and I thump him again. It's silly to be this upset over something I never had. That doesn't stop a lone tear from escaping, though.

"Knock it off, Pitchy. What's done is done." He pries my fingers from his shirt, releasing me without care.

I let my hand drop with the weight of his rejection. His use of my nickname is a hammer to my crumbling heart. I turn away from him to shield the hurt streaming down my cheeks.

"I thought we had something special," I whisper into the dark. Our chance at happiness goes up into thin air with my foolish dreams.

"It's better this way. You and I weren't meant to last."

My eyes squeeze shut, sending more sorrow down my face. "Don't be cruel."

He kicks the dirt and a rock rolls toward me. "Nah, I'm being honest."

Which delivers the parting blow. There's nothing left to discuss. If he wants to pretend our relationship is that disposable, I can play along.

I give myself two more seconds to mourn what could've been. The ache in my chest doesn't cease, but I don't reveal the cracks splintering through me. My heart pumps and air continues to flow into my lungs. On the grand scale of shitty situations, this bump in the road doesn't deserve mention.

My sandals grind into the ground as I spin to face him. I ignore the burn spreading from behind my breastbone. The grin I force to appear might as well be made from plastic. But I'm the picture of acceptance.

I swipe at my wet cheeks to erase the leftover evidence. "You're right. It's for the best."

Jake rocks backward. His lips part and press together to a disjointed tempo. For the first time, he seems to flounder for a response. "Yeah?"

My head bobs in agreement. "I'm leaving for college at the end of August. There's a dorm room on campus with my name on it."

And I couldn't get there fast enough after this relationship demolition.

"Thought you were commuting?"

"Plans change," I clip.

Something painful flickers over his features before he smothers it. Then he's the mask of indifference. "Right."

"So, I guess this is goodbye." My voice cracks, but I ignore the stumble.

Jake squints at me. "You're good with this?"

"Absolutely." I laugh, but the tone is humorless. "And congratulations. You're gonna be a dad."

His eyes blow wide, and he drags a hand through his dark hair. "Shit, that's weird to hear."

"You'll get used to it."

"Not much of an alternative, huh?"

"Good luck." My smile wobbles with the farewell.

He pauses to study me again. "Why are you acting so chill?"

"My pity party came to an abrupt end. You told me to knock it off, remember?"

A breeze stirs at that moment. He glances at the swaying branches above. I allow my gaze to follow his lead. What little brightness still exists on this day shines through the leaves. It offers us much-needed peace.

His stare is unfocused when he looks at me next, but determination squares his shoulders. "I'm sorry, Harper."

"Don't be."

"But—"

"You're starting a family. There's nothing sorry about that." Or that's what I'll trick myself to believe.

Jake's sigh sounds heavier than the elephant crushing my chest. My throat clogs as conflict pinches his somber appearance. He fidgets, curling his fingers into white-knuckle fists. Muscles bunch and twitch beneath his shirt. It almost looks like he wants to reach out to me. But then, just as before, his features return to their stoic state.

The sight is almost too much for me to balance on this teetering farce. I gulp to trap the hiccupped sob ready to betray me.

After a single nod, Jake turns away. His retreating footsteps threaten to weaken my willpower. I want to chase him. Beg him to choose me. But that would be selfish. His path is heading in a different direction. One I can't follow.

I can only watch him leave our love behind.

Read *Wrong for You* today!

And how about the book Garrett read to Grace while she was sick? *Leave Him Loved* actually exists and is available for your reading pleasure. Enjoy this excerpt from when Audria first meets Reeve.

A blast of air conditioning chills my skin as I stride through the sliding glass doors of Valley Market. The grocery store resembles a Hy-Vee, but on a smaller scale. That doesn't stop the space from buzzing with weekend activity.

A laundry list of yummy goodness forms in my mind as I wander to the cart corral. It's never wise to go shopping on an empty stomach. The meal plans stack up faster than I can track ingredients. I absently tug at a cart sticking out on the end. Nothing happens. That gets my attention, knocking me from my food stupor. I put in more effort but struggle to remove one from the bunch. They're all wedged together in tight formation. Kudos to the attendant for shoving them in with such precision. I giggle to myself, thinking about Vannah cackling over that last comment.

I shake my head and get back on track. With more force than I probably needed, I yank backward. Not even a single squeak of metal. The damn things don't budge. I exhale harshly, blowing stray hair off my forehead. Next comes a little mental stretch to prepare for war. I grip the handle and wrench with all my might. There's barely a wiggle.

On my next futile attempt, I ram an elbow into an unforgiving surface. Since I don't have a wall behind me, it's safe to assume someone just got jabbed in the gut. My innocent victim releases a muffled grunt, confirming the worst. I hang my head as a wash of humiliation singes my cheeks. My hopes of making a good impression are dashing off faster than the power-walking supermoms in aisle four.

"Whoa, easy there."

I spin on my heel at the gritty timbre, feeling like a spooked horse. *Is he trying to soothe me? Make sure I don't trigger a stampede?* Those thoughts vanish as I take my first decent glance at the man.

When I picture a hunk of farm-raised hotness, Scott Eastwood from *The Longest Ride* pops into my brain. This guy couldn't be farther from that stereotype. He's dark and broody without leather chaps or a Western shirt in sight. Broad shoulders, toned muscles, and a trim waist fill my vision. His white T-shirt is tight enough to hint at a set of defined abs. It's no wonder my arm is still vibrating from the impact. Without shame, I admit my mouth waters at the idea of tracing those washboard lines. I would gladly volunteer to scale him faster than a hayloft ladder.

The logo on his hat is familiar. Carhartt has a recognizable enough stamp, even to someone detached from country style. I'm pretty sure their apparel is made with heavy-duty labor in mind. Back home, the brand is popular with the hipster crowd. I have a feeling this guy didn't choose the label to be trendy. Maybe he's more purposeful about his fashion statements than I'm giving him credit for. He makes a ball cap look ultra-sexy, regardless of his purpose. As if hearing my thoughts, his stare bores into me from the shadows under the curled brim.

The chance to offer a polite apology and salvage my manners is vanishing with each stilted breath. I nearly choke on the buckets of sand lodged in my throat. "Shit… I mean, shoot. I'm really sorry. Are you okay?"

Painful silence is all that greets me. It seems the stranger is too busy giving my body a full scan. I shift my weight from the blatant perusal. The need to fidget needles at me. *Is he sizing me up because I'm seriously lacking in the height department?* A tiny nudge from me certainly wouldn't result in serious damage—to his flexing physique or otherwise. To be fair, anyone over six feet makes me look like a shrimp. I wait several seconds for a response, but he remains disturbingly quiet.

Taking the hint, I creep toward a stack of small baskets and prepare to sulk off without causing further injury. "Um, okay then. I'll just be moving along."

He blinks at me, drawing attention to his alluring gaze.

"Wow, are you wearing contacts?" I squint at him like some sort of stage-five creeper.

If possible, his frown dips lower. "No."

"I'm aware that it's super weird for a stranger to randomly ask. Your eyes are just really blue."

"And yours are brown," he deadpans.

Speaking of, I'm not scoring any brownie points with this guy. "Solid observation. Isn't it rare to have light eyes with dark hair?"

"Can I question the same for your blond hair and dark eyes? Unless you use dye."

I gasp, twirling a loose strand around my finger, holding it out for inspection. "This color is natural, thank you very much. And I'm really leaving now. Sorry again for the bang."

There goes the remainder of my dignity. I press my lips together to trap more nonsense from spewing out, futile as it might seem. The damage is already wreaking havoc on my pride.

The man's harsh mask cracks, a slice of amusement twitching his lips. I catch a twinkle in his eyes while that slight humor grows into a crooked grin. My earlier assessment is no longer valid. He isn't the hardcore, surly sort, other than his resting dick face—also known as RDF, for future reference. It's almost a relief to see the expression I came across so often in high school and college. Without having to mutter a word, these guys would receive a wide berth from most. That skill is essential in chasing off unwanted attention, for themselves and others.

A dimple dents his cheek as he graces me with a full smile. The oxygen meant for my brain fizzles into a puff of smoke. As if this fella needs more ammunition to reel in the ladies.

"You're not from here."

I slap on a grin of my own to cover the undeniable scent of lust wafting off me. "Why is that so obvious?"

"Any lifer could sniff you out in an instant," he drawls. "We don't get a lot of visitors in our small section of paradise."

"No?"

"Not that look like you."

I almost recoil. "That's not very gentlemanly. Do you make a habit of being rude to women in the entryway of the supermarket?"

My word vomit erases any progress I managed to make, not that he doesn't deserve it. But the stranger surprises me with a raspy chuckle.

"Nah, you're proving to be a special case."

"Should I be offended?"

"Not in the slightest, darling. I meant that as a compliment. You're so… shiny."

I glance down at my outfit, noticing an obvious lack of sparkle. "Like a new toy?"

He scrubs a hand over his mouth, hiding a smirk. "Not sure I'm bold enough to cross that line just yet."

Read *Leave Him Loved* today!

about the author

Harloe Rae is a *USA Today* & Amazon Top 5 best-selling author. Her passion for writing and reading has taken on a whole new meaning. Each day is an unforgettable adventure.

She's a Minnesota gal with a serious addiction to romance. There's nothing quite like an epic happily ever after. When she's not buried in the writing cave, Harloe can be found hanging with her hubby and kiddos. If the weather permits, she loves being lakeside or out in the country with her horses.

Broody heroes are Harloe's favorite to write. Her romances are swoony and emotional with plenty of heat. All of her books are available on Amazon and Kindle Unlimited.

Stay in the know by subscribing to her newsletter at
http://bit.ly/HarloesList

Join her reader group, Harloe's Hotties, at
www.facebook.com/groups/harloehotties

Check out her site at www.harloerae.com